EMPIRE!

Science Fiction by

RED JORDAN
AROBATEAU

EMPIRE!

Cover Photo by Dr. Sam

ISBN: 978-0-6151-6687-2

Published by RED JORDAN PRESS
484 Lake Park Ave. PMB 228
Oakland, CA 94610
USA

1.

EMPIRE!

(Novel to which JOURNEY is subtext.)

Part One: The Unity Of Utopia

*What follows is the account of Star1.vax, citizen of the new world order, The Unity of Utopia, living in year 2054, on a continent once known as Am-Erica & his/her study group focused on fragments of a found journal (JOURNEY) which had survived the rubble & chaos of the old world. ---*Editors note.

A writer's art is a tool for justice.

PASSAGE Volume 1

Chapter 1.

THE UNITY OF UTOPIA. Year 2054 AD.

Red had been last living in a day, 2040 AD, when parts of the world were still free. Of course this had come to an end entirely under the first dynasty, that of Kim Sun II., second dictator of the 21st millennium, and current world ruler of the new state of Utopia. Free reading material had been stamped out, banned, and now all there was were prescribed texts-- approved by the authorities, and marked by the great Seal of Jun Kim Sun the Dictator, which were embellished by that big red seal baring a golden rising sun in blue on in its middle. --- A situation which would have amused Old Red we speculate, for practically all he wrote about was his infernal religion-- and a thing called freedom.   His texts now of course were banned but still available in odd places of the galaxy here/there--for a price, and the greater part of that price was the manifest danger in acquiring & possessing them, for one takes the risk of running afoul of cyber police, corporate/industrial military soldier forces—and, or, of the espionage agents of governmental world control.

Old man Red Jordan had been, according to these forbidden texts, transsexual, in a time, not too far back but of the last dispensation (information about which has been banned and is gradually being eradicated out of memory banks of all current data) in a time when transsexualism was still illegal in some part of his ancient world-- a laughable situation if the policy makers of that day could compare themselves to the present enlightened times, 2054, we now have---when nothing is thought of this condition whatsoever. Further, some choose to emulate its symptoms since mostly, being trans is High Fashion--tho they themselves are not truly genetically born transgendered.

This Old Man, Red Jordan was, by profession a writer/artist who had apparently left many fragments of his literature upon his death not only in his condominium (one of the old fashion kind, self-owned, and not property of Utopia) stuff which was of course sealed--as he had been declared an enemy of The Unity. Some paintings of his too had existed but were publicly destroyed in a grand conflagration in People's Square before a multitude of 2 million citizens beamed in by satellite to numerous wide screen viewing portals strategically positioned, as well as globally to the satellites, and ships on voyages in space--however there exists some reproductions of these done by cybertech that still float thru the new state of the Unity of Utopia---as do his texts. Sometimes to be found under the very noses of the Authorities themselves! So there is a lot of paraphernalia still available to the intrepid, the gambler. Collectables of the Old Prophet. –

This being only under the penalty of severe repercussions, so that only the most daring, or disillusioned with their life may attempt the cultivating of his memorabilia. The following of Red, which rumors say is growing, has become an underground cult. So his legacy--his idea and works can be acquired, but only at a risk. And further, the people who seek them are assembling themselves together to study these works collectively. (Again at great risk.) Red Jordan's ideas are studied as a sort of jigsaw puzzle whose fragments are divided from us by eras, decades, not to mention already being rendered into pieces, but when all put together present a very unique philosophy indeed---that of revolution. That of resistance. And these are getting harder and harder to get in their original (done by the artist himself) slowly being stripped out of the culture by ever-present cullings done by soldier/police, etc., on one hand, but, being declared contraband, thus have now a soaring value which has generated full scale underground factories of reproduction; small covens, or cults of study, and subsequently tiny flares (like fires in the night) of *acts* preformed in sympathy with his radical ideas. These will be documented further...

Red Jordan's times were for all account different then ours today. The world was still free in places. Individuals could write and say whatever they pleased in some separate areas called nations. Oh yes, the world was divided up in a haphazard fashion with many states--called nations or county's-- which no longer exist having been swallowed into the grand total, the Unity which now reigns, in the first dynasty. The Unity of Utopia. Under Jon Kim Sun, I.

Chapter 2.

"CITIZEN!"

A tinny voice blared out of a speaker, which over hung the speedwalk.

S/he corrected his-her mistake, fast walking, and retraced steps back to veer off to one side, and enter thru the weapon-detector scan, passing thru to eyes of a noncommittal uniformed soldier, female, and of low rank. He/she thought, 'They're so low paid many of them are not getting nutrition to eat, just regulation daft'. Instead of being foul-tempered many soldier(ettes) had retreated into a lethargy on medications. 'Well' he thought 'it's better then being at the front in deep space and being killed by aliens. Even at 3 times the pay.' He-she passed thru the device with no problem. Continuing on his brisk walk thoughts drifted back again to that afternoon. A letter had been miss-delivered by the mail robot—baring the wrong address. It was to the actual owner of the building. At 887 Pine Street. Where as he was on

Sacramento. A $2,214 electric bill for their whole slum place, which still had not been reconverted over to any of the nuclear systems, and did not even have individual meters for each unit. 'I knew all along it was still a private owner, and not the Unity at all.' One of the old guard. Owning anything as substantial as housing was still out of reach of the average person. And no matter! Under the Unity of Utopia housing domiciles were guaranteed for everybody, no matter what their salary. Let the rich upper class and the powerful Unity battle it out! In their fight for supremacy over each other. The Unity would win... it always did... And slowly, ever steadily its tentacles were encroaching throughout once-private holdings of the rich.

Picturing the dull witted soldierette he thought; 'She is miserable inside that Unity uniform I bet, working a 12 hour shift and probably medicated.' Star1.vax contemplated momentarily how if only the soldierette could have realized what was inside the briefcase he carried—something more powerful then a-bombs or fireswords! Fragments! He understood the soldiers. Because s/he personally hated & resented the fact he hadn't had the opportunity to become more middleclass---thus able to command the respect of professional people, expand his shabby circle of friends & maybe get a wife/husband. And was usually just treated like a lower-class drudge with little intelligence, who could be satisfied with mental fuel fed out of public media outlets by the gods of Empire. That was until he'd met others like himself, those seekers who collected fragments.....

Here his feet falls pounding on the sun-cooled speedwalk of Utopia, he walked thru a maize of people congested to try to rush someplace by different directions. The few stumbling super large males---- omnipresence with their bottles of illegal darf liquor inside a brown paper bag, going nowhere; these were the manly workers back from the frontier in far outerspace, who were sorely needed, difficult to replace, and had impunity to do just about anything they liked while back on leave...

Star1.vax stopped for a moment, exiting the speedwalk once more, went to the base of a gigantic edifice that sprung up in a thick metal grid of mirror-like surfaces & windows from roots which plunged down deep, 50 stories underground. Here was the remains of somebody's homestead, broken, put out on the stationary sidewalk outdoors. An Exercycle, compartmentalized shelves for a dissembled cyber bookcase, a few empty jackets off cyber books (all baring the nauseatingly familiar Utopia Official Media Logos; a yellow sun-dot within the blue circle, which beneficently beams its rays). Boxes of stuff--- used jumpsuits, kitchen utensils, computer parts... lots of junk attachments for a failed robot, a cheep household gadget of a design who were more trouble then the amount of work they could actually do or

10

time saved... These caches frequent, but once in a while contained a rare find—one of the real printed books of pre dynastic Utopia, which were by now all banned, illegal, but still turning up after a change of government from the last dispensation, which wasn't very long ago. Star1.vax let his greyblue eyes gaze quickly over the remnants. It was obvious they'd been picked thru already. Then he was back, moving swiftly on the speedway out of the City.

The heart of Utopia was a well, in reality, about ten city blocks wide and seventy long, which descended in an in a incline to its oceanic tip, surrounded by huge enforcement walls one hundred feet in height, twenty-five feet thick. The City was below sea level, which had been rising steadily since the turn of the last century—nearly fifty years ago—a well from which skyscrapers of immense proportions grew... strange steely surrealistic creations.

A few things were the same as in Red Jordan's day tho much had changed. The same sun shone, but around it, now 14-recorded planets orbited. —In Red's times there were only 9 of knowledge, Pluto, the last, having been discovered when he was just a young Transchild of tender years, then being demoted into an inferior status when he had arrived at old age. The Unity had diligently been cultivating several of these planets for human habitation back 3 decades, even before it was The Unity. There was growing necessity that the human species and animal companions find other habitats to house and feed their increasing population. Space ships containing workers, travelers and cargo were a daily occurrence to be seen across the sky flaming out of the atmosphere into outer space. So much was the same, but different.

The glaring/blaring moon reigned high in the heavens in these times above modern compounds of downtown mega-story domiciles as it had over the squat ugly low building tenements of yesteryear, as it had in ancient times shone down upon castle turret top —so all was still in some respects, unchanging. The City was on the same geological configuration but had mushroomed up and up in size for those last fifty years unfolding its grandeur in great height and streamlined modernity, as the average apartment building now was approximately 300 floors tall (these topper-most floors having great appeal for sky pilots, outerspace workers and airline stewardesses)--and 20 to 50 in addition underground, with mole dwellers; where as in the older years, at ridiculously low level of 5 or 6 stories no buildings could exactly be called tall, nor the basement dwellers who still had the light of day immediate at eye level on the street above their heads outside not exactly deep enough to qualify as moles; likewise those laughable so-called 'immense' skyscrapers of yesteryear zooming up to 150 stories were now tripled in size 400, 500 floors taking approximately 15 minutes to ride up/down in the elevators, and requiring great climate control.

A strange surreal nation had begun to emerge, sadly, much like a script from one of the many prophetic novels such as 1984, or, by Adlous Huxley, Brave New World. All these rumored texts which few had actually seen, reduced to shreds now—yet still available & being reconstructed by the ghosts of Empire who haunted its deep underground sewers of discontent.

Back at the early turn of millennium 2000, after domestic terrorism increased to such a level, that whole wings of government espionage & surveillance were instituted, given new powers by which decades later thru their new-given iron grip, plus by other erosions into the Am-Erica Constitution by collusion with its puppet government they had done away with House and Senate—a governing body once elected by free vote of the citizens. Many devices were used to keep an eye on every individual in the nation to guarantee these 'free' powers never reasserted themselves among the masses.

Early in the new millennium, 2010, government agents had begun to track all citizens—that job made easier thru advent of computer use, which was by then ranging over most of the population who had finally caught on to the ever simplifying machines, greatly reduced in price.

Both the pupils of their eyes, and imprint of DNA could be scanned by screens stationed at strategic check-points upon all main thoroughfares leading thru and in or out of The City. All government buildings and most domiciles compounds had instant recognition. And everyone had got use to this.

If any one point was obvious about Utopia, to historians both official and casual, it was that it was the Newest Empire in a processional of others, which had by time been reduced to dusty ruins, & this had not been good thing to be in bygone days. So, to compare Utopia to fallen Dynasties of past millenniums was troubling. No matter then the Dictator glossed over this fine point. There had been the Roman conquest nearly 3,000 years past—with the splendor & might & conquest that was Rome, (an Empire), only to fall in its end times. There was Egypt. The Maya-Aztecs. There was the British tentacle hold on its foreign colonies. The totalitarian Soviets sweeping across the Balkan states, which boarded old mother Russia.

His group had studied this history. True history. Which was no longer taught in the many fine, free schools of Utopia.

Population of inner city old San Francisco was swollen from 700 thousand to 9 million on the strength of these 300 story monstrosities. And all over the arch dome of the ozone free-air shield. The wind was picking up now, the moment he passed out of the ozone free-air shield... He walked along on an antiquated contraption which lacked the acceleration of inner city speedways, and soon to be on his own, by foot power alone propelling him to the final destination. And he thought frequently about the warm coziness of his study group. How soon they would be reading together! 'Maybe aloud! I hope I will be called to read from a fragment!' His mind wandered back to how he imagined the ancient days. 'Did their parents sit reading to their children just as my parents programmed the robot to do for me?'

Star1.vax had often declared to him/her self "I can't hold on much longer! I gotta get out of here! Get out of this hell hole! But then would arise the question, 'to where?'

In a backdrop behind him, SF steel & glass casework rises like a castle fantasy of old, only gigantically taller.

'Maybe I'll just dig myself in deeper, and be like the mole people. Get a unit 40 floors beneath earth-surface, and live out my life on medications.' --- These were provided with the luxury units below. 'Few people can live buried that deep without drugs. That would be my excuse to jump off this miserable planet, but not be dead.' Maybe he'd become a mole person and go underground. Old prophet Red.... He had written: 'I know it is hard for people, deformed, mentally ill, my loneliness is temporal, theirs, lifelong. 'Yeah. Huh. I'll crawl deeper into myself. I'll go down, down, down...'

Empire!

How high she looms—driving people from her, then compelling them back in!

1.
The beginning of JOURNEY, so here it is like PASSAGE, with quotes from everything from the Maoist International Newsletter to the Holy Bible.... I am biting out great chunks of life, and the Bancroft and my fans & buyers are purchasing little pieces of it. A sample, 1" thick, on my desk for preparation: **E-MAILS CONCERNING RED'S PLAY PORTRAITS FROM A GHETTOIZED POPULATION, FROM THE CASTING CALLS TO THE FINAL END, 2006.** Going to arrange them in chronological order, bind them and sell to the Bancroft. A copy goes to

Dalila too who wants to see them-- her schedule was too busy to read when they passed by her at the time-- then that is done. Can't publish that on the public market tho, real names in it. Oh, also have stolen a kiss from Rosa Salazar---not on her mouth of course! As she quickly snaps her head away out of reach of my lips when I try. The kiss lands wet, SMACK, on her neck.

What a great gift God has given me! What a magical book PASSAGE is, what an eternal scent wafts in from its pages! Maybe this Journal of days-- this JOURNEY is what's gonna put me over-- into the limelight of public discovery---and into fate. "Red will be read," as the Madame of a quaint fetish brothel once stated, proudly at her mastery of puns, (see Madame V. in her 'ho house in the Outlaw Chronicle Series).

Saw a fellow traveler yesterday-- a bum from whom I turn my head at first glace assuming to be an intrusive insane panhandling pest, but as walked by with a quick step noticed on the sidewalk at his feet an oversize attaché case covered with duct tape & streaked with color, --- and a tell tale folio bulging with painted-on paper of an artist!) Another special being of God, another 'set aside' out of the common realm and work-a-day-world. Suffering quite obviously.

I realize now God has filled the sails of my desires with inspiration-- it was my great love to see things in a super interested way and jot it down in verse on paper or a quick sketch in a drawing book--- provided by my Good Father who bought me art & writing supplies on his daily wages as a working man (a desk job, buyer in an office run by Jewish people). Likewise this starving watercolorist on a bench, he is gifted—as well as afflicted. He must persist thru the adversity! And also I am here to inform you that the great artist does not really desire fame—but for their works to survive—if that takes fame, to push their art out of the impermanent shadows of obscurity and invisibility into the blazing light of day within some spotlight, so be it! A great commotion might be needed!

There is a wise saying; 'if de bird gets too big s/he breaks de perch and all de other birds falls down!' Meaning if this bird gets too full-of-itself, puffed up ego, etc., and I don't want to be like that, nor to harm anyone by my works left behind me! *Wise saying just invented by the artist.

Had placed an 8-foot by 4 curb-found mirror in his studio which gazed at him. In it were reflections of surfaces of self. Now it has been replaced by canvass upon which, from out of the depths of his soul will come imagery captured in color. To see what he can draw out of that.

I will begin painting soon! (Sat. Sept 24, 2006 Autumn Equinox.)

***

My document might be considered subversive by agents of our current government! Does it say somewhere in the US Constitution that treason means *disloyalty to the nation itself, but not necessarily to a current body governing our nation?* Again, this thing about patriotism and what's going on in leadership occupying the White House today! Because I am a patriot, but loath, hate & detest almost every single thing this stolen-presidency puppet has done! Anyway I must speak politics—a dry subject usually, except in times like this when it's become inflammatory because America's wounds, ills, grievances, & world-trespasses have begun to bleed and ooze pus so badly over our universe! I must speak truths observant to a social scene! Any great work of life is to prepare the children, the next generation, for what will come-- so they will feel safe, secure within the danger, and hence their security and survival will be optimal.

> **To end the evil wherever it is.**
> **To comfort crying people.**
> **To protect.**

Dear Children, my readers to come, (cum) our world is composed of flowing waters, oceans, land masses, mountains, there is a starry sky above, there is gravity, and there is God. Yes, a Creator ---Who is just all part of the thing, and we might as well accept it now, for our journey will be easier with Her (Him) available, and in a hairs breath of a prayers reach-- concerning all matters: IE; the pervert (a good pervert)* and her/his lover having finally found themselves in bed together after a long persistent courtship; the pervert having finally convinced her-him what an exceptional lover he/she is, has gotten the trade to bed! —But finds after 2 laborious hours using every technique said lover has failed to have an orgasm. The wise pervert raises up his/her head to the heavens and utters a silent prayer-- for Creator to intervene in this sad, tedious fiasco and grant the lover an orgasm! Upon which returning industriously to the task of fleshly manipulation (use your imagination Children) about five minutes later, the lover comes and comes indeed! Copiously! So you see our Creator is ever at hand, present in all situations, ready and willing to come (cum) to the aid of those who ASK! She is aware of all our politics, our sexuality, our very lives breath!

*There are good perverts, and evil doing ones, who are described, but not endorsed nor applauded in my texts--in fact the opposite, they are

15

placed very low upon the human scale of value; those who do damage willingly or unwillingly mindlessly or mindfully to any other life forms, human, or animal or the environment. Especially concerning during sex.

So as illustrated already, JOURNEY is a full-scale wild-ranging beast.

This torrent of words!

JOURNEY will just be that, with no attempt at weaving a plot thru the thing. Tho several are certain to appear..... It also is a continuation/outgrowth of the finite AUTUMN CHANGES after which came PASSAGE, which also had an end. –They all departed from my prior 40-year herstory of fiction.

You know if I decide to continue JOURNEY into still another dispensation---ending the journal part-- and like I did PASSAGE, with another series (which essentially moved from the Unofficial Semi-Autobiography of Red Jordan Arobateau, into PASSAGE) an account; views and observations of daily changes, passages towards reconfiguring myself again as a fine-artist, out of the 40 year drudge of novel writing, short stories, back into oil paintings. I will call it passion. PASSION.

Every humanbeing leaves a trail of detris, excrement's. Emotional stuff, things they say, mistakes they make, which has to be cut off & discarded. Stuff which doesn't endure so there's a stream of rubbish behind their life as well along with their good works that more or less stand the test of time. One goal? There's a sort of criticism, an elimination of stuff no longer necessary, stripping the self bare to go foreword in spirit, not be flesh-bound.

JOURNEY! Passion!

Now onto something still topical....

Sexy TS muy simpatico Mami Rosa has showed Red, illustratedo, on her fine curvy body with pinches of golden tan fingers tipped with long red fingernails accented against her soft yellowish-white flesh how she pulled and tugged at the skin of her male chest repeatedly, first beginning as a 14 year old girl, to encourage the extra skin growth necessary for the 'de implants of las tetas falsas' which she would not be able to afford for another decade, then, how she likewise just pulled & tugged at her scrotum-- got it so it hung down half way down her thighs, this preformed over

16

another 20 years --so necessary for the construction of the new labia lips of her vagina which she now has!

A deep, dark, mysterious, pungent, many-layered hole to fuck. Mami has one!

Her panties: She wore the type, lacy, satin, bikini style, which were easily pushed aside by finger tips of golden tan fingers reveling her new pussy to me. Opening her legs in her desk chair at office in the storage room of the Sex Shoppe of her employment she spread her labia lips (once hairy scrotal tissue). "Best pussy I've ever seen yet ... On anybody!" Transman Red exclaimed delightedly, licking his lips and clapping his hands.

His mad impulse was to lick her pussy! Get right down there on his knees on the storage room floor but restrained himself. He knew he could strap on his cock & give it to her good—any size she wanted---- & told her so. But was denied entry.

The new transsexual woman must learn the rules of living female, to become fully integrated into the normal social world of gender successfully.... But most especially as a New Woman whose not able to pass successfully. She's not going to be able to get answers. She is not listened to. When she speaks she is ignored. She is ridiculed. She is ignored at best. She is ill-treated.

Again, like the starving artist, we must persist! Remember, all the peoples of the world are Gods! All belong to God-- first because She created them. Also secondly, because some of us have committed ourselves to Her.

Why I have become a literary activist, and take this awful risk of unpopularity, of tomatoes, eggs thrown? I have nothing else to do with my life! That's why! This malformed society has taken from me everything people hold dear, starting with my mother at an early age taken by segregation, incest, systemic abuse of women, (not by my dad), and by schizophrenia. My mother, a beautiful, intelligent, Colored woman (that's 3 strikes against her in a row) missing in action.

Repeat as I said before about me being a bewildered citizen who belongs in a nation which the rest of the world denounces in fiery rhetoric night & day all spread across the tabloids, podiums of the world... and increasingly in actuality burning the effigy of America and its ridiculous U$ President dummy doused in gasoline & lit with matches from a dozen hands similar to fragging of US America soldiers of their own higher ups in the military in another unpopular war—in some peoples memory, Viet Nam. Upon my journey daily find it easy to search at a glace passing, news rack coin-return slots for a forgotten quarter or dime; can't help but see headlines big black bold print these foreign diplomats criticizing our U$ policy. They really say what it is. Information of how that we have propped up our economy by going over to other nations and grabbing stuff from them—stuff which belongs to THEM, not to U$!!

When I was young, times there was no food. —When living at dads house our refrigerator was always well stocked—but I still might not eat, so I could go out on inspirations wings.

Lets talk about transexuality, homosexuality, being an artist, a political activist—all of it! Let me tell you what it is—a driving imperative. You know how tumultuous sex can be? Longings, desires, lusts, some thwarted, others over-indulged. Especially in the beginning teenage years the unfamiliar coursings of being on the threshold of adulthood after having had a brief decade simply learning the lessons of childhood—you know how tumultuous sex can be? Then imagine what its like for sex, double-crossed as it is for us as transsexuals, being on the interior a woman, finally presenting as one, but still having male lusts, a frantic scrambling to find & situate oneself in this society like a survivor on a raft of mishap, set adrift… sometimes an individual who has lived almost from their first day as 'Quaint Irene', an odd character amidst the milling norm, their dissatisfaction being both inward from the sexual misfiring angst, plus growing greater outwardly due to them ill fitting inside the established social frame. Finally the dream vision lays close ahead, hormone therapy, surgery, transition itself! But upon completing their Sex Change find life is far from perfect, maybe at that point some begin to go slightly insane.

I look at the effeminate male; the naturally-occurring mannish woman; we are such a delicate construct- different from the norm, pushing gender boundaries further--not completely by our own decisions, but what biology has bestowed upon us from before our birth. An impoverished street trans woman forced back into boy clothes, her wig (too ratty) combed out with vigorous strokes, yet in her bald shaved head, an effeminate flounce of hands, Alors! She bes wo-man! Shining thru! Two lesbians in leather & starched bluejeans. Very masculine vibrations---of both the smaller femme and the larger butch, dressed identical--- not just their chaps/vests and short haircuts, but their mannerisms, the voice tone, the lack of 'feminance and something else different too... we are such a delicate complexity, a mental hard-drive programming of computer or clock-work intricacy by which God has made us! And locked back somewhere in the archives of genetic history, is our key!

18

Visited the East Bay today, to the Bancroft's temporary location while the library on campus is undergoing a drastic retrofit, which will last 3 years. Hope it survives all the shaken' & quaken' yet to arrive! Am delivering the stuff mentioned—via a metal roll cart, there's so much.... Out the window of the Bart train look at a nostalgic sight ... Our old grim stone cement walled hotel. Freeways cuts air at distance so that just a slice of it is visible, grey cornice that fronts on Oakland's 14th street on Jefferson, 2 blocks below Broadway ... Life was there was hard. Warm bodies, her & me in bed; a sagging hotel mattress with old cigarette burns------had only the dream of my art, her of her dance & so little security at my minimum wage jobs. Now have a permanent income & have established much in this new studio in a good neighborhood—yet am alone. Back then had 2 warm bodies, a dream, few scruffy possessions, and the misty future.... Oh. Want to thank you Husky and Mew--- for both of you accompanying me as long as you could hold on. That meant each going into illness & pain, before we made the decision to release you. Thank you for holding me in your love. Your grasp on this earth was very strong (16, 17 years apiece). What will I feel at the hour of my death?

> *Hail Mary full of Grace,*
> *God is with you,*
> *Blessed are you among women.*
> *Blessed is the fruit of your womb, Jesus.*

Did I get a few of the things I wanted? Have I achieved my rights? Friends whom I've made, will they hold my soul between their human hands? Will they miss me after I am released from this earth?

Well, these days California is being sunny, but not too hot. A whiff in the air of long-ago times. Sun drenched summers, barbeque picnics, soda pop, watermelon, '50's hit music soul station remember, can taste it in my mind. For instant stirring in the air it's just like home. Those time won't come back again. I existed in a totally black life then thru the 1940's. '50's then beginning 1960 began to escape from it into the racially mixed artist areas of Hyde Park, Near North Side, Greenwich Village.

Down in the TL there's grime, dirt, and as curtains of a street-front rented room are fluttering in a breeze I see the same sofabed pushed aside against a wall like I did to make more painting space. I well remember the poor days, everlasting and onstretching, with pencil and paper, easel and brushes, typewriter ribbons and stamps to mail out a hundred solicitations which all received NO, but am proud of my work, have overcome and actually get a few sales per month!

Where the dream lives, the people prosper. At least in their hearts.

I should not hear one single clink of a tin can in my garbage can, because am now turning all the empties into flowerpots. That's right. Using a great gold mine, two bins of found earth in humongous planters wheeled home in the dead of night after a terrific windstorm dislodged them from a fancy deluxe hotel lobby. Cuttings from friend's plants. (Rosa Salazar.) Surreptitious 'home-birth deliveries' of minor shoots. Seeds of stuff. Potatoes purchased from the supermarket set in water to root.

Me and Doctor Sam discuss our respective vocations over coffee at STARFUCKS after a Chinese food dinner on Polk Street, & browsing in a going-out of business bookstore (where purchased retrospects of Picasso, O'Keefe and Masaccio-- for $5.70!). We speak of in-the-closet polticos who veto gay marriage bills. But I will not criticize politicians, lawyers who lead double lives---evading prying eyes of their clientele and constituents. I have chosen a life work that has the least restraints imposed upon it from without--- how else can a creative spirit truly be just that? Artistes are notoriously iconoclasts, scandalous, doing stuff, which embarrasses their families and gets them run out of town.

My God, I am going to quote this---its taken from an anarchist pamphlet published in Andalusia, I found it in that book about Picasso by John Berger ('65, Pantheon Press) who lifted it originally from a quote in Spanish Labyrinth by Gerald Brenan (Cambridge University Press 1945). By an unnamed radical, 1900'rds:

> **On this planet there is infinite accumulations of riches, which, without monopoly, are enough to assure the happiness of all human beings. We all of us have the right to well-being and when Anarchy comes in, we shall every one of us take from the common store whatever we need: (men), without distinction, will be happy: love will be the only law in social relations!**

So can you believe the Anarchists of the distant past, a century ago were speaking the same language as us today? — That of revolution!

Terra Viva! Young punks of Mexico City are starting gardens on top of cleared-out garbage dumps. Their feverish call is for punks to plant this permavegitation around the world! The People must abandon the errant ways of plasticized civilization and go foreword into a higher degree of civilized integration of nature back into life, once again. Just like in the beginning, when we lived exclusively on the land, dwelled in tribes, and were closer to God. Closer to The Garden. A radical re-integration of

20

nature, science, progress, into societies advanced civilizations, and lifestyle. With regard for Sea Turtles, Elephants, and all living beings. Instead of murder, genocide, and brutality wrecked against the lower life forms. Whose revenge against us has been mad cow disease, obesity & a few other strange virus's.

Terra Viva! punks look the same as punks worldwide with wild pink/lime-green/chartruse/blu/violet hair, piercings, tattoos, sawed off slacks, safety pinned clothes. They are young, fierce, idealistic.

***

Well, must tell my ongoing fantasy ever since that day a few weeks past when finishing up PASSAGE, as noted had found fortuitously upon 2 separate days, looking into abandon cartons of books put out on the street first Il Nuovo Dizionario Inglese Garzanti (an Italian-American dictionary) AND, next, a travel book written in 1965 about Venice! So, its been Venice in wake-dreams ever since.... (Hence the Masaccio). Perusing Italy travel books at Borders Free Reading Room. If I win big at Indian gaming, $12,000 or more, we're on our way! I'll pay for Laura, Dalila, and me, Semi-Non Professor Turnip and Dr. Sam. Would pay a friend of Dalora's to watch our brood of animals and plants, and be gone 1 month! Of course Sam couldn't stay that long being a doctor and everybody else would loose their jobs... *Oh well...* Venice has many streets which are actually canals and not solid at all (except if they freeze over to ice in winter)... how romantic. It has a low crime rate, because it's too difficult for thieves to escape! There's a canal or bridge blocking nearly every turn! Maybe there are sail-by shootings, don't know, but a drive-by shooter couldn't get further then a couple of blocks on a paved street before they'd have to leap out of their car to cross some footbridge or jump into a canal and swim for dear life!

Streets of heaven are paved with gold so they say—for my whole lifetime 60 years I've heard that refrain—which means that the material, the cheapest the most ill-considered, that is valued the least, is what the Saints use to walk on Up There—where as here on earth, Gold is all we think about! If earth streets were made of it, folks would be out frantically cracking apart the roads with jackhammers, striking it with pick axes, digging frantically with shovels, prying chunks of gold out of the street with their fingernails till their fingers wore off into stumps of blood and they still wouldn't stop! —I go on and on!

Dear Children I hope these books are something all of you can use—use not simply in the manner which was suggested that poor recluse Henry Darger might have indulged himself in his own private art collection, (self illustrated by drawing, painting, and collage of magazine cutouts found by scavenging trashbins at night); but also to uplift and to inspire you, and to illustrate agappi--- world love-- for all creatures from the sea turtles to the butterfly to the mother orangutan who looks down with love at her newborn baby orangutan cradled in her arms. To imbue the hardened hearts of the children of this world with greater love. To put you in touch with spirituality as a constant reminder.

God has given each one of Her/His creatures a voice. A throat. A sound issuing out of a mouth. All animals have a voice. Here is mine:

Grey fluff feathers
merging shimmery haze.
Sleek of wing,
Pink feet,
one, hobbles briskly;
two crippled, gnarled nubs.
Pigeons dine at curbside
Chinese rice,
spilled out of a white carton
decorated with red dragons.
Stuff your beaks!
Stuff your beaks!
Stuff them full my Birds!
Of your lucky largess
in gratitude!

On the corner of Post & Polk; midway down the block world-famous Divas, spawn of the now-gone tavern the Motherload, home of tranny hookers, transwoman shows, and general fun hangout for a sector of our trans/queer demimonde some artistic diva has tied a long purple scarf which blows in the breeze to summon in the trans-starved wayfarer, to call back all sistas lost at sea. For a sea change. *Read: Calling tricks. Just got out of jail. To have a drink among friends.* As the small stocky Transman stomped wearly up the incline, his heavy sack of art upon his back he thought thus: 'Oh again wish there was more love between us brothers and you sisters.' Well, isn't that the way of this human race anyway? Dividedness is a certain commonality among our species.

Well saw Rosa Salazar today on a short pitstop at the Sex Shoppe. She was busy with her catalogues, her bespeckled face stuck inside lace & bondage.

Couldn't bother to talk. Recoiled at my touch upon her bare golden tan shoulder. Again I will abandon the pursuit of this crazy, beautiful, temperamental tranny girl. It's a lost cause. She don't think of me as a man, just a Transman. She wants raw dick on the hoof! AND, get this! She don't want that dick inside her new pussy, no! Mami wants it up her original pussy—her ass hole! That manpussy she's been fucken' with for 35 years! She takes 8 or 9 juicy inches of cock! Why 'in de asse?' Because it pounds her prostrate gland, which she greedily relishes! The male prostate gland, its theorized has a corresponding site within the biological born female body—but inside the vagina. The "G' Spot. Stimulation of this leads to female ejaculation as well as orgasm. However, Mami's new pussy sadly does not come equipped with this spot, so, the old Prostate will just have to do!

Red's little flirtation with the buxom senorita has little hope of ever flowering into a romance worthy of being novel-length...

Although her hard work in life and diligent self-betterment had availed her of a vagaplasty; XXXX still had a big dick; she carried it right between her ears, in her head. Male thinking. No, this is not another character of whom I'm speaking, but yes it's our beautiful Mami Rosa with whom you are familiar! Sex change women are not always de facto woman-identified, nor feminists. And many, if not most remain in an all-male world as much as possible. Preferring male-born individuals for companions, lovers, and compatriots. If they really wanted to be like women they'd try to be around them. But something about a true 'fish' they internally find repelling. Problem is, some of their male lovers are no longer accessible—as the key to those old boyfriends hearts and beds is for the woman to possess a biological dick between her legs he can grope or fantasize about while giving her pussy butt a good pounding with his own dick. Also, their poorer sisters who cannot afford SRS may be so intimidated by the presence of their friend, The Queen, who now sits upon her Throne of gender perfection, that they can't stand to be around her! Find it too threatening! So the bewildered new woman may suffer loss of old friendships as well. The objective of the antiquated Harry Benjamin Standards Of Care was that such new females should go out into the world fearlessly as women, assuming a totally new identity in some new city where no one knows them and blend into the scenery there among normals, which mostly doesn't happen. Many girls (and boys) still wind up eventually being attached to the trans demi-mode in some way.

Speaking of men, emotions and differences, must know about men, men cannot cry. Women accuse men of holding back tears, to gain power by not showing their emotions as if it was totally voluntary occurrence,

Men on testosterone can't cry. Do you know how hard it is to really keep from crying? Men don't 'fight back the tears'—that is something which is visible (a bit of water in the corner of an eye, a watery look a gritted expression)--- the tears just aren't there! My greatest release was to be able to cry when sad, depressed, in despair, when in sympathy for someone else's problems! What a cleansing of soul! Once on testosterone I noticed my ability to cry vanished within a month or less. Me who use to break down and cry several times per day, or every other day! Fully. Deeply. Heart wrenchingly.

***

'Wal, let me tell yuh! Speaking of painful inclines and huge sacks of art ... I rather have my life be a gradual incline and no decline whatsoever— except in old age physicality which is inevitable--- but not my spirit, my art, nor my popularity, nor my love, nor my friendships, nor my prayers to the Creator! Hope they increase with fire! By the way...I really don't know God, I know God is good and God is great and people struggle a lifetime to know God, but I don't really know more then that... I pray, I pray often for what is right for me, for better things to come of my life and then I'm waiting for an answer. Just like everyone.

Wiggle your toes in appreciation of God!
For She is great!

Yuh know, looking back at some of this stuff just written, see all the foolish daydreams, which will soon melt away, into the mist.... Like Venice.... Well, just as long as my higher values don't die! My great inspirations!

Gonna come a time when God is gonna come for us and take back our immortal soul with Her, or Him back to heaven. Its Gods soul who S/He gives to us, and one day She takes it back. Its gonna happen to all of us. People don't talk about that in the political field but they should because its just as much a fact of life as water, earth, wind and fire. The soul--and its ascent after this life on earth is done. Then we enter into a new dimension. Che Guverra got assassinated--at the moment of his death his soul soared beyond radical politics and was reclaimed by Creator. Mao Tse-tung, the great Chinese leader who liberated women, and brought education to the masses while liberating the poorest peasants from under rulers economic yoke.... All of them had to die and all of them have souls & spirits which don't expire with the body but which travel on--so this needs to be mentioned from time to time in political circles as well as holy temples and

24

mystic religious places. It's the final end of the human phase of our souls dispensation.

For the second time this week; 3rd in 5 weeks, have done an interview for a reporter re: ftm transition. Bolstered my ego. Also it gave me an opportunity to wander into the past with memories ordinarily would not have had. The 2nd interview, radio, for KQED got my voice live answering direct questions about personal transition how it affected me; relationships etc. The first was fellow Transman Marty's film; similar, more centered around the nature of our trans community and how it has evolved. During the 3rd, a reporter gathering data for a proposed article to the Bay Guardian asked who were the first transsexuals I remember seeing before taking the plunge myself and this really got my mental wheels spinning because had to push memory further and further back, realizing each successive memory actually wasn't the first, and, the one before it hadn't truly been the actual first sightings, etc...and the list grew greater the further back I probed my memory.... the shocking ftm on hormones who was explained to me in private by his ex-girlfriend; about the procedure he'd done....guys who subsequently left the community and started new lives—so this started me thinking.... back even further then that. Don't forget all this time thru the 50's, 60's, 70's, 80's, I'd been dwelling in ignorance, in the allusion I was a butch dike. Fini! End of the line! When actually I'd been impersonating a man all that time. Some of us not yet realized transsexuals were more passable into gay society or lesbian, and there we perched, in our dis-ease. So let me tell you the way it was 'back in the day' in the gay clubs there would always be this strange fringe element lurking slightly apart and not among the crowds of gay women & men, all the non-gay hangers-on. Cootchie-cootchie mans, sneaky voyeurs, middleaged tricks, etc. Plus there was these ultra radical freaks who went to the very few social havens they knew, the clubs of their 'cousins' the gays. These strange creatures only meeting place was a gangster run tavern, alleys, slum or special bohemian streets, or afterhours dive. They'd be so far gone weird we normal gays shuddered at the sight of them! We mocked, jeered, pointed our fingers at them behind their backs, as if they couldn't hear us! Half women's apparel, half men's; lopsided wigs, ill-fitting men's suits but not doing this as a lesbian or a gay, but actually trying to BE the sex they sadly weren't born. Realize now these monsters were transsexuals set out of time with no place.

There's an on-going list of them in many of my old books. (See STORIES FROM THE DANCE OF LIFE Vol. 3, the end piece. Also some of the novels from that time like HO STROLL'S depiction of the black gay club Soulville.

Day Comes To Ten Thousand Studio Rooms
  Poetry by Red Jordan Arobateau

Day comes to ten thousand studio rooms.

The bell, which rings summoning humans, cries out.
BBBRRRRRRRRINNNNNNNHHHHG!
The enormous cat is dislodged from place
under his armpit, amid the blankets & sheets.

He brushed his head like you would shine a shoe,
 and out he went.

Upon another days journey over this blue planet.

The tip of San Francisco, Chinatown, is surrounded by
 water; blue. @ X of Sacramento/Mason can see down
 both streets in both directions to lands end, —water,
 curve of the peninsula where the city sits. Look down
 the 2 separate streets to the water! Water! Blue!
 While walking up Sacramento to the top, Huntington
 Park, stop @ Tortoises fountain. See the spooky
 carousal children at play in bronze circa 1942,
 a year before his birth.

& he goes round about the town
upon various and sundry errands
of by now forgotten meaning.

A pigeon spins whirling, one wing upraised. Shows
 its soft white body down; it spins two erratic
 circles in succession, POP!
 Sheds a feather. Fluffs up,
then upon two pink/red feet
proceeds upon its way.

A feather for her hat!

She murmurs softly:
Drink greedily my birds!
Drink greedily the water

I've poured out for you
into the crevices.
Let your throats warble!
Drink great gulps
of life!

"I'm sick"
cries a homeless man covered by a blue blanket
laying in the street.
"I'M SICK."
He means look at me somebody!
Can somebody help me?
Take away the pain!

> *It was a magical time,*
> *& so uncertain.....*

Jours sans. (Days without.) No matter! Despite
poverty, loneliness, and non-success follow Creator
Children—it is Her way, which is best! Even if it be
living humbly and simply in a trailer park. (Nowhere to
rent, no where to dance, no where to paint, no where
to write, no where to live in San Francisco.) Rather
then a mansion on the hill built off somebody else's
mistakes. Live with your conscious clear!
Free in Her Arms!

Like radical author Jessica Mitford (not a single
biography; only one book in print today).
I will write/paint my expressions & they will BE until
the shroud of time covers them up.

***

Photocopy another page.
At end of day with the janitor.
Closing up at Trans Space. Downstairs, outside, night
has fallen; the pavement is sparkling with some
infinitesimal tiny specks of silver rock so the street
has glitter---fitting for a clientele of divas (many of
them fallen stars themselves).

Night comes again to ten thousand studio rooms.

Setting the stage for his masturbations he typed the following on his minor computer (to be printed out later on the major one):

She was stretched out on a dais, clothes in disarray revealing her nakedness. His penis was hard and hot and slips easily into her tight vagina, plunging up to his balls. He moaned. Great was his enjoyment of her. He had pulled out her enormous breasts from under her brazier, under her half-open disarrayed silk blouse. He licked and stroked her titties nursing greedily on her taut nipples. He rose over her now pumping his turgid organ inside her pussy as she lay beneath him, open, receiving his fucking. He rose and fell over her stroking and moaning, petting and sucking her big luscious breasts.

This is pornography and a welcome addition to JOURNEY. This sex act can be simulated by Transmen everywhere and is every day during their acts of copulation. But let us not dwell on the least of the bodily functions! Let us drop the subject and move on to more uplifted topics! (This sudden 'dropping of the subject' is reminiscent of the lover who, even during the moments of ecstasy as his hips are pumping involuntarily, chest heaving breath, still manages somehow, by wildly thrashing, to throw off the paraphernalia of his stimulation towards that height! ---The falsies! Tears off his frilly nightgown! Kicks off his golden backless strapless high heel pumps! So that he might instantly revert once again to a somber masculinity-- after the fun is done! How necessary this is so that he might fully enjoy the remainder of the ecstatic orgasmic crest, as a man once again, his true self!) So! What follows the smut? A Christian Homily? A didactic political diatribe? No, since this is a sort of my diary, what follows is somewhat personal.... A brief revelation—who is it I dare not name! S/he has surfaced in my dreams! Three times so far! Heshe is sinister; gazing half behind the mirror in kitchen, larger, sturdier in nondescript clothes covering him, obscuring her, twisting a moustache of one who is sinister or mysterious; who posses a plot for self purpose which may well be used against others to achieve what s/he wants. S/he offers a cash dollerbill of some increment, -- but it is printed green and perfect only on one side, the other is blank! Portending that he-she will pretend to give, but will only take! A vision of the Florida Keys on a map and money. The key to him/her is money and little else. Whatever other truly decent emotions feelings s/he possesses, money is key.

Later on this subject. I've begun to pray against it already!

***

God is great and God is good, and before the rise of advanced civilizations who left records chiseled into stone; dead languages scribed on papyrus scrolls; organized communities, city states with priests, shamans; there existed small tribal groups of early humanbeings who worshiped God without formalized religion, without language, nor words even, who raised their heads to the sky and hearts up within them, and hands outstretched to something above-- they called upon this Being who had created them (tho they didn't know it) this Being who made their heavens and their earth from the beginning. These early humans are with Creator right now in Paradise! They weren't numbered in any particular book of records, took no sacred oaths of allegiance, they did not plead the Blood of the Lamb--a very sophisticated concept of redemption of sin--nor did they call upon Diana, Allah, Buddha, Jesus, Muhammad, Vishnu, Great Mother, Goddess or God by any other name, these early ones without language or words or religious creed. All this established protocol which we need so much has evolved over 78,000 years. There was no special numbered group who would make it to heaven, no chosen peoples back then. God was God then, God is God now. God worked Her dramatic unfolding of the human pageant, the miraculous unfolding of heavens and earth. And we need just praise Her by any means or names, and forget about just who is 'getting into heaven' and who isn't! Or what name must be invoked! Or what tradition honored! One belief done in faith, love, devotion, and prayer is the same as the next! And remember those gurus, priests, ministers, mullahs, those clerics whose pompous titles evolved out of the masses of common peoples blind belief, those appointed religious leaders sometimes, they're having gaining a high position in that spiritual institution has little or nothing to do with having faith at all but what text one memorizes and how one maneuvers themselves among their peers towards the avenues of power. Some great unfeeling men who are essentially atheists have reigned from the papacy I'm sure, as well as sacrosanct thrones of many many other religious dispensations; passing down edicts, rules, restrictions upon the heads of the common believers often to their detriment, but above all for their social control.

Today one can see works of a great diversity of religions where cosmopolitanism has spread them to all corners of this globe. Wherever cities and towns are inhabited by many diverse types and cultures and practices of people, so that a person in need of a speaking to Creator, just might conveniently duck into any passing place of worship they pass, kneel down (in fact, or in mind-- while sitting sedately on a church pew or chair) or knell on a floor mat, depending on which brand of holy place it is and cast up their requests to the Divine Being in any possible way, language, or formal practice as they are in during that time! And God will answer for God is a miracle worker!

**Great is My loneliness
for My lost sheep.**

Creator gives us these words, so we will be not clueless on the erratic path
stumbled thru wildly like the grace-less, uneducated ignorant masses
wielding a caveman club; ignorance. Furthermore regarding another sin
(while we are on the subject) greed—plain & simple not all our ills can be
blamed on advancing Korporate Mega-Kapitlaism. (That overworked point)
Its only human nature. It's in all of us... Greed, Ignorance, & the
aforementioned Lust! Furthermore there is the everpresent sin of
prostitution to material wealth; the obsession for possessing stuff! That line
between sanity, too real & raw, and insane infatuation with material objects.
Fine satin dresses vs. the progress of the spirit. Journey to the soul thru all
the layers of crap!

> A triangular piece of pizza,
> yellow, red, beige
> captured under a garbage can lid.
> Liberate it dear children!
> Toss it to the sidewalk!
> Dine birds! Dine!
> Feast on the engorgement of the human race
> overstuffing itself
> in their hungry sorrows.
> Dine!
> Then fly!
> Fly on your newfound strength!

Like Darger, Van Gogh, Proust, I'm ready to open up my treasure of
unknown art to the world! Where will come the break thru? The
illumination? The discoverer? From what direction does the messenger
ride?

God gives a person a head start that's all talent is, —or genius. Anybody
who works hard enough is gonna at least become an OK artist. Geniuses are
special constructs. But most anybody can produce something of merit if
they dedicate themselves wholeheartedly to the task!

There it is almost done, liberated from obscurity all 22 volumes of ancient &
forgotten lore written in my '30's; encapsulated into the Juvenilia Series.
However a blow of adversity is struck! Now the policy against my use of
the Trans Space copy machine has escalated! The door to the location of the
machine is locked. The staff person who unlocks the door for me must

30

stand guard counting EACH COPY spitting out of the machine—insuring it does not exceed 15! AGGGGGURRAHHH! Thank God my Re Xerox project is almost **Done!** Only 4 more books to go, but all of them double length—originally in 2 volumes each. However a new catastrophe awaits! Next day wearily the Transman Mounts the stairs to the infamous 2nd floor Trans Center, to be greeted by a photocopy CODE! Which means from now on all his copies will be **counted mechanically by the machine!** The high-quantity press is done! Fini! Thank Goddess he finished most of it beforehand! Now as far as making any money off this Re-Photocopying project, it may take decades! So it's always a labor of love, not profit, must say in my defense! For I might peddle only 2 books per year!

Transman Red glanced thru the ancient pages of the old stuff, a puzzling look upon his sweaty yellow face. Stuff he did at crucial times of change or upheaval in his life seem raw & pure and not as manufactured. I.e. books written immediately around his Sex Change; (STREET OF DREAMS, DOING IT FOR THE MISTRESS, AUTUMN CHANGES) circa 1998; HOW'S MARS---my first trip alone to New York seeking a gay world, 1963. Must say, am having a blast reading thru these ancient books—my Juvenilia!

2.
Attended shul tonight—Friday services—for the first time in awhile, and truly felt close to Creator. Enjoyed the service, and find am beginning to be able to stutter thru a few of the Hebrew hymns by memory. The food was appreciated afterwards, as was the hospitality. Realize I've missed this place, and intend to come back more frequently. Oh by the way, I forgot to add Rabbi, to my list of ministers, mullahs, priests, gurus, etc., while denouncing them all in the last pages! Equal opportunity! At library got an excellent book about the Donner Pass Party by a man called Stewart. A book for its author to be proud of. A book is a friend! Am just hanging in there for now, over this long 3 day 'Columbus Day' holiday—with precious little to do with self, and thus alone. Not fun. Must work to stay positive and not give way to the blues. Need a girlfriend!

> All the hope that remained was
> faint clouds of smoke
> from chimneys in the distant horizon.

'Thank goodness for my birds who are chortling upon me now', he thought, even as he wrote it. 'And for Little...' (huge) ... 'Mr. Fluffy, curled up in the bathroom sink sleeping, awaiting release from cat-jail when the feathered pets are returned to the safety of their home...' (cage) ... 'which

31

they truly love.' Everybody loves a happy home. All Gods creatures. Oh, an astounding happening at shule, a Jewish member has returned from a trip to Israel where he/she witnessed the destruction along the Gaza strip and was so moved that he wound up marching in a Palestinian Liberation parade in protest to Zionism! S/he proclaimed her beliefs from the bema (pulpit, Christians) to a hushed and raptly attentive congregation. Heavy stuff. Transman Red sat in a pew stroking his beard, gazing pensively as he/she told his story to us. Closing with the sukat parable---you know, the one about building a fragile house, which easily blows away, but not worrying about this because this is how our lives are here on this earth! Fragile, and the things we struggle for so long so easily blown away .... However, this does not necessarily mean powerlessness, not at all.....

It's surprising how many such fragile things can have such a strong even stronger effect then things attempted by force. Not by muscle or might. On the affluent upper Fillmore Street a grey head woman nods politely at me— knows me from my volunteering at the abandon dog clinic--- now I can't be seen hollering BITCHES and MUTHAFUCKERS! at the top of my to somebody at the bus stop who makes me mad. She might witness it! My father, too, was the first great reason. I lived up to his expectations, which was very basic. Don't just don't fall and get in trouble! (Meaning jail or drugs or something awful.) His wish was not 'be a great genius or university professor or a person of social affluence'—some impossible goal. A testimony about my Dad.

PS. As much as possible Dad tried to follow his heavenly beliefs...

***

Ever since their masculine beginnings, man-dikes have secretly looked at other butches & compared themselves, ranking on the masculine scale. Am I as much a man as her? Do I dress harder? Am I as stockily built? Is my chest flattened out enough? --Like hers? --Relentlessly, and cruelly comparing themselves. Gee look at that butch! She stood up and won the fight! --- While I ran away from it! Men do this. So when all begin to see the irrefutable, non-ignorable results of others transitioning-- which won't be ignored-- that new men are doing with their bodies it made any red-blooded butch eat their hearts out in tortured envy. Realizing dimly, for maybe the first time that we could do it too. Their strong, sinuous physiques, their fledgling beards, gruff voices, how easy they jockeyed with each other in public places—like wild teenage boys fired by their new found nuts-- with impunity, before the eyes of straight lookers on, who expect this behavior of boys—something we'd only been before allowed to do safely in private gatherings. Of course we ate their hearts out until we couldn't take it

32

& finally stepped on board the testosterone wagon… The ultimate perversion is when we go deep against into our own inner standard of what is right for us; when we bow, conforming to a scowling society who would, if able decide for us our own rules of lust!

***

The larger the baggage the smaller the soul. Steamer trunks & luggage & bags & baggage preoccupation. The bible says God will send you there. God will equip you. Take only food and clothing for two days change upon your journey. God will furnish the rest. Ironic, if at the later part of my life I ascend into a more spiritual plane; write about Saintly stuff openly, instead of disguising it, or tacking it on in back pages of already written novels, 'Sermons' I'd wrote giving you my philosophy like a pinch of salt to flavor the stew of stuff—pornography, plot, fabulous dialogue, etc, what if it becomes the primary thing? Well this world is waiting for help at every turn! It needs a spiritual viewpoint whenever possible, and people will indeed listen, just for a moment you'll have their ear!

***

& there it was, the moon rising from outer space beyond the earths crust; moon, majestic, ominous, threatening, stormy, it rose swiftly illustrating the slow turning of the world. A homeless woman secures her blankets in a tree while she's out forging for food--- in the garbage cans-- while richer tourists vacation in $100 per day hotel rooms which come with free continental breakfasts. We need a political jab or two to keep the world on its toes, moving in humane directions, but also practical guidelines for self-defense of person, home & nation. So I'll make a another rant right here—but this one disguised in a poetic coat.

A funland carnival
of affluence;
4 sailors in uniform black/white
amid 100 tourists.
2 army commanders show off stars/stripes;
are a class apart; they appraise
the fine establishments;
"I hear that place's an excellent restaurant."
This is the military,
 which enforces the affluence.
I see the mighty arches they make.

The truth is not here.
---That is all locked, deep

33

inside the monastery of contemplation.

The rich men's club on Sacramento and Mason gazes at Tortoise Fountain
Park from half lidded eyes.
All brains, wealth up inside that old rock fortress. Homeless sleep in the
park outside.
Grace Cathedrals tenants toss
intermediate prayers across to
Heaven where we will go someday.

> *The city sinks down again*
> *On both sides of this green square.*

2 things remember children,
resist! You resist and run
with all possible strength
towards victory!
SMASH THE MACHINE!
Struggle always.
 Follow your heavenly beliefs!

***

Transman stopped a moment from a fixed routine to contemplate his artistic
position. It was uncertain. Unlike years of dedication to a purpose
unchanging but for titles he wrote & increasing maturation of style. He had
broken off novel writing 2 years back, solely devoted his energies to the
different journals & plays, laboring over typewriter/computer while his birds
clucked/chortled upon his shoulders burning the midnight oil. The Re-
Photocopy Series was all but done. He truly was at a crossroads! This is
what he'd actually written in the Authors Foreword upon the last book,
Boogie Nights:

> *Think of his-her early decision at the crossroads of life, weather to*
> *pursue art; writing & painting, upstairs in those gutted-out rooms,*
> *or to cross over some invisible divide, going instead up a more*
> *secure well-paved path of a Civil Servant, and it's affects on my*
> *lack of fortunes today—but, a wealth of art! Think of the time of*
> *choices, and of risk, of expending energy towards some uncertain*
> *future! Well, this series-reprinting machine is winding down, and*
> *once again finds the artist at his hour of decision—to settle back*
> *down into painting once again along with continuing to write? To*
> *pickup brush, tubes of oil, red, yellow, green, blue? Holding a*
> *blank canvass, ready, the easel is waiting!*

It was now he realized he'd have to pick up the brush & oils once more---
while he was still able---if he was going to do it at all! Also it occurred to
him those 2 promised plays were yet undone... Maybe if I think about
Venice again, water canals, gondolas, boats, foreign aromas, dining with
friends in small cafes on platters of spicy Venetian food, picking up pallet,
smock, brushes, colors, and being a fine arts oil painter it will all come true!

Today Acorn bookstore on Polk Strassa is finally closing—after an
extension of one week from the date they planned. Got a Frans Hals folio
for 65 cents. Italian tenor emotes a dramatic aria piped into this vast,
emptied space. The shelves all gone, but for a few, which loom, leaning
against a wall waiting to be transported out by the highest bidder. And
books are stacked everywhere over the floor.

Must confess for the last year or so a gnawing pang has nagged me from
back corners of my mind, that having abandon the genre of the novel, (last
endeavor being STAGE DOOR, circa 2003)--- a fiction form, & putting in
its place the more easy-to-do journal/diary, that I'm cheating myself, and the
public, cutting short my abilities, plus limiting my range of expression....
Well this AUTUMN CHANGES stuff is easier to do! I attempted to
interject a brief whisper of a novel into PASSAGE with that Rondo stuff
which was excellent, spine tingling! A Murder Mystery! And now, it's
back! Come back strong! The yen! In fact a novel, is beginning to churn,
ruminate, asserting itself into my daily work routine! However, now am
also planning to return to oil painting as well! How in hell can I possibly
switch from journal to novel and oil painting, (not to mention finishing up
the two infernal plays) plus the stresses of daily necessity to procure food,
scrape up rent monies, plus try to have a social life! So as not to be so
godforsaken lonely! How can my tenuous artistic elasticity & stamina
possibly take on the discipline of:
1. Art
2. The structure & planning a novel takes.
3. Venting my daily observations, which have now become so
   necessary to me? In a Journal?

Maybe I will write a novel—combined with a Journal—a novel/journal!
Taking all the liberty in the world! A domain where verse can be inserted,
dreams recorded, my everyday political rants printed out, ---- combined with
my forte—fiction! All under one binding & title! It will flow much easier!
Then rushing back & forth from book to book. Thank Creator that I have
now switched to computer, much easier to use then oldfashion typewriter;
its speeded up.

I've been writing a long long time but at some point I also became a publication company, don't quite remember what date, but its reflected on my earliest chapbooks of poetry COME TO THE BLACK MARKET, that early '70's genre ...... I am leaving these words behind Dear Children so that you might understand more about my times, and be able to catalogue my art... Remember, we are all food for some other being. Green plants grow to become food to lower animals. Lower animals for greater. Humans are food for subsequent generations--their own daughters & sons feed off of them.... You are my dinner Dear Children. And I am food ..... I am food for you.

Chapter 3.

As he got near the end of his journey he had reached the outer fringe of The City.

For all its progress still, there were open fields around this bigger city of empire, which being 2 miles across & 5 miles in length meant its circumference was approximately 35 miles; the most developed part of which was under sea level.

S/he mused crossing the cement & steel easement over some abandon rapid transit rails twisted and rusting from yesteryear, and a gully clogged with debris, to one of the smaller cheep development cluster of prefab pods assembled in a gigantic jigsaw about 40 stories high, half a city block wide—had their been blocks out in this area. A cheap construct built out on the fringes. Hadn't the poet Red stated something about... the true believer in freedom, the radical, hungry for change.... How......

> *They'd immediately retreat back out*
> *into the cold, wide open spaces*
> *Of ultimate freedom.*

The country. ----There was a sense of peace in the undeveloped areas around The Unity's bigger cities.... but this was deceptive. If true revolution was to be found it was more likely to be in the gulches and valleys of the modern created steel and glass empire itself. In its immense labyrinth of byways and cubicles, not in the more wide-open sparsely inhabited countryside's, which was easy to scrutinize. Any anomalism was easier to spot. But hadn't it always been that way? Back in the ancient times, even then, poets and artists; free thinkers, anarchists, radicals, free women not designed for the yoke/servitude of marriage had fled their families, their small town gossips with waggling tongues, and pointing fingers?

Going down in a crate-like elevator, after pressing a blue light, indicating his destination was to reach a depth of 20 stories; he-she navigated a series of white industrial solar paneled corridors intermittently set with window breaks. Outside thru the thick bulletproof glass could be seen the structures bare steel girders of its skeleton; beyond that, by a few yards the view came to a dead stop at cement colored reinforcing walls, which held back a huge mega-ton press of subterranean earth. Passed a multitude of prefab pods. He entered into a particular unit, prepared to check in with his-her identification to be turned in perfunctorily to the Records of Gatherings Commission. (According to the statutes, 'no meeting of over 2 citizens will be held in Utopia without an attendance role, purpose of the group, location and date turned into the Commission'.) There at its station was greeted by an antiquated robot-- basically a computer on wheels with minor naive intuitive capability--- and was asked to give his name—any name. Preferable not his true name, but the same name he always used as to eliminate confusion.

H/she entered the room.

"STAR1.VAX!" A friendly voice called.

"Hi." He replied not sure of who had spoken and fell into a seat near the front.

On the board before them was written these words in laser script:

The revolutionary spirit is still alive!

Once he glanced back to the rows behind him to try to see who had spoken to him, but wasn't sure who it was… The voice had come out of the group of 40 or so comrades just taking their seats; opening their book fragments, assembling study notes. Two elegantly dressed women of the transsexual type were in attendance. Of course they looked beautiful. (A Nip and a Tuck is all it took—a lot of nips and tucks—to alter ones birth sex from male to female, or visa versa.) Men like himself were more difficult to spot. Otherwise it was a bland crew in blue work garb, a jumpsuit, of the average proletariat, a few professionals in their white or grey uniforms, some greasy robot mechanics, and outer space techs.

The group had 3 facilitators today. They were strategically stationed at different parts of the solar-lit unit. There was Anderson, Valdez, and Gojenko. Clustered around the latter a crowd was jockeying for position, peering over each other's shoulders. There before Gojenko on his desk was a box of ancient books. He was in the process of carefully removing them. "Red Jordan's Re-Xerox series." Somebody was telling another, in an awed whisper.

Thick stubby peasant fingers with oil under the nails indicated his trade as a mechanic. He gently opened a green covered book and pointed to a phrase in it. Then with a gesture indicated the laser board. To be greeted by 'AHHH!'s' And OHHH's!' As heads turned to look. For there was the statement written out. 50 years later seeing the light of an audience.

Anderson, the doctor, dressed in her customary white lab coat, thin and mild, began speaking even as the crowd was still assembling themselves in their seats. "We will delay our planned discussion of the political climate of the Old Prophets times as he wrote about in his journal. And instead we're going to jump right into that advanced reading of Red's novel STAGE DOOR. Because it contains a very specific *act*, especially after what has just happened, and I bet …" Suddenly a loud cheer from the audience arose and a shuffling of feet, momentarily interrupting Anderson.. A wan smile broke over her narrow face. She bushed a shock of blond hair away from her eyes, and continued. "I bet a lot of you will sympathize with Billy's *act*. Now we dedicate these next hours together to our fallen comrades in the Beneficent Rain Belt Northwest --in the old days a city formerly called", her final word was repeated by a dozen throats; **"Seattle!"**

Today in his banned reading study group they had been scheduled to analyze the journal PASSAGE, by that ancient author. Written half century ago in 2003. And were to have just briefly perused the next of his works on their study guide, this STAGE DOOR novel, for future homework. Of course a whole 30% was missing from this one, and they had had to invent filler between texts written down. One part of that book the authorities hadn't gotten to, to shred, sat reduplicated this afternoon on many comrades desks in its complete form. Probably because it was a greater seller in its time and more copies had been available. It was the 4th section, the books end, in which the hero Billy—a transgender male—takes up his pistol and performs an act of political warfare against the money- grabbing moguls of Empire.

The papers he was given to enjoy---at the cost of a confinement sentence in prison, or worse in a mental institution if he was discovered--- contained these following fragments. They were such a joy to read, and so refreshing after the pabulum drivel spooned out by empires media—Utopia World News--- that no one much noticed if they didn't hold together well, they still made sense. A lot of sense.

Time went by swiftly. Midway thru the class, as they'd been reconstructing this final book of that novel, the group could not help but see an irony. That all hero redhead Billy had struggled for was vengeance upon one of the Capitalist rich realestate moguls--- rich landlords! Something, which their very dynasty, Utopia, had disallowed! --This was a little embarrassing contradiction, one of several, which were libel to crop up between comparisons of generations and dynasties of rule....

Additionally, finally, after a 9 months of readings, his study group had collectively come to recognize several prominent points, which came into amazing divergence with realities of the present day. One, the poor Red had struggled so long, so bitterly against the hard conditions of poverty—a thing unheard today in modern times under The Unity—and had in fact devoted much space in his beautiful written works to the subject of being insecurely housed, having to dine out of public waste receptacles, and being so obsessively concerned over what life would be like for him in a poverty-stricken old age if he didn't become 'famous' or 'discovered' (which was one of his paramount goals, & that he was by no means alone, millions of other Am-Ericans were in similar straits) so all the things they had wanted and lusted after so far back in those dim dusty times had come true!--- But at what a loss!

Freedom is measured to the degree by which you'll compromise.

At last weeks meeting, on the laser board had been written 3 axioms, which he still had treasured, keeping them surreptitiously & dangerously in his illegal study notepad:

> 1. We believe in freedom.
> 2. In this big city many have fallen. & many more will fall. It is a risk we take.
> 3. There must always be a Resistance.

To these Star1.vax had jotted down with the electronic cursor some notes of his own. *Fight against the spread of normalcy, complacency—because it kills. It stifles the true spirit of humanity.*

He thought: 'Yes. Not enough people struggled back in those old times so in empire today, this dumb Unity of Utopia shit, normalcy has got the winning hand. It's already happened. And it does kill... We struggled then & then got killed... We struggle now... like the comrades in the Old Seattle... who've been captured.

Now, under The Unity all struggles are done. Everything is regulated. And anything else, which doesn't fit is killed.'

A hand shot up in the class. Somebody was speaking. "You tryen' to survive, you tryen' to survive. It's the most important thing on earth. Its this mandate. Age old pejoratives. It is the animal laws... keep yourself alive by whatever means possible."

And this is how comrade Star1.vax was doing it. For the sake of his sanity. His soul! Going to these illegal studies. And if that didn't work, he was dreaming about becoming a mole person......

They left the group that afternoon with yet another fragment to cram into their study, to be discussed in a future course:

> Like a torrent in flood our people streamed out.
> Locks, bars, gulags, ghettos, cages, cuffs, a nightmare scattered.
> We trod the long furrow, slaves, sowing in tears.
> A lightening bolt loosed us.
> We tread the long furrow half drunk with joy staggering,
> The golden sheaves in our arms.

From Daniel Berrigan. Hadn't he been a freedom marcher in the old Civil Rights days? Back in mid-century of the 1900'ds? S/he'd flunked the quiz on peace & freedom chronology. Well, he thought piling his fragments carefully into an unobtrusive pack, 'these are my golden sheaves, these pieces...' Pieces of the puzzle.

Empire!

Like a flame in the night, a torch upheld! Proclaiming itself to be the incarnate statutes of Liberty. Yet, slowly the military had infiltrated the U$ government on the interior, just as it was waging total war here & there all over the planet. The military in ties with industrial corporations for profit. Not only had this cartel taken over other nations, but crept into their own democracy as well, like thieves in the night. Yet they weren't in total control then. Nor were they in total control now. It was a balance of powers who constituted The Dictatorship of The Unity of Utopia. And now, still another force to be recognized with had arisen. A new insurgence was at hand. The times had produced unexpected results. Times like this of undo stress—from powers above, within the government's repressive crackdowns of regimes caused cracks in the very system, which supposedly was control-perfect!

When he got home, there was another message waiting on his individual wordhole in the Tely-screen:

People in trouble be strong & weather the storm. Heroes are instantly created. Strength comes in the most amazing packages.

All that week these little prods to the mind would come when you least expected it. Of course they were designed to erase upon the first glimpse. For the sender and the recipient were doing a dance of evasion between the dull slow eyes of the robotic and sometimes human censors. (Not that those dull soldier(ettes), medicated, underpaid and overworked weren't like robots themselves, becoming zombies of the walking dead because of abuses they got during their thankless careers...) A citizen might easily be called in and asked to explain the meaning of such an inflammatory statement.

Switched on the Tely. Dictator Kim Sun dadaistically table-pounding, spewing the daily Utopian message out of his mouth, and there it was! That word again-- Empire! Proclaiming the Unity to be just that-- this fallen thing, this cyclical rise then crash to the ruins of disaster... which the First Great Dictator of Utopia would have known, and which the Second, Kim Sun could have known, or at least his speech writers should have been aware, had they cared to open up the pages of history-- a dead history also a closed book non existent and primarily stamped-out in the great halls of free learning of this, newest in a succession of empires. Star1.vax let his gaze linger on the Tely-image of Dictator Sun; the soft folds of his face, his piggish cruel eyes which glinted firesparks. Idly wondered if he was digitally enhanced? As the figure popped off, to resume the dull memorandums of Utopia Media News there came an excited rehash, 8 citizens of the Beneficent Rain belt Northwest had been apprehended, stripped of their citizenships and were being held in confinement in an unknown location as was protocol. Their case was coming to trial soon in a non-publicized event, and a speedy resolution was promised to the public. Star1.vax stared solemnly at the screen. He would have been surprised how many other citizens of Utopia were also secretly sympathetic with their cause---not that they were involved in any particular action, or study groups or anything whatsoever labeled sabotage by the state, no, they were just in sympathy. Maybe its human nature to perpetually quest to know the unknown, to examine whatever exists anywhere. And anything of variance which pops up on the horizon...

Throughout the week Star1.vak would think back (between the windings of his fantasies about descending underground becoming legally medicated; going down, down, down into a trace-like asphyxia never again to emerge into the sun) imagining stuff about a history so close behind but so well sealed; stuff about that Red guy, a Transman like himself, for instance how happy the artist must have felt on the acceptance of his poems in the New Yorker. A major popular 'zine on every newsstand back in then in the olden times. Now these too were burnt. Scored fragments were all that remained. Even the antique files of that once-esteemed New York publication had been confiscated, and undoubtedly burned along with the rest of the past. The past history of the once empire Am-Erica. Indeed, the history of the planet.

After the amazing blasts of freedom glimpsed in fragments of those long ago diaries (the author just having deceased a decade ago), after being awestruck at the scope of librated speech, spoken ideas and revolutionary thought actually voiced aloud—publicly--even voiced back in that dim era in what they had called Spoken Word poetry events, a modern citizen of this new future 2054 must recognize, something a bit strange. --Between the lines were so many glimpses of common ordinary daily life, of the amazing predicament many Am-Ericans—(that being the name of the state or nation which Red lived, and where he/she Star1.vax now lived, in one of its more radical Cities—which ironically had been cursed with the trite, infantile name of Lovely Hillview Beside The Bay---formerly San Francisco)--- of the impossibility of survival there—because of a phenomenon called **Rents**, which were charged to its tenants, attached by a perverse legalese to each and every housing unit! Yes!

So in the year 2054, housing was no longer an issue—as the world state, Unity of Utopia owned nearly everything & everyone had a fair share of a domicile.

Would the old prophet Red have been satisfied with the current state of affairs? Yes everyone had a place. A pillow on which to rest their head. A freezer unit full of foods. At worst there was temporary housing until new units were made available—of course if you wanted to live with the mole people as deep as 50 stories (up to a mile underground) you'd be placed almost immediately in a luxurious suite with every amenity. A deluxe interior with every possible labor saving hi-tech robot operated device. An underground village of shopping malls, amusement parks. It was a longer wait for a satisfactory unit upstairs, on the surface of the world.

Red had written: '*I know it is hard for people, my loneliness is temporal, theirs, lifelong. Deformed, mentally ill.*' He had written so much about the homeless—a state he was perpetually teetering on just a few hundred dollars away per month from being cast into its pit. And about being alone, and isolated. About being disfranchised, and outcasted.

> *The churches of my faith are shut against us.*
> *The cathedrals are darkened.*
> *Gone stone cold.*
> *Large oaken doors shut.*
> *& the shul is dancing in Dolores street.*
> *Someone whirling with a Torah*
> *clutched in her hands*
> *They dance!*
> *In the joy of Creator*
> *and community.*

The changeover had been gradual & it had been swift. Galleries removed 2,000 paintings with political themes, simultaneously in every major European & Am-Erican city. They cut inflammatory topics for shows off radical media, finally shut the stations down altogether. Just before they shut down all free newspapers in which should have been a warning period of time, they first traced down upcoming interviews with divergent artists & writers about who articles were planned and stopped them cold. Bulldozers roared down, glacially, sweeping away utterly all opposition, by superior force. By the year 2030 all was completed. Motionless stasis in time. Until now. 20 years after the take-over.

Anyway, this Prophet Red's goal had been to stay alive until he reached certain plateaus of his life. —First receiving Social Security at the 62-year age level, and then receiving medical aid from the state, and then Social Security at its final level. This and to be received into the world as a great writer & fine art's oil painter. Ironically tho his first dream of being of world renown had not happened, he died only still having a small, but thankfully constant eclectic audience, his works had not died out but continued to grow, albeit now underground for a different reason, suppression by the authorities; but his second goal to be housed had come to pass more excellently then one could imagine. So much had changed. Scientific advancements in building materials; now new tensile strength atomically engineered on the sub microscopic level provided girders, beams, structures, & frames, even a glass like substance which constituted the domes, of such great weight baring capability and endurance that the size of buildings could quadruple itself without danger of collapse, and were even stronger then the prior 2030 buildings before them. Thus the last years of the old prophets life had seen him joyously housed in such a unit. – Provided by the very System he had so hated & opposed in the early days of the then-forming Unity. A mere 120-story height limit in his past age, now for every single low ranking skyscraper there had grown 500 of the new ones, 500 floors each, all necessary to accommodate the rapidly expanding population--- which was flooding into all the costal areas of the globe. — Since in the midlands, heartlands by now had soaring temperatures 140 to 160 degrees all summer, slightly less in spring & fall; thus huge parts of the continent, and all over planet earth had become uninhabitable to human or animal life. So another reasonable trade-off for its freedom---which endeared the new empire—Utopia--- to its citizens, was that it had been able, by being a totalitarian power that dictated public funds at will, to rise to the occasion of housing each and every citizen in a temperate zone--- meaning many of 500 million who inhabited the continent once called Am-Erica, were now spread out around the entire continents coasts, as and as the middle, its 'heartland' become desolate incendiary wasteland. They had been rescued before those areas had turned into sun-scorched deserts with not a green leaf surviving; The Unity had been able to transport and house its entire chosen citizenry effectively along what had become the new costal regions as rapidly rising waters had covered the old coast lines of prehistory to a 30 foot depth, some to the length of almost an entire state. And above all the many geodesic, tensel-strength enhanced ozone simulator domes, which shielded life from the suns more harmful rays and blocked out residual radiation from the III World Nuclear War which would continued to circulate for 180 thousand more years.

To the old Red having a house and remaining independent was his worldly paradise. Not being forced into the streets to live like homeless vagabond, or die in a isolated coach in some remote trailer park, or sleeping in a car or rotting in a nursing home…. It was his ever-present, fear, so he dwelled on this, but also, at the same time, being a prophet and sighted with greater vision had also known the shallowness of material things.

And, he believed in Revolution. It was for these last two reasons the groups studied his words.

According to Prophet Red: 'Every body, every creature, every soul of God has a place. Where they are in is their place. Some by de facto it's the only place they are able to go. Others have chosen; but chose to be among the fallen because they must abase themselves, loose themselves. Some build great towers by industry, cleverness, & fortitude, amass gold, and prosper in the sight of others. But at some point everybody will look up from this place in finality. Maybe not until their final end. All, questioning why they are here. What they have become. What they have done with their lives.'

So it had come about that Star1.vax was beginning to change.. As the Prophet had said, 'I'm ready for destiny. Today is the first day of my life.'

44

So now too Star1.vax believed as well this was the time of reckoning for him.

3.
Am just preparing the cast emails from my dead play. **E-MAILS CONCERNING RED'S PLAY PORTRAITS FROM A GHETTOIZED POPULATION, FROM THE CASTING CALLS TO THE FINAL END, DEC 2005 TO JULY 2006** for archiving at the Bancroft. Talk about drama! The crème de la crème of drama! This is some juicy stuff! Wonder if the Bancroft will pay me $50 for it! Samples:

--I am writing to inform you all that we finally have a full cast. As you all know we will be welcoming a number of new cast members into our family. Because of this we will have to start working from the top of the play once more.

---She's full of it! I could smell her elitist attitude from a mile away...that's why she got a small role.

--In the interest of professionalism and mutual respect refrain from ranting, accusations, and comparisons among cast members! In general the average adult does not respond well to this type of communication.

--I need to explain my blow-up the other night. If you are not guilty of any of the things I mention, I'm obviously not talking about you!

--Sorry about my attitude! I am not quitting the play, I never quit anything in my life and I will be damned if this is the first!

--Another one bites the dust ladies and gents Unfortunately we have lost Boy/Girl.

--I'm sorry to do this but I am just not at a place in my life right now where I can be a productive member of this cast. Believe me, this was a hard decision for me to make. I'm quitting.

--I am hereby announcing to you that I am no longer a member of the cast.

--At this point I am requesting everyone who is going to quit the play to reply to this group email, so that you can tell everyone. Please don't waste the cast's time by calling in Thursday or the day before the run.

---There will be rehearsal tonight as we planned. Don't worry. I have a solution for everything. ----Red.

Oh what a joke! Ha Ha Ha Ha! —Red thought in hindsight. It was later evening, after his rounds of errands and socializing to the best of his ability outside, he was back home fussing over a paper-laden desk. Well am assembling the latest packet. To be ready to accompany the first volume of my new novel-journal* EMPIRE! as soon as am able to close it. William Faulkner wrote this to Roger S. his publisher asking for a $250 advance: "It's either this or put the novel aside and go whoring again with short stories." Hence my whorings for the Bancroft for this trick ($100) & a few other collectors at $15, $20, $25.* Quick cash to help pay the rent.

* Journoval...?
*A whore will tell you the small-money little customer gets the same thing the big spender does.

He went to visit the abandoned dogs once more:

I've come to mop up the blood
of emotional wounds.
The all-but invisible cuts
that erupt surprisingly.
In barks and wolfs and a fang or claw
 marks on my arm---they are afraid
from how they were mistreated
 in puppyhood.
Come to comfort you furry friend.
 To pray you find a happy home.
I hold you in my embrace

***

Once past golden Gate and Hyde the crazy drug infested insanity starts. Stern & serene governmental buildings; museum, grey stone, the older edifices & modern, steel & glass streamlined are replaced by squat low ugly tenements and cheep small-room hotels. A visible population of hags, winos & jittering dopefiends who stay outdoors and crack dance their monthly welfare stipend away in the disco of the alleys in a single night.

Jittery hypes go cross the street flowing with traffic against the red light. Walk out in the middle between honking speeding cars, hurry to the needle exchange program. A hag babbles, rummaging at the corner gutter. It's a good thing ho's kain't fly--; cause that bitch would be everywhere! Traffic must halt! or run her over. And above all the whitestone cathedral gazes down O'Farrell Street in inspired stone.

The inhabitants respond to the rough demands of the street, which made life so untenable here,--- policy is if you can't take care of yourself the smiles turn to frowns.

An exotic dancer, bare legs; in black tight satin dress steps on her way to strip joint employment. "DRESS LIKE ME! DRESS LIKE ME! YOU AIN'T NO DIFFERENT THEN ME!" Howls she, defensively back at loitering men hassling her while walking from her car to work at the strip club carrying a costume bag. Its 4 pm.

> A lamentation song howls
> thru the night
> Softly & soothing.
> Jungle rhythms
> everconstant
> as a heartbeat.

Naturally the next day finds him at Trans Space. These girls, these girls. Money is their language. They banter on & on about superficial stuff—yet all want love! It is their basic heart-dream. Too bad they seldom get it.

We are very close-knit group---transsexuals—its such a small world all trannys know each other in any particular city if they participate in T-events at all, and aren't afraid to be known. Not stealth nor self-isolating. So we identify with each other, us men. Are even acquainted with our transgender sisters--the mtfs-- but we do inhabit 2 separate spheres. Apart from the occasional romance between ftm/mtf, few penetrate the veil thru into the sisters' real lives. Sadly, occasionally when one does get thru all their feminine allure, false eyelashes, the high-pitched voiced banter and real truly gets to know these new women one might be tempted to exclaim, under all that they're still men! ---There in the problem lies. It's not male behavior, but its not female behavior either. Oh well, won't abandon my fine idea of more love between us.

In this big post-millennium, pre-apocalypse big city one hears conservations like: "I'm not sure what her rent is, *but*...." Because greedy landlord moguls have made gold their God. We are all worshipers of strange & various fruits in our own way. Witness the vain Transwoman/Transman! Here is a brother Transman in love with his new self, moustache, bulging biceps, slim hips, male bulk, who can't distance his vision from the mirror too long.... Small minded people and very selfish. Consuming their focus measuring how many centimeters their dick grew that week. There's other things in life guy!

Well, Dear JOURNEY (title of my journal) am killing lonesome time by going to library, getting on line & books checked out, studying about the Donner party. It's a testament to human endurance & human will.

Whoops! Forgot to mention, was it October 15?—When finally put black typefont to white paper and began to write that science fiction novel! My newest project since finishing up PASSAGE. New creation and tending the garden of my old stuff—which means selling books/art prints in person, checking online sales outlets etc. Also archiving. My salvage of those 22 abandon, dusty file cabinet-bound-books has been running smoothly. Must mention that in front of each title of my Re-Photocopy series is a newly composed Authors Foreword, but they are not synopsis or little book reviews that describe the contents of the work, as one would assume. No. Just what thoughts each triggered when I held the book up in my hands & examined it for the first time. (Some, after 30 years.) Am pleased that it's almost over—results; a master copy cut for each, plus 2 copies, one off to the Bancroft at a reasonable price ($20-35), one to sell at higher price to any public interested whereupon to earn the cash to afford copying fees for any subsequent volumes--- given that this free-copying probably won't last forever and won't be able to do it here. Almost all of them are now done—minus 4...

Black hat upon his head, the stoic poet marched single-mindedly to Trans Space, up the stairs lugging his heavy backpack. Transman Red is in for a sad surprise upon gaining the door to the photocopy room. **AGGGGGGGGGGGGGGUURRRGH!** His Re-Photocopy program has run aground! It has been stricken! Fate, the great despoiler of fortunes has struck again! No more copies left on his 'account' and the director doesn't return for a week to correct the error! He'll keep going however! Pay for it himself! At infernal Kinko's Kurrupt Korprate Kopy center. That money comes out of food & rent however...

He was strong in his radical coat
of arms.

walked on beaches
of the universe.
He fancied pigeons.
And made his fate as he was.
Not pretending to be someone else.
Raconteur, idealist; hardworker.
A truly marvelous person.

People may accuse me of having a big ego, tooting my own horn, this is not precisely the truth. It is The Work I am tooting a horn about! This body of art to which I've given my energies, my time, most of my entire life in fact! Having the same desire as any parent to see that their child goes out into the world and finds her/his place! So I want my works to go out—out of myself, out of my person possession, out of my filecabinet & book shelves into this world and there find their rightful and deserved position—whither it be great or small, that is Gods decision! However mass-popular, or arcane this writer/artist becomes let it become a fact that he received his justified due!

History shows people in a different light then what they were. How history will view me; I hope I will have not been seen as idiot full of sound & fury at best; at worst malignant. My desire about the whole matter, ultimately I guess it's to leave this world a better place then when I found it --in some small/great measure.

Some people look at passionate artists and claim the only true passion is the love for Christ (read Mohammed, Buddha, etc.) Some people look at great leaders as if they were anointed. Revere them, deify them. And who's to say many aren't anointed? And who is to say a good work is not a true love? You don't have to preach the Gospel to be anointed you could be doing Creators work and so be blessed. I know I was led to art, gifted by it…. And by Who if not some great, wise and infinite Force?

Right Wing Religious Fundamentalist Bigot Asshole: *The end days are coming will you be taken up with God or will you be left behind!*

Red: *Well I'd want to stay around awhile then! I'd stay behind because so many people need help. I'd be helping people.*

God: **That's a Christian.**

Speaking of leaders what amazes me most, and is most disheartening, is not what a few stupid, crazy & insane men up in the White House can do, but

49

that so much of the rest of our nation went along with it, voted for him for a 2nd term!

> See the American city
> garbage cans overflowing.
> So much wealth.
> So much waste.

Often in these times with this terrible headline news I wonder: God, if it was worth it to create this human race. Answer from a wise religious leader: Yes! Because so many people have done precisely what God has said to, they have proved love and care for their own children, their own family and their own people thru undying effort, and have had sympathy, compassion & done good works for those not of their own. Untold billions of people down thru the ages have done precisely this.

> The grave lays open
> like it has lost its occupant.
> Risen on resurrection day

I think of the beautiful *'Hay-yah, Hay-yah, Hay-yah, Hay'* ritual religious song of the Native American Indians. I been to shul tonight, and plan to attend Eucharist at Grace Cathedral one of these Sundays soon. Think a person can worship Creator in all faiths. —And still be worshiping the same Great Being Who made us all!

Transman Red had gone to Jewish temple, to Native American spiritual ceremonies. Buddhist meditations. Other Eastern Religious sects. And dozens & dozens of different churches which fall under the Christian classification. He'd been accepted into this tribe of folks and that-- made to feel welcome--but since he had not been born into that particular tribe always had this little uneasy feeling in the back of his mind that he didn't really belong. He'd been like an orphan for a long long while and appreciated any hospitality.

Is Armageddon really here? Doomsday come now? Who will do the fatal deed? **Then the shot that killed all of human civilizations was fired—the shot before the end…**

> *--It is so hard & so much grief.*
> --Follow the stars Red.
> Follow the stars
> they will guide you back home.
> Follow the stars,

that's all I can tell you now.
The stars will point the way.

Chapter 4.

A wonderland of geometric blocks all stood up on end. White & silver.
He/she was returning into the city.

Unity Rapid Transit plummeted at speeds of 300 miles per hour over the
usual wasteland, uninhabitable soil baked by poisonous ultraviolet rays from
a malignant sun, & covered by a fine layer of neutralized radioactive fallout
from the last world war (III). Piled high with waste products of,
refrigeration, cooking, washing, communication. These labor-saving
appliances by which the citizen of the New City communicated, cooked
their food, enjoyed media; appliances, which had become outdated by
current technological advancements (which progressed so rapidly month-to
month) and had subsequently been dumped haphazardly into these abandon
acreages which were of course no longer inhabitable-- being outside the
Great Ozone Free AirDomes. Thrown into the numerous gullies, ravines,
and ditches left by the bombs, & excavations. The Great Domes covered all
major cities—where their beneficent shields did not extend ultra violet rays
grew instantly stronger and soaring temperatures in to the 140 degrees and
beyond shortened life drastically for any humans-- and there were a few--
who strayed their for too long.

Due to discoveries in technology especially those of reduplication of
material from the barest substance, and the 100% increased capability of
metallurgical tensile strength, new products had become available so
citizens, now more affluent under Utopia's simplified economic system,
could constantly upgrade their stuff. What else was there to do for a citizen
of affluent Utopia but consume!

As s/he leaned back in the prefab mini-module of Unity Rapid Transit the
slightly unhealthy pallor of his pale face with its already yellowish tint went
thru it's changes as the train compartment crossed thru the light spectrum of
electronic impulses which hover producing in the air; it reflected a
moment's impish glee due to a flash of a memory. Just hours before
Star1.vax under stealth clearance had stated 'Bossa Nova teacher'. A term
he'd garnered from his illicit perusal of fragments from the Olden Days &
none of the foolish soldiers(ettes) knew what this meant! HA HA HA! --- It
had actually been a dance craze, burning brightly for an instant during the
last century, 1950's. For his next clearance check he/she'd dream up

another one. —It was his small attempt at Revolution. Star1.vax had had a laugh about that.

'Revolution. Viva La Resistance. All that stuff we're learning... Can keep on that track. Or...maybe just drop out of the group, drop out of everything but my job; go underground. Be a mole. —The Unity gives you drugs down subterranean. So you won't be afraid no more from claustrophobia. Or suffer the artificial sunlight blues. And stay stoned forever.' Citizens needed it, Unity's leaders thought. So citizens who didn't just put on the claim forms that they needed 'medical adjustment', but actually took their meds allocation, peddled them on the grey market for something they could use. So any citizen could get them. Their study group leaders were very critical of the meds. Anderson particularly railed about its chemical debilitations. Valdez about it's social controls. They all preached that society must change in order to heal the individual—not the individual medicating themselves so they can tolerate being twisted into a pretzel by society. And direct social action was needed to change society! A hard concept to accept for the average Utopian who already assumed The Unity was a true perfection.

That week at his mandatory job at Depot 33 of The Unity Central Bureau Clearing House of World Statistics & Information progressed with the same gripes, headaches & complaints interspersed with little relief's like oasis's in a wasteland of shit. The 20-minute coffee breaks, gossiping with other workers in the cubicles near his, as s/he processed incoming calls from citizens. S/he looked foreword to the next meeting of the study group which had become during the last 4 months of him joining, an even greater oasis's in the desert of his life, just like the coffee breaks, the moments stolen at idle chitchat at the Bureau.

In seconds seized occasionally, unfrozen out of a mind dulling routine he'd cut off the incessant work flow by surreptitiously jiggling his fingers against the electronic nodes to unplug his wordhole so it could receive no incoming calls and simply sit, stare ahead into the now-grey sight board upon which an ever-changing Technicolor panoramic background ordinarily would be projected, and imagine. For instance how did that Transman, Prophet Red Jordan feel when he opened the envelope from that New York magazine, — maybe just like Star1.vax himself opening the latest offering of printed material? In all excitement---his heart fluttering like a little bird!

How often do citizens really know about other citizens, the intimacies of their daily lives—that's why artists & other 'characters' in history stand out, --especially forbidden history--- not only because of what ingenious works they've done but because of who they are. It's fascinating to have a glimpse of another's humble daily existence; how they brush their hair, eat their food, have sex...

And at other times he/she thought about Revolution. Not the frightening part of it, nor the lethal potential consequences of attempting it, but of being a hero. Had thoughts. Dreamed. Felt these imaginings so hard that it rushed him thru the day's mandatory work. And soon physically these became the main focus, while all labor was done robotically without much thought until evening. Labored briefly as possible at each call, then stamped out *processed* on its form. He dreamed he'd rescue political prisoners from hidden detention centers just like another more simple citizen might vision they'd rescue little dogs in trouble lost in a maize of Utopia's skyrise building pavilions, barking frantically among it's hanging garden. Saving citizens from the occasional Dome malfunction pressure fire! Or, maybe he'd go be a mole they didn't rescue anybody. They were souls on ice.

People are empowered by the struggles of those who went before. But what was the struggle? What had been left behind? In the Unity of Utopia everyone's wants were provided for. & of course nothing had been left behind—for there was nothing—no history. Nor why should there be? For what reason? Everything was the same always. Everyone one was equal (almost) with no problems. No want. No struggle. That was the end of the matter; any further questions would be labeled treason! Dissention—and a matter for the soldiers to remove.

***

Morning.
Star1.vax's eyes came unstuck. One then the other opened.

The study groups next meeting was moved back into the City. Their location was constantly changing so as not to arouse suspicion.

A bright sunny day, standard under the ozone free-air dome in this, one of Utopia's premier cities, saw Star1.vax going down the speedwalk towards Unity Rapid Transit, which would take him up-island.

The artificial atmosphere was exceptionally mild today, the usual stench being completely filtered, and the walks weren't too crowded. Already there were interesting things to behold—sights slightly out of step of the mundane routine.

S/he paused a moment. Here was one returning! Star1.vax paused a moment to look up into the sky.

A space shuttle from deep outer space was returning with its laden cargo from the next galaxy 60 million light years away. Star1.vax strained his eyes as the vessel arrives far up in the atmosphere. It slowly turns & turns itself becoming more visible as it enters the material plane. 'I hear those grunts aboard get good money, but their bodies can't process the light year mileage after more then ten earth-years worth of trips. Unity don't send young men or women, unless they've already had their children. Or at least frozen their eggs in sub-zero storage. Because of genetic damage.'

And the second sight immediately following the first was more rare in these progressive times.

Dressed in traditional ethnic clothes—alien to the new Unity of Utopia. A strange costumed émigré, multi colored blouse, unmatching dress, & absurd footgear. Probably one who'd climbed up from out of the barren, uncovered wasteland zone. "'Scuse me, for sale, for sale!" she whispered, upholding two stolen glasses, along with a fistful of eating utensiles---property of a Unity free cafeteria.

Occasionally you passed one. A strange outcast being. One who was probably insane. Utterly crazy. *'Some are little in size, tho not in heart.'* The words of the Prophet came back to him. These homeless were of that sort s/he thought, charitably.

Citizens seldom if ever saw aberrant people on the streets of this new empire. This one must have recently crawled up out of an unincorporated area over some viaduct. For most, gradually over the last decade, had been picked up by the soldiers, taken in to confinement in hospital where doctors experimented with various psychotropic drugs to see what worked most efficiently to stabilize their minds, set them straight, into conformity with The Unity, & reintroduce them back into Utopia's society where they would do some mandatory menial work, and live luxuriously underground. −And out of sight. Even the worst off could be permanently housed in special facilities and given simple jobs. Ones too severely ill or who refused to remain on their meds, these had been removed to one of those top secret, unknown facilities. And look! Even as he was watching, the soldiers have arrived and are handcuffing, anesthetizing this mad creature right now! Wrists locked behind the back, feet being shackled; to the industrious grunts of 4 soldierettes. A wheel less handcart opens up out of pocketsize, put into place to carry the body—now growing limp in a twilight sleep... the person is already being removed! Right in front of his eyes!

So the streets of the new cities of The Unity of Utopia were very clean, safe, free of insane or homeless derelicts once so prevalent -- to be studied in now-forbidden photographs of the Old World and still immemorially etched in dim memory of very old timers, of which they dare not speak. Nor could many of them remember to speak of it---being so pleasantly ensconced on medications, so beautiful (cosmetically enhanced) living out their remaining stay on earth fussing about at necessary jobs delivering hardcopy email memos between The Unity's Bureaus, counting inventory at Unity Supply depots, doing census counts at the Unity Morgue, or some such meaningless drudgery.

Along with the absence of that homeless, insane & criminal class however, had also gone---or that is, been removed—the protesters, picketers and human rights marchers.

How sad, the STOP TORTURE & DEFEND YOUR RIGHTS people of the last century were gone. Swept up under the torrent of paid soldiers/ettes of a new empire, The Unity of Utopia, who had been sent out scouring the city for them and anything else which didn't fit! How sad! ---And how ironic! For wasn't torture still going on deep in the subterranean bowels of Utopia? The Unity's dark side. Surveillance was everywhere gathering intelligence about everything. Flashes of this constantly rushed across his work telescreen as a reminder. It was spawned out of a single brain, centric of hundreds of thousand officious tentacles, which reached out globally to pry under each ozone dome around the world. This brain center was housed in that strange geodesic pentagon located in the original capital city of the old world, once named Washington after the founding father of 400 years past, George, a revolutionary General. Foreboding black-painted stealth edifice. The ancient, ordinary Pentagon building of past times had reconstructed itself from the simple design of the old days in it's primitive form of 1 dimensional to sprout into the 4th dimension of 2054.

Morning was passing quite briskly with excitement which did not have to be invented by his own mind. Something else was being removed. As the slim youngish citizen Star1.vax walked briskly into the transit station any attempt at tranquility of this pleasant faux sunny day air was broken by the hideous shrieking of faux hawks, a predator of smaller birds. It rose and fell unexpectedly at every rapid transit exit to chase away what was rumored to be the few pigeons who still remain, tho in greatly reduced flocks, raising their brood despite the heartless cruel metal spikes of empire. Despite the gutterless streamlined buildings without ledges of empires austere cities. And this method works efficiently, because he'd never seen any.

2 soldiers, the police variety, buffed, immense, wearing dark blue uniforms strode aboard the New Utopia Rapid Transit today giving Star1.vax a brief qualm. Both over 7 feet tall, 350 pounds; the white one, largest, bullet head, shaved close to his skull, short cut sleeves revealed his thick, hairy, muscular arms. The Hispanic had a slightly softer look, like he'd give you a break—but probably too quagmired in adhering to the protocol of Utopia to be understanding of anything above and beyond its Rules.

Stern, the solar badge shining perpetually, lethal 3-effect ray guns in holster; stunner, striker, killer, this last being a fast-draw death. Stun was for the mild approach. Strike, for a knock out punch. It was a sad proven fact that some gone-insane citizens clinically did not respond to the stuns or strikes electric charge & kept on upon their maniacal assault putting the soldier's life in jeopardy. Better shoot to kill!

After appraising the two soldier police apprehensively awhile her-his mind wandered off to his new passion. In Star1.vax's study group a very interesting paper had been presented of the writer prophet; of particular interest to him because it was about home & family, so Star1.vax had paid special attention, not letting his mind wander at all through that discourse.

So far in her/his young life she/he had not received a permanent domicile and was being shifted about from one unit to the next. In favor of family's--- those with children, even families containing just 2 citizens. This was OK, as he/she was never in fear of a place to stay—like as in the old prophets time. It was an issue Red had spoken of un-ceasingly.

Old Red had spoken of this God Thing in his diary—a journal named JOURNEY—he'd given little lessons in it. Here was one. *"Do I want to be rich, the richest man? Or do I want to have what I need. There's a difference."* Later in these pages he'd referred to being 'called' or summoned by this God Thing—called like one invites a friend on email in their individual wordhole; to make a voyage of some kind into a new geographical region, and that the God Thing would pay for this trip and finance living expenses once he/she'd arrived, that the trip was very important and it involved Red going to live somewhere near a very ancient people who were a collective. A tribe. The Indian citizens.

So there was another of this Transman Red's secret idea, to establish a sanctuary in the woods for himself and a few loved ones & friends plus animals. His family. *'God sent Noah...'* Fleeting dreams!

***

When he/she entered the room it buzzed with minor chat, much of it involving those comrades taken prisoner by Utopia's soldiers in the Beneficent Rain Belt Northwest.

"The rain. Nobody goes outside the dome ever, because of the rain. Life stops."

'You come to the study groups for fellowship & that's why I'm here', s/he thought. Not just the political part. All though he liked that too—and was a fast learner. S/he took a seat & began to unpack his materials.

A fragment of the old Prophets writings slid out of his stuff and floated gently towards the starry Astroturf floor:

> *Having disputes,*
> *having despair.*
> *And still nothing*
> *is happening here.*

Now what was that suppose to mean? Life was awful in the old times too? Yeah. Well as far as Star1.vax was concerned life is awful now!

But how the world had suddenly enlarged! Come alive! Now, thanks to the study groups, Star1.vax could dream in a bigger scope! Could vision back into the ancient times---as seen thru his reading materials—to those lives, pre dynastic upheaval, before the atmosphere had got so fouled up that all the citizens of each global hemisphere had been forced to pick up their things abandoning their homes at mid-land and migrate out to the shores of their continents, the cooler zones, wherein they were packed from sky high to deep inside the underground womb of earth; participating in one of the largest mass evacuations & relocations of the human race since its early ancestors had marched out of the African continent along the land bridge some 80,000 years before when the human world was in infancy. It was a good thing the tensile super strength building material had been discovered so as to accommodate them all.

According to the study groups readings, for all the big city business & the metropolitan bustle major cities of the old world had, still they were provincial, low key sunbaked leisure a day/night city's of midnight repose— not the 24 hour non stop mega dome city's of the new empire where one work shift replaced another at five pm and still another replaced that in wee small hours of morning—a round the clock enterprise.

His-her reverie was broken by the sardonic voice of Valdez. "Comrades, the meeting of the Red Jordan Arobateau Reading Society.... Chapter #33, Lovely Hillview Beside The Bay will now commence. Or should I say *San Francisco* chapter to this crowd." The medium size dark haired man, professorial in demeanor stood, slightly hunched shoulders, serious. Students chuckled at his little joke. All bustling and whispers ended; faces gazed at him, expectant. Valdez was a character. Of interest. He spanned the old world and this new one. His face had not been sufficiently doctored, and was a highway of rough living, which kept people away; at other times it bes friendly, inviting a chat or a jocular exchange of communication.

That day's study involved a special reading, and then they were to be privy to some archival footage of the original burnings. Sadly Star1.vax was not called upon to read, but a pretty, pert young blondish haired woman in Utopia full body service uniform did, and she was quite pleasing to the eye. "Mable473.vax will honor us with one of the Prophets poems."

Round body, hips and bosom, sturdy build, her plain blue Utopia uniform embellished by a pair of sexy fashionable pumps (not regulation wear) which she had carried in a canvass bag and just wore to the study group, but would then remove, replacing them with regulation gear, in her way out. Fancy dangling earrings poked beneath her bountiful blondish hair. With a commanding click, click, click of high heels she made her way to the front of the room, stood before some 40 comrades, shaking out the fragment pages with a flourish, and began:

> *I will tell you the tribe to which you belong.*
> I think what is happening there
> is much more horrible then people know.
> Half of a whole generation has lost
> the old teachings,
> the old ways.
> They have lost themselves.
> Where are the elders?
> If they would just stay among us!
> Where are the soldiers
> who would stand among us?
>
> Stay & do service my sisters
> & brothers.
> Lead them on the spiritual path.
> Tell them of the ancient ways.
> Do service.

Answer them.
Answer their questions.
Fill the young peoples hearts
With hope
Make your people be My people,
says Creator.

A brief discussion, in which this work was dissected. Originally intended to be about a specific group—the Native citizens of the once Am-Erica, this poem now was applicable to citizens of the Unity. Valdez cast a look at his starclock from under craggy graying black eyebrows, then on to the archival film footage.

Star1.vax recalled the burnings. He'd been young then—a Transteen of 15.... The afternoon had been mildly cool, of course, under the free air ozone dome, which arched triumphantly over Peoples Square. The vast faux lawn stretched for blocks & blocks. He emerged with a pack of other Utopian transit riders from underground to view the tremendous space. At first there was a surprisingly small turnout but simultaneous from all directions citizens were constantly arriving, moving in, in big clusters having disembarked the speedwalks and rapid transit outlets which fed into the great Peoples Square. They had timed their arrival to the event by their starclocks & thus made it painfully noticeably that in great volumes the citizenry of vax #33—The Lovely Hillview Beside the Bay-- had not intended to arrive for the first opening speeches of Utopia Leaders, which was bad enough, or worse did they bother even to arrive en toto until the middle—rudely---of the Grand Declaration of Jon Kim Sun the great Dictator of the vast empire of The Unity, but had actually just come to witness the Degenerate Art burning itself which had been so widely announced. Which promised to be a grand spectacle. And, so each could fulfill their de rigueur gossip/chit-chat pertaining to this event in the next 24-hour period at their various occupations, thus not arousing suspicion of the cyborg enforced soldier/police. But gradually as the time approached they all, finally, 2 million strong stood there in the cold and by beginning time had completely covered the square like a layer of ants.

Arriving among the first wave of the Rapid Transit outpourings young Star1.vax had seen the spot where the burning was to be preformed there in distance. He approached the elevated stage, which was hung with decorative banners of red & gold. 25 shrouded oblisques occupied it—site of the forthcoming conflagration—and soon found himself only a half block or so from the very center, among the first few thousand citizens.

Not only paintings were to be destroyed but other of the prophet's contraband works as well--- books. STAGE DOOR in its 4 homemade sections; a controversial denunciation of the former government, that old empire proto Utopian Am-Erica. With volume 4 in particular emphasis because of those *Acts* inherent in its time-yellowed pages. *Acts* of blood. Also a jaded document by the master of perverse sex of many descriptions AUTUMN CHANGES. And not to discount the poet-prophet's now infamous PASSAGE. Which had originally been made available by her/his own self-publishing in 9 parts—making it even harder for the censors of Utopia to track down all of them for subsequent removal. (Although that probably had not been his intention.)

Party music was blaring out of the sound amplifiers, played to entertain kill time until the spokespersons did their spiel. The growing crowd engaged in stray mischievous conversations buzz, in an enormous hive.

Next, live musical bands played. Spotlights searched thru faux clouds in the artificial sky. Festive, illusionary, in a light show. Stalls had been set up along the fringes by enterprising ethnic groups (those under the protectorship of Utopia), which peddled food of every description. Whose delicious aromas wafted thru the air. Turning the event into a bazaar of international flavor.

Star1.vax remembered it. —The press of the crowds around him had warmed up the cool day. Now in hindsight, a decade later Star1.vax secretly could gloat that those very paintings he had seen, supposedly, draped in funereal shrouds— those art work depictions of anarchy, rebellion; those great artistic inspirations of poetry and perverse sex, were securely in the possession of a number of individuals. Many of them within the study groups which had sprung up throughout the Unity in global proliferation, rumor had it. Somewhere those words of liberation & of freedom continued to exist! ---Thanks to his chapter, and dozens upon dozens like it— tho at this juncture he had not yet met with the study group. That had happened in ten years after the actual fires were lit.

Finally, here came Kim Sun's voice frail but sound-huge, and a bit tinny, artificial, like Star1.vax's own; his face super large impressed globally upon 3 billion eyes---eyes staring back, each with their individual recorded DNA scan in the memory banks of Utopia's Unity. As usual nobody had seen him.

"Huh. Our Dictator still ain't showed up. Not even to this event! Never seen him as I can recall…" Murmured a voice nearby.

"No one ever sees him." comments another citizen.

"Old Timers say they remember seeing him in person."

"Is he alive?" Joked another, but in a whisper.

"Mommy is our Dictator dead?" Asked a child, innocently.

"Shhh!" Hushes its mother.

To kill time, now while the porcine Kim Sun spoke, young Star1.vax, tired of standing, shifting from foot to foot, rebelliously had gazed skywards. Blithely observing the grey blue/white canopy of adjusted atmosphere inside the dome. Outside the real true poisoned radioactive atmosphere still limped along alive or rather more in a state of semi existence which was still frantically being doctored with by the principle research scientists & engineers of The Unity on all it's global fronts. The complete demise of it would be the end to everything & everyone on earth. End to the human pageant utterly. So atomic particles and radioactivity which bombarded the great domes on their outside skin were still bouncing around planet earths once pristine air. Thus salvation of all green things and living beings was delicate work. Restoration fumbled along at an excruciating pace. The temporal civilization now primarily existed inside a grid of domes, which proliferated over the world into the tens of thousands, and, out of necessity, were still multiplying.

Starting with the last speakers, the huge numbers grew dense. As the crowd pressed foreword compacting itself they obscured sight of the stage where the actual event would transpire. Soon no one but the tallest citizens could see. So hundreds of thousands of eyes lifted to the monitors set at 3rd story height to view. Good thing for telescreens.

Their Dictator was just ending his declaration. The calm tranquil face of Kim Sun flooded into ethers---probably hurrying on its way to appear on the other side of the planet, plus planetary colonies repeating his trite message, then vanish; only to reappear at another gathering in another day or so— televised--- but never in person. Who ---in fact what was Dictator Kim Sun? Some propped-up electronic dummy robot? A cyber simulated animation?

Gazed upwards, following the action, which was relentlessly transpiring on the stage in distance, his heart rose within him. Maybe the paintings would somehow fail to burn! By some kind of mishap! And –that's another thing which was the same… Which persons of 2054 AD had in common with the Prophets days…. A human heart was still beating in their chest.

Voice of the last invited speaker, some dignitary with seniority in the hierarchy of The Unity chosen to narrate the burning now boomed over the immense Peoples Square; **"CITIZENS! FIRESWORDS HAVE BEEN LIT!** Her breathless step-by-step description with subsequent echoes of the crowd, presently including his own tinny, transsexual voice (scientifically engineered by hormone therapy); thundering thru the great Peoples Square from East to West, North to South; and, over the entire globe via satellite telly in simultaneous ceremonies held at any/cities which had Great Domes. S/he heard himself yelling, yelling along with the rest, "TORCH IT! TORCH IT!" In denunciation of that long dead poet-prophet whom he did not know!

Emerging from reminiscence, to the words of Valdez elucidating some obscure reference from his radical flock, Star1.vax's last imaginings were of Red Jordan 'partying' in the expression of yesteryear. He could almost see their figures, those ancient citizens of the past millennium, 1975, shuffling, dancing to the music—slow/fast beat; pressing palms of sweaty hands together making a camaraderie salute in the dark. Black-tan discos of yesterday. They had some good jams back then, some even with political messages such as, The World Is A Ghetto, or, War, What Is It Good For? -- Its chant-response being 'absolutely nothing.' Of course that same music was still listened to by citizens of these modern times. --- Tho the words were forbidden by today's rulers of the newest earth empire, Utopia. And just then, a most amazing happening occurred! He was just day dreaming, lazily following Valdez's talk, but enriching it with memories of his own with fantastic visions … When young Star1.vax upon opening his eyes could have sworn he caught that pretty Mable staring at him! --- And she … she WINKED! At him! … Or did she? And now wasn't she was laughing privately to herself!?

So consumed was s/he by this, being caught in a moments escapist daydream, and by someone so pretty, shocked him out of his secret enjoyable memories that had just been triggered by the stark photo-doc images of that burning ten years ago. 'Did that redhead comrade WINK at me? Did she see me not concentrating on our teacher? But why was she looking at me?' The remainder of the study group passed by without Star1.vax paying much attention to anything at all but the turmoil inside his head! And the class filtered out into the ordinary Utopian world once more.

Before they left Valdez's last words by now etched dully into his mind, were as usual: "remember, comrades, the more you are hooked up into this

62

system, the easier you can be traced. Don't use a computer to communicate sensitive data, its plugged directly into the Unity-- don't use any cell phone, it can be traced; your wordhole, the same."

They left out into a strange more drastically cooler air then 4 hours ago when they'd entered, that atmosphere outside the protected Great Dome. Hills shrouded within themselves were mysteries. The real moon drifting steadily across the sky, now full, a spooky galleon on the sea of night, and tonight totally apparent, no longer blocked behind the ozone shield dome, its each detail utterly splendid, in a dazzling wonder.

The moon had expanded itself from ¾'s to full in the days since their last meeting. The study groups of course were not scheduled every 7 days nor in any regimen fashion but held at random. Haphazard, in strategy similar to that used in the old Am-Erican Revolutionary war back in the 1700rds fought essentially by what would be named 200 years later, guerrilla combatants—so forbidden history told them.

Now the departing comrades moved out of a loose knit band into pairs or separately. Star1.vax walked by him-herself. Not by choice. Leaving the large building conglomerate of their meeting place which was like an island, they came across a clearing, void, beside which gouged ravines and heaps of War debris still stood, with nothing of civilization but the antiquated walkway grumbling along towards an outpost of Utopia Rapid Transit.

Quite alone now, young Star1.vax continued her-his astronomical observances. Moon was so much clearer here out in the old atmosphere of earth, tho it would kill him slowly if he remained, like it did the natives, wild people who dwelled in the canyons and gullies of the ravaged terrain living on scraps and charity discards, whom one seldom saw; who occasionally straggled back into the City, diseased, unkempt; out of desperation, and at great risk for they faced instant arrest by soldiers.

S/he marveled at the full moon! Lovely! A face crossed with jet planes effacing its calm stern ageless surface in their constant paths crisscrossing the planet. For Utopia had developed into a global society. This plus the occasional trajectory of space shuttles supply cargos to Utopia's space stations & the planets under cultivation. Rarely did one see the awesome sight he had witnessed earlier that 24 hours, the materialization of a deep space vessel returning from outside the galaxy.

Mable473.vax was aboard the same rapid transit car as him! Just a few rows away. And again Star1.vax thought he saw her mirthful face staring at him, but she didn't hold his glance; flitted off behind her wordhole pod—in defiance of Valdez's edict. The short trip transpired uneventfully at top speed; but then once back inside the protective dome of The City, as he-she raced along the speedwalk eager to return to his pod something terrible happened! Ahead having stationed itself on one of those nefarious ever-changing Unity Homeland Security Stations was an elite military cyborg. A gadget of Utopias Internal Security Forces. These giant monsters of The Unity always brought a chill to ordinary citizens---that's what they were designed to do.

Larger then even the most giant soldier, these robotical machines began at 8 feet in height, and, depending on their model, grew as tall as 9. Pre-human like shoulders, massive, ox-like, the girth of 3 football players stuck together from yesteryears war games.

The cyborgs entire body suit made of metal skin was dotted with porous holes, which at glance one might assume was part of its design to render the ogre lifelike--- until it bristled with rage when its commands weren't obeyed. Then the person saw horror–struck for what nefarious purpose they were; out of each hole first protruded a glint of metal seemingly like coat of armor which suddenly covered it from head to foot, but within split seconds it became apparent this was actually a spike emerging out of each pore; these gradually grew from one eight of an inch to 2 inches, at which it was usually sufficient to bring about compliance, but if necessary to 6" just for sheer terror and greater –to a length of several feet, now with the ability to impale any disobedient citizens right there on the spot. All ruses of errant citizens had been pre programmed; it was a well thought-out cyborg design from the ingenious minds of Utopia.

Suddenly the minor qualm in his stomach turned to panic, and the bottom of his stomach dropped out! The monstrous cyborg had turned stiffly in the manner of a being so gigantic it can't make too quick an adjustment in angle—just deadly direct ones--and was beckoning to him. **"CITIZEN!"** The monsters voice boomed.

It was the most hideous voice a human can hear--simulated human but not human, in a basso profundo so deep it almost cracked down beyond the range of a persons audible range; no human being could make a sound so low, and this was part of the cyborgs design, to install terror in any citizen who crossed its path.

"CITIZEN, HALT! COME OVER TO MY STATION!"

-- In a society where feminism was more revered and androgyny actually encouraged, what better way to go—to the deep end of one gender or the other to pass the boundaries of the familiar, the usual? In the case of the cyborg programmed with a male spectrum basso profondo voice hollering at top-most velocity, which rattled windowpanes of buildings nearby, and bounced in terrifying echoes into the distance. Having this distorted human feature was actually the worst, most frightening element. That it was a combination of human plus metal & steel wiring with tremendous, potentially lethal strength.

Immediately upon approaching the terrifying monster, all his statistics were being scanned, recorded, even as Star1.vax started shuffling, weak-kneed towards its station; and wasting no time, the cyborg was also approached him, clearing the distance in gigantic steps. It took a millisecond to process & file his data, retina laser, DNA print, plus access The Unity's central memory bank. Of course young Star1.vak turned up clean. For his spotless record he was rewarded by the monsters creaking jaw opening in a hideous artificial smile. -- A printout of his cleanliness was soon forthcoming out of the ogre's belly. A frightening indignity followed as slowly from out of the plastic perforations of its artificial skin emerged the metal spikes, one of which impaled the data sheet with mathematical precision into one of its perforations, and thrust it at Star1.vax to take. Then the ogre boomed once more in bone rattling strength; **"THE UNITY THANKS YOU STAR1.VAX YOU ARE FREE TO GO ON YOU WAY."** Then the cyborg nodded politely, lumbering swiftly back to its station.

Shaken, the slender Star1.vax, trembling like a reed in the wind, moved his suddenly numb feet back towards the speedwalk.

Out of the corner of his eye he saw a young woman approach. It was Mable473.vax. Hailing him she exclaimed, "I'm glad I saw that! I was just waiting for some sign… About *you*…" She smiled pointedly. To which Star1.vax stared dumb. "The reason is, I wasn't sure if I could talk to you before. I wanted to make sure you weren't an undercover cop."

To this Star1.vax replied, "what a nice compliment" in his iciest voice. — For all the momentary panic, which had been caused to him, but her simply, blithely tossing this off. The pretty comrade began to talk, friendly, about nothing in particular. As she spoke he observed Mable close up; hair which grew out abundantly from her fair complexioned skin was defiantly yellowsh-brown, --- and appeared that she'd added some yellow coloration to it. He thought then immediate to her crotch, about her pussy was it the same? —And nearly died. His mind now in total confusion, whirling!

They traveled a distance together. Him returning to the downtown area, her further out; at the point where their paths would diverge; they stepped off the speedwalk and parted on a dimming streetcorner of Utopia, saying goodbye, promising to meet and maybe sit together at the study group, soon. For some mysterious reason, his heart grew boyant after this. He smiled. Dazed. Happy. He gazed up at the heavens.

WOW! There it was again! The full moon! He'd been too blind to notice! Evenly framed squared like a thrift-conscious art student frames her canvass with only inches to spare between their subject and the unearthly looming government constructs of Utopia at one side, and at the other 2 low squat prior dynastic edifices still in the clutches of private domain.

The full moon was lovely; its face crossed with jet planes effacing its calm stern ageless surface in their constant paths crisscrossing the planet, as Utopia had developed into a global society. Plus the occasional trajectory of shuttles of supply cargos supply ships to space stations & planets under cultivation. Rarely did one see the awesome sight he had witnessed early that 24 hours, the materialization of a deep space vessel.

Entered the lobby of his (*temporary!*) lodgings in the Sacramento Street compound; building N. A drone was housecleaning the large range of grass-simulated flooring.

The drudge, most likely a mole, passively went about the vacuuming of this synthetic grass, eyes intent on its job and pointed stupidly to the young man who entered with a careless gait, indicating its machine so as s/he'd not trip over it; a pig expression on its face like a Halloween costumes perpetual mask

A short ride up to the 30th floor. He-she entered the confines of his efficiency home pod.

What a day it had been!

A wave of his/her small hand across the video ray activated the Telly. News from Utopia across the planet.

Utopia had developed into a global culture. There were advertisements for foods from places he might never visit: *"Go to the ethnic section of the store you will find the hair care products you want! Right here in Mumbai, India!"* And recruiting ads for soldiers(ettes) blaring their usual mundane propaganda. No messages greeted him in his individual wordhole. He thought about Mable, the bond, curvaceous, all womanly inside her blue

66

Unity standard regulation uniform *for the citizen with refinement* —dolled up by earrings and fancy shoes. "She's a 473. Huh." Blinking. Somberly considering Mables prestige. Wondering how she got such a low figure. Maybe she's a freak like me! ---Huh! And that's why she's in our study group! Or maybe Mable just wasn't a popular name given out back in year 2034…. He'd have to look that information up.

Wearily he waved off. Scenery on his telescreen of rolling solid green covered hills which actually no longer existed slowly slid back into ether.

Time raced along over the starclock set at real Utopian time.

Outside his tinted window the huge wonderland metropolis of Unity's 33rd vax, Lovely Hillview By the Bay, stretches in a panorama. Night sky above the dome darkens our world below it, but the mighty nuclear powered lights of empire shine steadily out of 20 million windows, streetlights, advertisements. The City bustles on & on non-stop 24 hours. Other skyscraper domiciles rooted in 50 underground levels chiseled into bedrock, zoom up into 300 levels; all happy homes of citizens permanently domiciled, but here he still was, on a lowly 30th floor. You could still see people from the 30th floor! —Like ants! Which could not be seen on the 300th. It was in an ancient ruin, a reconstructed skyscraper of only 50 levels; awaiting his name to be called from the Housing Authority List so he could go select an available unit to own. —Unless he chose to go underground, and then a vast opportunity of subterranean living was available for the taking. To become a mole was his last resort. The slim figure drew in a deep breath, nostalgic; admiring the austere city in evening's dark, then went about necessary chores before going to sleep. As s/he set out the next workshift's blue uniform newly cleaned/pressed by the drone, bathed, did dental care—using the instant dental automatic--- s/he mused.

Study groups were not dedicated entirely to just Prophet Red certainly his work was formidable, but the groups were about the seeking of truth and there had been a multitude of prophets speaking it. So there were other studies too. Other fragments. It was only since Red had been most prolific, a voice from the underclass & not the intelligentsia, not of a rich or affluent group—a phenomenon much more common to his time --- in fact he was from triply afflicted minorities; which made his material far more compelling as multiple lessons could be learned from a single reading all at once. He-she was: 1. Part black. (& to make this more difficult the back then-unwanted mixraced individual of black, white and Indian blood). 2. A transsexual. 3. Poor. Thus it was decided upon that particular prophet (one of many, many diverse from many nations & eras) for whom the societies would be named. So, during the course of their studies, the Red Jordan Arobateau Reading Society was perpetuating that name and those ideas.

Star1.vax was drawn to the works of Red Jordan because Red was also a him-her, just like him/herself.

Star1.vax was mixed too, but in a different sense. Star1.vax had been first of 'his litter', hence a noble 1. A brave 1. A prototype 1. Because he had been taken in to Utopia.

Often people ask jealously; "How did yuh get to be a 1 Starvax? A 1 out of 2,000 plus Starvax's, and those out of 10 million inhabitants of The Lovely Hillview By the Bay—designated by vax. And these, --out of 300 billion worldwide-- numbering according to statistics at the bureau where s/he was employed, 23,679,041,582. Star1.vax was special. He had been adopted. He wondered what Mable's history could be.

No accident Star1.vax was orphaned at an early age—3 ---his biological mother being an outcast, when the infant had been accidentally discovered, was seized, removed, and taken into the Unity for humanitarian reasons; so he had no family, and that made him de facto a looser—an outsider. An outcast. Because of this, due to the process of extemporized reasoning he felt, is why he had no girlfriend, and no permanent domicile, but was ever shifting, and his sexual relationships had all been essentially one night stands with seldom anything of permanency evolving from them. All, which conspired to make him feel lonely, somewhat blue perpetually, blue as a standard regulation uniform, and without having his feet on solid terra firma. A situation which constantly broiled over in rage; for instance the time at study when he'd confronted a classmate about some unfortunate remark they had made before class began, while comrades were still shuffling to their desks: *"Whadda yuh mean I'm not oppressed in Utopia? Look at me, I been waitin' for my name to come up 12 years on the Housing List! Since I was 18! My life's wasting away! Its 'cause I'm single, 'n don't have a family! There's prejudice against single citizens!"*

Primary identification 'Star' had been given young Star1.vax. However he/she too had a last & even middle name—but since they were no longer allowed to use it on any legal or official matters s/he'd all but forgotten what they were & actually had little idea of their proper spelling. So, the child her-his mother had named 'Star' after those glorious orb's set dazzling in heaven which shone far above the wasteland pure & beautiful had these odd anomalous appendages on his names primary proper spelling. Once in the raw beginnings of Utopia this 3 part designation had been printed on Star's official citizen identification—even at his young age of then 7 —which was after the edicts had gone into effect, laws stuck inside alongside thousands of others in a 12" thick Official Manual of Rules & Regulations of The Unity Of Utopia, back in 2040.

Just by having been given his birth 'outdoors' that is outside the civilized of areas and incorporated lands of The Unity, little Star was forever destined to wander the known territories as an alien.

The Unity owned and controlled en toto planet earth and its sub planets in outerspace, but admittedly for the sake of thoroughly policing and cultivation of these major and minor territories all throughout the old empires of Am Erika, Rush Sha, Chine Ah, Indy Ah, Aff-Rica, U-Rope, which had since become incorporated into the global Unity, had to forsake its outer areas, those abandon to radiation fallout and debris. ---Hence they remained wild. It was here the infant 'Star' had been born. By natural childbirth. Pushed bloody, painfully out of his-her mother's womb. That practice which was definitely not standard by now in the 40th year of the current millennium, 21, but anything goes on outside the proper jurisdictions of The Unity, sadly, which we know.

Near the beginning of the end of that ancient dynasty, oppressive headline news of war gave great rise to protest in the literature of radical students. It was an era in which underground 'zines, & graffiti scrawled on public walls and other acts of expression plus more violent ones, proliferated. This had been officially stamped out, but continued to raise its arm in acts of resistance.

Long before Star1.vax's newly emerging underground times wo/men had sought to subvert the social order. Even as far back as 1145 AD, fragments of readings well-illustrated. For instance one by some obscure author Amy Ruth Kelly about a royal Queen Eleanor of Aqutaine, a social revolutionary in her own right. 1000 years ago! Wow really ancient!

So it seems by their studies that there had always been a revolution in various times and places.

Back in the dark ages near end of failing Am-Erican oligarchic, plutocratic dynastic-controlled empire which essentially dominated the world, an unfortunate series of catastrophes both occurring naturally and man-made, in concert, bankrupted all the nations. They were natural occurring. (This is debatable). -- Global warming created super-size hurricanes, floods that engulfed entire costal states, & from this turning point on also arose the unbearable hot temperatures. And secondly, the nations had been damaged or eradicated utterly by decades of wars and terrorism. Debris of the old civilizations could be seen all over the face of the Middle East, U-Rope, A Sha, Af-Rica and The Am-Erica's. By now all the rainforests & many animals had died, so it was really no laughing matter. Sadly those higher primates, Apes, Chimpanzees, were almost vanished; pre-ancestors connecting our world with theirs of a million years ago, that brief ephemeral bridge, instantaneous, which soon dissolves in the small fractions of millennia's.

Man—made holocausts, the expense of war international, and domestic terrorism, had bankrupted every civilization extant. No more tax revenue could be 'wasted' on anything-superfluous not necessary directly to national survival.

For example, no more city streetlights. Only brief 2 hours of them, one before dawn, one right at nightfall—this to accommodate workers, and school children. And none on weekends. No more 'recreational vehicles' which meant nothing not licensed by city authorities for Fire, Police, Health emergencies, sanitation and government.

Dark cities impassable to ordinary citizens of that now fallen empire were slowly slipping away out of memory. That practice of groping a path along thru by now impassable territories become foreign—feeling their way down the front of stone buildings, so that no one hardly ever went out at the dark of the moon when it had waned; when there was insufficient light to see your hand before your face! Houses of course were dim inside with no electricity. People burned candles, if they couldn't afford constant supply of batteries—and this increased dramatically the amount of fires.

That old workhorse Social Security had been coughing its last breath subsequently terrifying one quarter of the nations desperate senior citizens who depended on it for their lives. They stampeded polling centers of the-long-ago, now forgotten vote, and overthrew governments across both seas.

Soon followed, by necessity, the great global takeover, the intermediate phase of the dictatorship pre-Utopia.

Now, the only parts of the world left unpoliced were the outlying territories not reclaimed and left outside the Great Domes, which still were subject to periodic incursions by soldiers, and subsequent 'removals.'

His new-found histories was teaching them that with the break up of the Roman empire owners were unable to stop their slaves from running away & the plantation system broke down. In Copan the Mayans escaped their self-aggrandizing feudal kings and escaped silently back into the jungle;

without its workers the cities soon fell to ruin and decay. It was the end to the pomp and regality of the dynastic Indian kings.

So was it the same? Would this empire crumble and fall too? This Utopia, which everybody basically loved? Including old timers who no longer had to grope down the streets at night for want of light, (these problems had been solved by instituting the cost efficient yet occasionally deadly nuclear power plants). Their lack of housing, under slavery to landlord's rents. For almost all struggle had ended. Everyone has a domicile. Everyone has food. Everyone's medical needs are attended to. But what price freedom? There is no history attached to these people of the new Utopia; it is like we've sprung straight out of the earth fresh with no beginnings, no roots... who are we? Where are we all going? Maybe it took an outsider like himself, like the others assembled over contraband fragments studiously piecing together the Truth at secret study groups, which were springing up everywhere. For whatever reason they'd come to ask that question, and in so doing, challenged The Unity of Utopia!

At some time in life you begin to learn the lessons that what you take into your body can kill you fast, it can kill you slow. Poison is an obvious thing, but so are the doctrines and teachings (or lack of them) of the Utopian empire!

Star1.vax held an automatic hypodermic injector in one hand, withdrew amber liquid from a vial of testosterone. When the substance hit the 2-milligram mark it shut off, being set automatically. He proceeded to give himself the 2 times monthly shot. Ah. Manhood. He grinned slyly at the sexual boost, which he knew would follow later in the next 24 hours. 'Maybe then I'll fantasize about blondhead Mable...'To accompany his pumping hand. If he hadn't forgotten her.

Artificial evening ends, night begins. You lay your weary transgendered body down. --Sleep.

Inside his unit in vax 33, between buildings modern, and old, an amalgamation of both, young Star slept.

Moon wanes over shining ramparts of a new age, and turrets & towers of yesteryear.

4.
        On the other side of the world

71

there is a fishing village built into the cliff side
of the sea wall.
People must scramble up &
 down steep cliffs
for all their needs.
Casting their nets for fish.
Drawing water from wells.
Cooking.
Building shelter.
Birthing babies.
God it's so poor.
& so hard.
It is so poor & so cruel
 for so many.

The rich are getting richer.
We know. The poor people know.

Jesus, Mohammad, Elijah, Buddha, The Great Mother, all walked thru this
world with the greatest simplicity. Michael J. Fox the stricken movie star
appears on Television, a jittering spastic puppet diminished by the disease
Multiple Scoliosis. I use to hate Michael J. Fox. To me he was a privileged
twerp. Now I don't hate him. I see his compromised body shaking before
the cameras pleading for stem cell research to continue- research, which will
benefit untold millions of other human beings to follow. Mother Teresa
wore just 2 habits, it was the only clothes she had. Her nuns lived in
simplicity, eating meagerly, dwelling almost without possessions of any
kind. Washing and bathing in cold water—not heated-- in order to share in
some measure the adversity of the poor & disfranchised of this world. I
don't hate her. I don't reject her. It's because of the degree of suffering.
I'm sick of people who have so much!

These folks, these folks. They want masters. They want kings. They get
war, poverty, starvation. They don't want that, but that's what they get
when they won't think for themselves! And this is what we're getting right
here in America, greatest nation on earth! Greatest ever seen! We're voting
for the wrong leaders for the wrong reasons---and flushing a nation down
the toilet!

As you rise higher in the body of Christ/Mohammad/ Moses/The
Eternal/Great Mother/) some of the old stuff must fall away. Self! Self. ----
The putting aside of self—that is The Way. The Path gurus speak of.

To use the higher path first throw away mirrors---- then the higher way opens to us.

> The nuns prepare my way for me.
> With a humble bow.
> Attired in severe black/white habits.,
> They take my full length mirror;
> lay it lengthwise on the ground
> so I can walk over it.
> Thus my Journey begins.

The poor artist must live the monastic life of a saint in self-deprivation. Accept physical hunger deriving from a hunger to know the Divine.

You must hold to the Way. Yes, isn't The Path putting aside of self? So that one might see more clearly? This self & all its desires needs & fears.

Noticed I'd gone to church, prayed a prayer that day, went to shul that evening and continued the same prayer that I began that morning in church. It's the same God, the same faith & the same prayers---just in a different language.

Church, shul, mediations---I've had difficulties with all of them.

But make no mistake you believers! God has extended Gods-self into every single nation, every people, in every single time and place and by many different Names!

The Lord(ess) God most High has thrown a wangdangle on me. God of all Creation I'm moved to tears! Fighting faucets of water back as we exit Grace Cathedral into the black night; in a clear sight (for there are no tall buildings) there over the park square, way, way above, set in a dark black blue sky;

a blaring flaming and furious moon! MOON!

God is always outdoing Gods self! A huge circular stained glass window cemented in stone shone like a precious jewel set on the face of Grace Cathedral, lifts its breast up to the moon in heavenly offering!

An unusual stratus of clouds formed to look like an underline for emphasis under this full moon, or a reversed eyebrow beneath an eye.

God is sending signs & wonders in the heavens!

A day later in a different part of the city I continue my astronomy. Veils & veils of white/grey clouds above the moon (but none of them upon it) being now like an eyebrow in its proper place.

No more copies at Trans Center. The new director has forbad it. —In her again-changing-of-the-mind. It's a good damn thing I did what I did while I could!
Have come full circle back. Returning to the printing of 7 copies of each new work as I did 30 years ago in 1978. From now on. At the height of free copying it was 16 (of PASSAGE). So my station is removed to Kostly Korporate Kinko's. As far as the restoration project, am now making the Re-Xerox Series at one sheet (1 copy of 4 pages, back-to-back) per day of those ancient originals. The next day return to Korporate Kostly with the new master to make additional 2 copies. Because I said I'd do 3 copies each of 22 titles. Such a painstaking pace now! Like how in that movie with Morgan Freeman some white celebrity star dug, dug, dug, tunneling his way thru prison walls to freedom 2 spoonful of soil at a time over 20 years! Excruciating! Lucky ELECTRO SHOCK DOKTOR was almost done upon the largess. Too bad I had saved almost all of the double length books until the end.

In JOURNEY I, at 7 copies, continue my progress thru this world. This diary of days. The latest dresh* is this: I said I wanted to write/paint things of beauty—here is a quote pertaining to that very fact: *'it is only though symbols of beauty that our poor spirits can raise themselves from things temporal to things eternal.''*

Abbe Suger, De Administratione, circa 1126.

*--Hebrew; a commentary.

Chapter 5.

S/he was reading. Fragments. Star1.vax found it highly amusing how old Red who has, essentially taken the vow of poverty; living in his priest-like cell/studio under the barbaric tyranny of the old empires rent moguls in simplicity, had been stricken by consumerism. Star1.vax's lower lip tucked into his mouth, his nostrils flared with suppressed mirth. Prophet Red had inherited the cast-off furniture of his ex wife & her lover, a certain Ms. Laura A. The couple having purchased new cabinets, shelves, TVs, VCR's & DVD player (an ancient form of home-movie entertainment which was outfitted with 4 excruciating interlocking parts with many criss-crossing wires connecting them, which has been replaced as we know, by the modern singular module, completely tensel-strength-lightweight transportable and without any wires at all in which 7 medias are featured. And how the confusion at the sudden glut of his good fortune in material goods drives him wild! A humorous portrait of Red frantically darting about his small space moving stuff around discarding his 'old furniture', which wasn't furniture at all—just a bunch of plastic something's (*Milk Crates? What are those?*) Which the reading fragments didn't explain.

While pondering over this curious volume of forgotten lore the young heshe began to nod, small chin fell to rest upon the collar of a blue fabric uniform around his neck, and soon fell completely asleep.

Transman Star1.vax had a dream he was living outside, on a grassy hill. He was a sheep. A Shepherd was watching him. This Shepard's voice spoke. S/he looked up at the vast sky above and said to the sheep: "The stars are big and deep out there in My heavens." Then this Shepard pointed with his index finger, and smiled so wise and kind & full of love. "They cross heaven. Then they turn back around." He/she said, indicating the whole wide heavens, and made a big circle with her index finger. Whatever the interpretation, upon awakening it had left him with an extremely hopeful and positive feeling. Did the Shepherd mean, that all lost things will be found? And people too?

So when weary Starvax snapped out of a nod, in the too-comfortable media/reading chair-pod, realizing s/he'd have get up from his ease and go thru tedious preparations simply to go right back to sleep again, this made him even more weary, pissed & disconsolate. To entertain himself while he lethargically moved about the unit; setting out a blue uniform (standard fit for size small Utopian male) ordered next period's (morning) breakfast via internet to be delivered by drone & ran bath water, s/he envisioned the past as they now had a view of one thru the studies. How back in the ancient days of 2006 Red was piecing together his little life—husbanding his few dollars, placing stuff into the jigsaw puzzle of survival under the antiquated Kapitalist system (like how long he could use his bus transfer, what he could afford to eat for the day, etc, etc) and in reflection it occurred to him that maybe who he'd seen in the dream was that Great Shepard the Transman had referred to in his lost, now found documents. And because of his own discontent, subsequently was so moved by this discovery that he actually stopped mid-way into the bath, foot poised over whirlpooling blue waters; his jaw dropped. '*Is this what he was trying to tell us about, us citizens of the future-- this Great Shepard?*' Was the old prophet calling Star1.vax from beyond, from his time & place? Or, (another idea swiftly formed) was it the same Shepherd who called them both?

***

The next 24-hour period proceeded in the familiar. A mundane pattern without event. Waking after 6 hours regulation sleep (for the dutiful citizen), plus 2 more out of sheer laziness, he prepared for his job. Trying to bolster lagging confidences, the young man spoke aloud as if someone else was nearby inside his unit, which no one was.

"You'd be surprised—these little snail steps of mine have gotten me a long way." He chuckles, yellow tint face forcing a laugh, his slanted eyes half-closed. S/he had made snail steps all the way up to the 30th floor—tho it had taken 7 *years!* Star1.vax originally had fought the intent of the cheerful intake workers at The Unity Housing Authority to place him speedily underground: One such worker had peered at him over her pod desk; just a glimpse showing of rapine teeth behind a lipsticked smile: "I can place you here! Immediately this next 8-hour period! By afternoon! In one of our lovely tri level shopping mall-centered units, with 2 baths, deluxe kitchen, built-in media centers in both the living rooms and bedrooms—oh did I say in **both** bedrooms! Two! —All for the single **individual** citizen! --- On the 40th level, ...*subterranean.*" She had added that last part inaudibly. He had fought it then as one battles a terminal disease, --descent underneath the earth; stamping that alternative out of his mind just like a sickness. And Utopia had conquered most all sickness, including those which affected the body of society, such as poverty. He had clamored and demanded in the offices of the Housing Authority to get a unit well above any sort of common 10-floor range. And got it. Floor 19. A tiny efficiency, 1 bedroom, living room, smallish kitchen, and a single bath.

Still talking to himself young Starvax took his breakfast at the unit door not acknowledging the drone who brought it & carried the hot-trey back to the kitchen.

There was hardly any dwelling units below the 3rd, 4th or even 5th floors in the reconverted skyscrapers and new Utopian super structure skyscrapers alike. These were reserved for supermarkets, shops, theatres and such. The ancient mall structure of the old iron/steel edifices of the now dead Am-Erica, U-rope, and A-Sha, leant itself to this. And their blueprints had been carried over into the future.

Yes, he had proceeded on to the 25th floor just 2 years later. From then it was only a skip & a hop to the 30th, with its more airy, lofty view. Yet

76

Starvax was disconsolate, blue as the blue uniform he was now stepping into.

In addition to being a mixedrace fondling saved from the wilderness but at the price of having no family, Star1.vax had experienced the denial of not being a male born man tho appearing to be one. To his great embarrassment, & hurt. On several occasions this was illustrated. All of them bad. Once, when he'd first started out at Depot 33 of the Unity Central Bureau Clearing House of World Statistics & Information in an entry-level job in the mailroom delivering wordhole hardcopies. S/he'd been so proud to capture a regular schedule job out of the aggravating chaos of endless miscellaneous work assignments here & there all over the city. It had given energy! Inspiration! The employees on the fourth level called him "Romeo" because of his then-flirtatious way with women. On the 3rd, he was that "New guy— Mister One." Because of his swagger and good-humored greetings. Cock-sure. Braggadocio. That was some years ago, before his confidence had begun to shrivel up like raisin under ordinary sunlight. Shortly after the remembrance, of those women of the depot having found out his true birth gender & subsequent transition thru a leak of security upstairs in the Personnel Department/Human Resources, and how they'd shunned him after their shocked discovery, ---turned so cold, because of having been so totally fooled-- and the unfriendly, bitter stares from co-workers, who although not supposedly prejudiced, were incensed at having been deceived; a time when he almost feared violence (almost unheard of under the Unity) and having preferred to leave this position, to be transferred elsewhere inside the gigantic Depot; flashed a vision of a blond, shapely in formfitting blue standard Unity Uniform, jangling earrings as she marched along the streets of empire. Trailing a scent of perfume. That certain walk she had. Mablevax. '*Mable473.vax & her pussy.* I want to die.' He knew, at the very thought. 'Yeah, I'll really become a mole— underground. I won't think of sex again. I'll get myself *neutered.* And crawl down along the emergency exit all 40 floors stair by stair and stay underground. *Forever.* Just work the mandatory job at minimum requirement of 20 hours per week via telescreen --- at home in my unit, curled up inside my pod. A Mole. ***Dead.'***

As Starvax prepared to go to his meaningless job in Depot 33 he switched on the Telly with an angry snap. Feeling he had nothing to look foreword to in his cheated life—but maybe some shocking global news would come on; this would give him a jolt of energy and ersatz happiness.

Maybe there would be a report about the latest exploration in deep outerspace that had just returned, which he had seen materialize with his own eyes! (That same fateful day Mablevax had first lighted her beautiful eyes on him!) It should be emerging from top-secret 10-day quarantine.

The Telescreen did draw his interest briefly with these headlines barked by an announcer. ALIENS HAVE BEEN FOUND! SPACE CRAFT BEING TOWED INTO SPACE STATION ASTROS IN THE EARTH GALAXY!

Immediately after this excited newsflash, came a loud bulletin; Unity's shrill calling for all able bodies of 1A clearance to volunteer to report to a new space mission. This strategically poised after the excited announcement of the alien space ship. A good recruitment tool. Too good. So maybe it wasn't true.

Within a few minutes, via super-speedwalk he arrived at destination. Work at the Depot. Monotonous as usual. *'Does it make any difference this job I do? I think my new studies in the group is thousands of times more important then this shit! And we're not really doing nothing. No Actions. If the other comrades in our study group feel as frustrated as I do…'* Her-his mind blanked at the ominous thought. But it was something like, *'so, they would never be in short supply of revolutionaries!'*

So far the study groups goal of seeking revolution was thru studying truth, chiefly thru the examining of history & documents indigenous to past eras and places. There had of yet been no talk of acts to be committed. Acts, which to which penalties were severe at best. Death at worst.

Time revolved precariously close to anarchy at a very tedious pace right there, stuffed into his pod.

Once near the last hour of his shift, at the thousandth dull citizens request for information whining into his ear, Starvax shut off the headphones, switched off the monitor and collapsed back in his pod. 'Goddamn the Unity! 'Goddamn the mother I never knew!' He'd damn them all! 'Goddamn Utopia! GODDAMN THE UNITY!' He screamed inside his skull.

His-her slim body unhooked from the pod; in blue uniform, sweat wrinkled, strode rapidly off the floor. S/he took a short break to gather his mental state. In the employee cafeteria s/he paced in front of rows of shining food/beverage machines, giving his inner self a pep talk. Only the thought of the upcoming study group however, in finality, seemed to relieve tension. Returning to his station Starvax cuddled into the form-fit pod again with a sigh, pacified. Yes. He was somebody! Somebody individual! Somebody wonderful! Hadn't he worked his way up to the 30th floor! And here at the

Bureau of Statistics he'd gone from a trial entry-level rank to this station before which he now sat, peering into a green lush telescreen. In a *permanent* position!

It had become apparent that one of the few things to look foreword to in life nowadays was the group. The next meeting was called practically on the heels of the last. What a joy!

Again their clandestine study was held outside the Great Dome, but in a different space. Mildly conscious of the fact that he/she now walked with determined strides along a creaking antiquated speedwalk thru an atmosphere where the noxious gasses of yesteryear still cycled hastily Starvax picked up his pace.

Sky outside the dome was a powerful blue with grey clouds rippled, a sky everlasting, ongoing, far reaching.

He entered the designation, a cubical— in a cement structure, unheated. The wan yellow-tinted face of the young Transman peered about—quickly, as if looking for someone in particular, who he couldn't locate. At which point her-his expression grew grim, mouth pressed into a line. He turned and sat down.

The discussion that day was age, & disability. —Something most of the beautiful subversive Utopian comrades knew little about. As one being they stared foreword at today's teacher with rapt faces.

Valdez opened. "In the Ancient Days there was great respect for the aged. Tho often their society allowed some of them to starve in a state of malnutrition because of the imbalances inherent in Advanced Kapitalism. You should remember, even the so-called aged of the past were only, sadly in about their 70's or 80's. Definitely nowhere near our current 200-year span. This reverence was despite their physically disability for unlike a true physical disability, so prevalent in those days, which as we know is seldom and only briefly seen now in Utopia, old-age infirmary was the eventual outcome for everybody. Respect was given to these Old Timers. Supposedly they had more wisdom."

Dr. Anderson chimed in: "Old age was not a specified condition that only some people got. If you live long enough you'd get to be an old timer too. Hence no judgment, or disparagement can be cast."

Star1.vax didn't think it remarkable that he might well live into 200 year range—even as a lowly transient low-rise dweller in a meaningless job.

Only how well he'd live, was the issue. Especially if could ever change his status under scrutinizing eyes of citizens of the Unity. Become Somebody, instead of Nobody.

The pleasant drone of the liberation class comforted him immensely, even tho much of the time he wasn't listening. Mind wandering off on its own thoughts. Eventually he returned to attention about the end of the first hour.

Gojenko: "How many of you here have ever seen a disabled citizen?"

The room of 30-odd students remained silent.

Valdez immersed in a pile of notes, as usual, professorial. Was preoccupied.

Anderson: "Do you think there's a reason for that?"

"Well of course not, because there's.... no way for a disability... to be. Disease has been eradicated, so there is nothing to make us disabled, and unlucky citizens who get in accidents get immediately outfitted with a prosthetic device. It's life-like. The doctors use sub atomic human flesh simulators. Nerve, and stem cell regeneration. So the public can barely tell the difference." Volunteered one comrade, a big fellow, bio male. Sounding immediately different then his appearance, which seemed at surface not overly smart.

Anderson nodded agreeing. "Good answer." Then turned to another corner of the room. "But how about people who are born with disabilities, not related to any disease---which as we know by our studies happened in the olden days."

A comrade mused. "Yeah, I think ... there are disabled people.... But... if you don't see them, well...." scratching his head... "maybe they've been... removed."

Anderson probed. "Removed? Well wouldn't you notice them a little bit of time? In the city streets? Your neighbors? For a while before the soldiers took them away?"

"Huh. Yeah... Guess I never thought about it."

Gojenko had put down his papers and entered into the conversation bluntly; pushed to the crux of the matter. "Maybe its because they have been removed before they get a start to grow up. Did any of you ever stop to think of that?"

"Huuuuhh...Ohhhh...." A mass inhale of breath, groans of disgust and sounds of disbelief filled the room.

"You mean killed off as children?" Cried a female comrade. Starvaxs full lips pursed, he tapped his electronic pen scribe on the surface of his desk and silently mused; *'where is blond-head Mablevax'?* But the female comrade was irate. As she yelled, to the agreements of other members who made noises of discontent. And Starvax only frowned. A grimace grew on his countenance.

Gojenko wrapped up the matter with finality. "As you know all new mother womb simulators are scanned by modern ultrasonic investigation from their first impregnation. If an anomaly is detected, the embryo is aborted."

"That's the first stage. Understandably." Anderson added.

Gojenko: "The second level is the observation of nursery schools and kindergartens, from which all aberrant children are culled.... Removed, as we like to say in Utopia."

Anderson added one more chilling statement to discussion. She raised her head somewhat, replacing her atomic penscribe in a pocket of her white lab coat. "Somehow we feel that not all of these anomalies are detected early enough, in vitro. However the subsequent progeny is spotted fairly early in development, in the beginning education level, pre kindergarten. And yes, they are removed."

Students were dismayed, outraged, and disgusted.

Starvax had missed much of the discussion.

"Well, it prevents some of the horrible crippling of people we saw up as late as the early part of the century, and all down thru history. They lived horrible lives." Said somebody.

Gojenko: "Mental illness is removed. But sadly including some artistic geniuses. We believe, in fact we have knowledge that children will be culled out who somehow begin to develop into what eventually will become to be too small adults, or too large, or too fat, or too skinny. Children who are too aggressive, too shy etc. etc. The culling out of any extremes from Utopian Society."

The last hour, more quotes from more long-dead folks. That was disgusting too. How the people of earth once had free societies. With things called library museums where all books and paintings were for the public to consume at will. All this had been removed. Once all the people of earth had freedom as to where they could live and travel and go and be— admittedly if they could afford it. All these free choices were no longer available. The whole humanrace was a monstrous disgust... "How had they given it all up, thrown their freedom away back then? Why wasn't anybody awake at the switch--when the train of suppression came barreling along down the tracks, and so wrecked them? Resulting in this present society we know today? Weren't there any protests against the coming storm-- well we know by their documents there was! We know by the writing of this prophet in his journal!" Anderson shook a copy of the old work in one hand fiercely. "There was! Fighters, just as we are today, here! You," she pointed to one corner of the room. "You there," she nodded in another direction. "All of you!" Anderson was a good teacher.

Sitting back in his chair once more Valdez smiled a weary smile, face upraised for only the second time since class had begun.

Starvax completely ignored the reminder of the study. Some interesting quotes from the Native People who had survived so poorly, dying early, back in those long ago days, as written down by the Prophet Red in his diary JOURNEY. The descendents of those people who rumor has it still lived out in the uncharted territories. Some of it was very poetic. He-she felt it had meaning, and made a note listlessly on his electron slate to peruse them later that week.

The usual announcements followed, amid warnings to not walk out en masse, to avoid sending personal communications of a damaging nature via the internet, wordhole, and other somber indicatives.

When they got outside the cement building Starvax looked as usual up at the sky, and noticed something. It was getting prematurely dark. So he picked up his listless pace.

Going back towards the antique speedwalk Starvax's steps somehow joined him briefly with a triage of students, who stared at him suspiciously, the large man, and two women. One woman looked at him a moment then said; "oh you're Mablefax's.... friend!"

"Yeah!" His manner energized instantly. "Where is she today? I expected to see her!"

The two women cast a look at each other.

"She's on a mission."

"Oh." Starvax took a sharp intake of air. For he knew only too well what danger that meant.

"We can't talk about it." Cautioned the large man.

"We don't really know much about it ourselves." Replied one woman.

"I don't know *anything.*" Starvax said. He hesitated…"No one ever says anything to me, or even talks to me…" And immediately felt foolish.

"That's because nobody knows you!" Laughed the smaller of the woman. And blushed slightly.

"You just started dude." Said the large man in a deep voice.

The four kept steps together a few more paces. Then even they separated. Starvax thought that those people laughed, friendly, more with him, then against him. And now… he knew…. Mablevax had told them he was her friend!

His spirits lifted. But clouded too, wondering if she would be safe.

Lighter in step, the young Transman walked along like the rest, alone, yet in a loose band of his comrades, slowly breaking apart far enough apart to seem not connected. A mass which slowly separated further & further on their trek back to the rapid transit. So as not to arouse any suspicion from the few passerby's who were also outside the city limits for whatever purpose. Soon they took the slow antiquated speedwalk which moaned and groaned numerous complaints. He could see the gulches and gullies and the debris of what remains of another ancient transport—called the railroad. At quite a distance away its rusted rails traveled, then turned off into the end of seeing between some demolished buildings flattened by the 3rd World War.

He boarded the transit, but not without first studying the sky. He hoped he'd be in time!

At a speed of 300 mph they arrived in moments. Lovely Hillside By The Bay (San Francisco to the historian) the view was the same, long hills rising/falling, ultimately rising into the very top of the dome, then plunging down on the other side, into the deep unknown ocean.

The real sky above the dome is darkening—the inside lit now, artificially, by nuclear powered light continues to blaze blithefully as it will until proper even-fall at the 3rd trimester of the 24th hour block. But outside of it the sky grows prematurely dark. A grey billow of clouds has massed. It was then young Starvax took an hour (which was precious to him) out of his regime, to make an important detour.

He knew the way going directly there.

He was already pressed for time, having attended the group and that at such a remote location. But once he returned back into The City, Starvax did something out of his usual routine. Took a valuable time to head onto a speedwalk down-island into the dense cluster of super sky-scrapers, those 500 floor megaliths. Stepped off the walk and fairly ran down the streets toward one ghastly giant in particular of several dozen. Amid throngs of citizens part of the night shift. The city worked 24 hours.

Entering a cold white stone lobby full of citizens, he snaked his way thru.

He didn't hover at the multiple elevator banks, but went directly to the special ones. —There were only 3. All the elevators designation were perpetually lit by a sign over them. One section; floors 1,2,3,4,5 to ten. After them, that bank of elevators which began at ten and went only to the 50th floor then stopped. Next those which zoomed straight to the 50th then proceeded on at a numbered sequence to 75. Behind those, the bank going directly to floor 100, then incrementally to 125. And so forth. He found that special few, those express which shot straight up their metal shaft for $1/8^{th}$ of a mile sky high to the absolute top!

Raced now along the semi busy lobby! Did not want to miss the show! Ran into the first one. S/he had it all to himself! The panel for buttons designating floors had a single choice. Pressed the button to the 500th. Impatiently as the silent elevator rose up along its monstrous shaft never with even a wobble, ten floors each few seconds, speeding past the 150th floor, 200th, 300th without a single jolt.

Metal doors slid open. He had the place to himself! This upper level, a huge city block square, a free public observation deck, with only a few hundred other citizens—divided by so much space—so that he heard almost only his footfalls! The observation deck was entirely glass windowed to the exterior on all four sides, filled at its center with shops, stores, souvenir stalls with maps, skycharts, binoculars for sale, a top of the world restaurant & bar, a tee-shirt shop. **I GOT THIS TEE-SHIRT AT THE TOP OF THE WORLD!** And so forth. Ordinary stuff of Utopia.

The young Transman rushed to the observation windows.

Here at the 500th floor, well heated inside, freezing cold permeating the triple pane tensel strength windows a solid 5 inches thick to the touch of his fingertips, and the view outside was unobstructed around. About were only a few other building tops as high. Sound of spacecraft up this high, could hear them roar as nowhere else lower down to the surface.

He wasn't disappointed! Thunder and lightening! The performance began! As great a lightshow as the heavens could provide! Lightning white, jagged cut amazing daggers thru the real sky above the outermost arch of the dome.

This spectacular view could be enhanced by the use of high-powered binoculars, at no cost, positioned every 25 feet around the deck, which he had often availed himself of, to bring up in bas relief grids of the city below like a printed map, his eyes eventually following the long hills rising into the very top of the dome, then plunging down on the other side—into the distance! So many times before Starvax had ridden the elevator way way up here to look down at those distant areas—even buying a pair of binoculars to own, in order to see that distant terrene, the place of his savage birth— where rumor said existed one of many tribes of humans, not part of The Unity. Those remaing residuals of tribes were that were lost; somehow creeping back in through the tunnels & sewers of the old city which lay beneath the new one; living & dying outside in the surrounding territories like a mystery haunting him-her.

5.
S/he prayed at nighttime. So tired, so exhausted, shuffled to bed found himself uttering the words, which were: "Mother Jesus! Mother Jesus!" Stammered out of his mouth.

He/she prayed at eventide: 'For those both domestic and foreign who's fate has been to be murdered, maimed, destroyed by our nations military adventures.'

He milled around while in the common ground of the park--then went up up the cement steps of the mighty Cathedral.

This edifice is castlesque. Minds eye can see back in ancient eras, falcons who inhabited castles of the early and middle ages, living in rafters, who shat everywhere, even upon the heads of royalty; nobles & vassals alike and the hounds who bedded down with the soldiers in straw on the cold stone floors; falcons swooping down to receive their portion of bread and mead, the hounds baying up/down rocky stairwells; these ill lit unventilated fortresses where smoky firebrands lit corridors and smoked up the interior, and warmth was scanty, provided by sections of tree trunks burning in huge fireplaces taller then a human stood, and heat was retained by thick rich tapestry's indicative of unparallel wealth which had been captured, seized as some prize which adorned the walls.

Approaching this vast stone fortress of the Cathedral, he prayed upon each of its steps:

(A step.) 'For all those whose hearts is so heavy.'

(Another step.) 'For the innocents. The children in orphanages because of war and domestic spousal abuse. The animals tortured in slaughterhouses to feed us.'

(Now clutching onto bronze railing.) 'For the environment, to save our air, our water, so that all of us animals and humans can have a future goddamn it!'

S/he prayed at nighttime, that all his/her gifts to the church (synagogue, other religious centers) be well-blessed and deeply received.

(Last set of cement steps, speckled grey.) I approach the last step hobbling on one leg, just as the Cathedral bells begin to chime their last note. Its 6pm.

Entered the massive gold gilt doors, he prays: 'I bow deeply from the heart to the majesty of God.'

Congregates dressed in their funeral clothes, those walking corpses--- wearing smiles on their moribund faces. Smiles of the dead. Drinking up inspiration from the angelic choir at Grace Cathedral sung from gifted throats of the choir. Pure--- awestruck we listeners are being purified.

The Transman let his gaze drift upwards, up, up, to the loftiest part, those arches which uphold this great ceiling—then vision fell again, to observe the well-heeled crowd in which he was sitting.

Behold the church straining at its weakest point! Its breaking! From sheer wealth! There's too much money inside here! In the pockets, purses, checkbooks of this congregation! Too many houses are owned between them! More then their share! It is breaking down the church of Christ!

Thought that out of the congregants, 700, 800? No, over 1,000, that Sunday afternoon only the woman who sang the chorals had the voice of the very finest angel, and that he too was very gifted, prolific, spiritually sighted--- that how few people out of this thousand were a specialist in their own field! To whom the other 999 must come to hear the angelic solo, read the fascinating novel, or receive benefit from the surgeon, master in her/his own domain.

***

Attended the two-spirits Harvest Day celebration. Native American GLBT. Ate fry bread, succotash, turkey. Partook of Native prayers. It's a way of life to which all are invited, Indian, white, black, Asian, all. In a changing world.

Colorado Indian musicians were striking the drums with fury. The drums are sounding danger! People must change their ways fast—for there's the inheritance of all blood spilt & hurt done to the red peoples. — The ancient chants speak truths. That a cycle is upon its returning swing—so listen, it's of importance, these red prophets:

> We walk as warriors.
> In a powerful & spiritual manner.
> Walk in a sacred manner
> Walk in a sacred way.
> Walk as a warrior.

Yes people, —that cycle is returning. You ones who love Creator must do the right thing & set food back on the tables of the poor from which you or your ancestors once amassed their great wealth! Set foot on the right path least we be caught up in the flood, the far-reaching destruction which is sweeping over this world--- returned with a vengeance! Go in the right direction! The Path.

The terrible part of it all is—this is not a work of vendetta or vengeance by human hands, which is thus more easily combated by human minds, but a work of justice set into motion by Creator Herself. The God, the One who made us all.

The emotions of human hearts grow hard.
Times become so vicious, so cruel,
that it becomes unbearable for the human soul.

& that's where God steps in.

***

God *is* good.
All others are pieces of good.
 (If they're smart.)

God: Make your people be my people.

Red: Well OK… (Begrudgingly) If that's what you want…

God: No Red, that's what YOU want. I'm calling you back home you must
hold to the path!

***

En-route thru the TL this afternoon. Junkie hype—skinny lounges against a
building. Vamp. A Dracula cloaked in narcotic shroud, invisible but oozing
out of her aurora like death. Explosive insane stalk the Tenderloin babbling
frothing hate. Grown up fast into adults stumbling druggies on the street are
crazed unhappy children laughing over 3rd grade jokes

There's all these food places, little cheep eateries in the dive environs.
Somebody has money & in junkie spirit of generosity takes everybody to
eat. So the fires of human charity are not burned out utterly.

> *Their young life being so bad,*
> *such a cruel upbringing*
> *that they've lost part of themselves.*
> *Too much gouged out. --*
> *So they must have a blood sacrifice*
> *Only spilling of blood—human blood*
> *Will ease the torment.*
> *Their blood—*
> *Or someone else's.*

I see my other toothless could-have-been-self in one of the dwindling supply
of cheap crack-ho hotels (the other residence hotels slowly continuing to fall

88

before affluent yuppie gentrification) a soon-to–die not transitioned transbutch hustler, welfare chiseler sometime part-time phoneroom worker living on the lowest rung scrambling with half pint of whiskey in her hand.

A young Red, angrier back then because he didn't understand how things worked, even buying a cup of coffee from employee behind the counter without creating an argument with the proprietor.

Suddenly, as if in finality, the grimy streets themselves make the final pronouncement of their fate, as the further out of dead-center of the TL you go the streets get cleaner; no stray newspapers, fewer wandering disheveled bums w/vacant stares staggering to nowhere or doomed dopefiends on intent purposes of criminal stratagems. It's all coming to an end! Being sanitized! Gentrified! It's outcasts removed!

Alcohol/drugs are not the worst offense the offense against the self, it is the giving-up of hope that is worst. These others spring from that.

***

Look up 1930's painter on Internet—Thomas Hart Betran. Writer Painter. I must pick up the brush, pallet, & oil colors! Maybe this will let me into a very elite group that of other writer/painters---in heaven at least (so all could be there including past, present, future) all of us down the ages or right here on earth. Must start, or be without it forever.

You've seen them before, ersatz, poseur, failed, or procrastinating artists in whose 'studio' (4 walls only being used to live inside) the same canvass stretchers sit unmoved from storage, unused brushes stuck by size in decorative vases gathering dust, and others, once too-briefly used sadly sit aside of the sink in a glass jar. Their fine sable hair stuck together in a non-rehabilateable qlucky glooy mess of by-now evaporated turpentine solvent once meant to dissolve oil paint and now the very adhesive which binds them in their death throes in an oily dried up Sargasso sea— if the artist ever regains her inspired balls she will have to go out & procure a passel of new tools.

When you're young you have all these desires, yearnings, that drive one out to explore the world, to search, to fulfill their inner longings. Full of energy. But as you get older this dissipates… For some it lasts quite a while, but eventually those longings do modify, cool. And it's a good thing, because those yearnings and desires torture a person to the death!

89

Oh by the way must add once more about AUTUMN CHANGES*—this is a total fabrication! Lies all lies told but thru using the voices of a conglomerate of other folks for instance the following case study....

Case study #450:
Some peoples live lives very difficult because they can't locate themselves on the sexual /gender chart. Sex & gender and how that is acted out in society and in bed. A case history comes to mind—most strange, that of Signore Serpeggiarevere Calvin Lezzardo Consigliore Di Poitou, a military officer of substantial degree and a high-ranking director (Consigliore) of the committee internal affairs.

Signore Calvin was stocky, well built, masculine in demeanor and attire—but in a female range of height. Handsome, well-groomed, well-mannered male, circumspect, moderate in actions and in dress. Not remarkable whatsoever---except by one thing he did. Which was, he was seen in lesbian taverns of the late 1960's and all thru the decade of the 1970's that heyday, age old since the tenuous rise of woman's taverns back in the 1800'rds, when they finally began to wane due to the clean & sober movement which swept thru the dike community when lesbians stopped going to bars, stopped drinking; this not-too mysteriously coinciding with the opening up of many more avenues for them to go, not in a small part thanks to the women's liberation movement. Signore Calvin would come in to some women-only bar—in uniform-- in his leisure hours after his duties as an official di Poitou and stand or take a barstool. Legally he could not be kept out since as a public place by the state code they must serve any customers who gave them no reason to be ejected. And as he never posed a threat (other then that, in the suspicious women's eyes, of his actually *being* there), over time he was just regarded as a fixture around the place---like a drably decorative column supporting the ceiling stuck off in the corner somewhere gathering dust. He would sit silently and stare at the crowd, but not obtrusively, watching the dancers, the revelers, and sip 3 or 4 alcoholic drinks during the course of an evening.

After the death of nearly all of the Lesbian Bars, which had come and gone by name, location, usually numbering about a half dozen in any given year, he was lost sight of. But a decade later the Signore, graying around the temples and having added an extra 40 pounds to his girth so that he now resembled a roly-poly soldier boy doll in dress uniform was observed in the following situations: #1. At the office of Dr.------ a notorious physician whose clientele was almost exclusive transsexual, a little on the shady side, who administered injections of female hormones for the desperate trans female population of those queer-unfriendly times and also testosterone to the intrepid sparse few ftms who might make their way upstairs to his 3rd

floor Tenderloin office. But under slightly dubious circumstances came these hormone treatments. First, they were sold at high prices to the desperate & marginalized transsexual clientele, and, the Physician was a renowned tranny chaser, trick, surreptitious tit & ass groper, & proved later to be a cross-dresser himself, who had secretly been titillating his fantasies on the parade of bedraggled showgirls in nylon hose who swished and sashayed up his grimy steps—which was the true purpose of his 'office' from the start. #2. 2000. On numerous occasions, after dark, in his car pulling up to the curb of Post near Larkin Street picking up a transsexual sex worker, the finer sort, passable, and dressed in diaphanous veils and silks of the highest quality which clung to her body and high pumps on shapely legs, this not a happenstance encounter but a call--date, prearranged. Finally, #3. Now, having arrived full circle, the Signore, was seen, by witnesses, frequenting a modern day transsexual clinic, the reason being a consultation on his own potential transition, to female!

*--The Authors Master Work, his Semi-Unofficial Diary.

***

Grace Cathedral also has rats. Some ugly big ones. —6" to 8 long. See a shadowy rat slithering out of a raised flowerbed, climb down side of its stone retaining wall, scurry underneath the rain/sun weathered wooden benches with curved backs & disappear behind the perpetual water fountain. The two-legged rats are worse. Every religious institution of every faith on earth has them. Those in clerics costumes. Who have worked their way into the church and climb up thru the scaffold of its inner workings. Worse because they destroy My fabric. Says the Lord(ess). They eat away at My Body.

Now I am poor, I am busy picking up dropped coins off the streets of Babylon in its Last (falling) Days, dimes pennies nickels & dreaming meanwhile of giving millions to inter-faith institutions that help raise up the plight of women, children, and the poor.

Recall those just before holidays how I felt like God was walking into my life. And Christ, literally. Tall, so beautiful, in the finest array of incalculably rich fabric so full of peace, radiating inner light. Felt the reverberations of God, so thick with substance unshakable.

Well I'll be honest about it, Creator had showed me, upon moving into my small studio, that it was in fact a cell and I was a nun-priest, a devotee, living nearby a Christian church where I could do service and be connected into the flock of the Most High, so that was 5 years ago, and tonight after

91

Grace Cathedral (2nd time in my life there) am thinking, when the minister cried *follow!* Meaning the Christ is calling us to follow, which means giving up everything, monies, desires of self, etc, that I am in fact a nun-priest in the service of the Most High, by my own self's choice, and so here we are!

When I was a new Christian I towed the party line. All I knew were Christians in my church during that era—broke off from the other friends of different faiths long ago as a transient person may do over the progress of time. And believed then, as my church taught, the only way to heaven was thru the one Christ, now I believe many others of many other faiths who worship Creator in spirit and truth and love, and need and sorrow and even joy will see the Great Heaven open to them!

All this worship at various venues, am learning a smattering of Hebrew! To go with my poquito Spanish as learned from the lips of the lovely Rosa Salazar.

> The kind Mohammad came to me
> because I was weary & so worn out
> He comforted me.
> I am the same. Same
> As the Christ. I Am
> Buddha. Mohammad. Christ.
> Our Great Mother.

Walking from the Animal Shelter where I heard great news! Two dogs I'd visited, prayed for have are going home! They've been adopted!

> *When a lost animal gets a home*
> *it's the most wonderful day in the world.*
> *Greater then the Coronation*
> *of Kings & Queens,*
> *with all their pomp, circumstance & gold.*
> *Because it's from the heart.*

Walking past the green hill park see homeless huddled there. It is truly justice that, given the painful climb to civilization's peeks & heights some lowly humanbeing carrying ragged backpacks/bedrolls would crawl on their hands & knees thru the city streets so grand & built up & richly heralded, towards a green park to hide themselves under leafy boughs of trees, bushes, taking a place on the damp soil, putting themselves back into the human race's early forest beginnings to survive mentally & economically among the sky scrapers and towers of this fierce empire.

God: Red have I created people to be like beasts?

Red: You created people to be people. Beasts to be beasts.

God has presented her/his case with the opening statement.

These well to do people who pass by, who have taken over SF turned it into a high rent capital of the U$A---- they won't be dancing they won't be singing! Those who have forgotten about their infringements upon this bitter world!

God I want to go everywhere and do everything, in Your heaven! I want to sit on the perches with the birds to be near them! I want to run with tigers! I want to go all over Your creation and see everyone and greet all animals and people with love, and dance with joy!

> It's a beautiful place
> A marvelous place
> Where animal families are restored
> mother and child,
> and human families live in peace.

We are crossing some kind of great plane divided from heaven & separated out of chaos. We are passing from an opening end to a closing across a landscape full of rising & setting suns, moons. The Good Shepherd/ Mohammad/ Great Mother/Buddah leads the way and comforts us on our journey.

> *I am the alpha & omega*
> *I am with you until the end of days.*
> *--Jesus Christ, 2006 AD.*

'God my work is a lonely work.'

He was known as 'the prophet who went by his own way.'

People laughed at him because he was different, but very soon they were to listen to him with an astute ear, nodding their heads in deep reflection.

93

'I'm such a mess.' Thought the Transman, but under the mighty arches of Grace Cathedral he saw the world in its pain—how much more of a mess! So much imaginable wealth held in the hands of a few, a few who seek to control the world and seize power! So much misery of so many untold masses of suffering others. This richest nation on earth—the most affluent time in history.

The bells of the Cathedral chimed their last note high in the cement tower like pronouncement sealed, judgment given.

Just one shake and I'll set it all straight! Says God.

Chapter 6.

In One Shake the world had fallen down. The different religions all claimed they were put on earth to help spread the light & fire far reaching. This, their holy people said. But it wasn't this kind of fire, which had rained down upon the early quadrant of the 21-century, it was the 3rd World War. Not spiritual fire but war.

On his regulation 24 hours off he/she was setting back inside his pod killing dead time with sour expression Telly-watching with a faint hope that something horrible would come over the screen to shock awake his dulled senses. Having filled the first quadrant of the 24 (free) cycle judiciously by making little trips across his small living room floor to check the wordhole repeatedly, and at 14, and 15 hours respectively by holding a splendid live simulation interface with his only two friends in the world, then, realizing the rest of the cycle would be spent alone, now sat sad/blue. Across the nearly wall-sized screen there came on a documentary film of a latest foray out into the unincorporated areas. A wildlife probe. With usual fanfare Unity vehicles, coated with the protective white colored shields which marked them as explorers-outside-the-domes, and manned by a retinue of health workers etc, clad in white puffy radiation free, germ-sanitized jump suits went crawling over the terrene, seeking to rescue any of the bizarre inhabitants there that could be found. –Or wanted to be. Plus gather any important data they may have missed on the last of these regular scheduled expeditions. They went out in a caravan of 3 large white-covered vehicles carrying 24 personal each plus de rigure military support, it was a showy display like many of the Unity's endeavors, designed to bolster morale, build confidence in the Unity, and create patriotic zeal, thus increase productivity among citizens at their meaningless jobs, and to distract them somehow so as they would remain satisfied with their positions in life. And thus subdue any restlessness or rumblings of discontent about the system.

All the health care workers, investigators and archeologists were covered head to toe in saggy white paper coats, booties over their shoes & white coverings over their heads made of the same material; it was super-reinforced and would be discarded after the outing. Many of them also wore the uncomfortable white facemasks. All wore inhaler ventilator systems, a clumsy device which they must breathe into, which claimed to filter out at least some of the foul particles of the ancient poisoned air of earth. All this regulation paraphernalia made Starvax laugh because ordinary citizens now traipsed into the unincorporated areas wearing no protection whatsoever, at least on its fringes, for the Unity was in dire need of more space, and new facilities were being located there in hastily-put-together cement cubicles, some a city block long, for sheer lack of elbowroom in the crowded conglomerate of the hard pressed built up areas in which so many millions of people had had to squeeze together under the Dome. Hadn't s/he been to 2 study group meetings held outside there already the past month? When you are only 30 and have a life expectancy 170 more years ahead, you don't worry about mortality. Suddenly his toes poking out of the bottom of his lounge suit twitched! His slanted eyes narrowed as he studiously watched the screen. The soldier(ettes) were finding something! The accompanying vehicles, land-roving monsters 20 feet tall, in back & front of the caravan which held the guard soldiers, had disgorged their occupants in a war-like maneuver. They wore regulation olive green and no environmental protection in favor of being less encumbered as military forces. It was one of the risks soldiers had to take at their jobs. They had all gone running towards a destroyed grey mass of twisted construction and were digging frantically with pick ax's and metal pry rods, even using their bare hands! While others stood by, weapons aimed at the pile of rocks!

"Have they discovered an alien?" Shouted the announcer of the film excitedly.

'That's how they found me.' Starvax said, to himself. S/he was on the edge of his seat.

Mostly these expeditions outside the cities of earth's Utopia turned up empty handed. Never any alien space monsters whatsoever. And evidently the humans who still remained there didn't wish to be seized and brought back into Unity at all. To be reprogrammed, maybe even removed, but preferred to live out their drastically shortened lives 50 years (maximum) in the desolate broken places with almost no resources but a earth rainfall for water, and scavenged food remainders from the dumps, where the effluvia of Utopia was discarded. Plus any small wildlife kills including rodents, which they could mange to trap and cook.

But occasionally a new captive turned up in custody somehow, maybe like the stray s/he'd seen lost and babbling on the streets under the dome a while back, having just tired of their deprived life and wandered back inside— caring little about what their fate would be. Their reddened & puffy scarred radiation sick faces were evidence of the indignities visited on them from living in that environment.

Starvax winced at the thought. To not dine regularly----meals robot-prepared and brought up to his unit by a mute drone shuffling on silent soft feet. Restaurants, the lavish abundant of choices on Utopias numerous bi-cultural menus. Rodents. 'They eat rat soup so I hear.' A sickening liquid boiled in found tin cans held up by pieces of twisted metal over bonfires built in the grey rock crevices, those glowing radioactive stones of the uneven debris strewn terrene. They lived in old bombshell craters, and cave-like excavations, which once were buildings foundations of that old mighty empire, now all reduced to rubble.

'It was here that my mother gave me birth. Aw... how horrible…. How painful for her.' For him as well. What a sad beginning. What a challenge.

What a challenge to overcome.

As was mostly the case the caravan returned later, empty handed of any survivors. There were no stragglers left in the old world who wished to 'turn themselves in' to the Unity, but did bring back sundry 'fragments' of their own; 'evidence' (so the authorities claimed) once again of extraterrestrial war which had been waged on earth, which had in fact brought about the massive destruction of the planet of whose ravages evidence could be seen everywhere. Thus 'proving' at least by Unity's leaders that the ancient lie of divided 'nations' of the past which had been so ferociously at war with each other, earth people themselves, which had practically destroyed themselves, had brought down the towers of their mighty empires spread out allover earth-- the wars between their own peoples-- a lie which all the old timers claimed was truth, but not as the Unity had it, wasn't true. More 'evidence' brought to light by investigating wildlife probes, of these alien weapons of mass destruction obviously designed by far superior minds who hovered in undetectable space craft just outside the Unity's recognizance, thus accounting for the bombed-out buildings, the radioactive count clicking of Geiger meters. What the excited soldiers had found would be duefully returned like all the others, those strange oblong parcels wrapped in radioactive preventing safety material, marked 'Top Secret' to be categorized, filed away and gather dust in Unity achieves.

96

For now that the world had come to terms, to peace with itself-- thru the assertion of the absolute dictators, the latest being Kim Sun II., the Unity had turned its aggression as one collective being towards any living aliens of the entire galaxies known and unknown, wherever or whoever they were!

In 14:00 hours of the 24-free cycle, going quite mad with boredom, young Starvax donned his blue uniform, took the elevator down, and went for a solitary walk.

S/he proceeded along the streets of the mighty Utopia so friendless and alone. Having exhausted the conversations of his two friends, then realizing dimly in the back of his brain the study group was due to communicate its next meeting to him at any moment! And by any means, par their method of stealth, to avoid detection from Utopias secret police. And thus savoring this thought in his mind awhile with delicious anticipation, he found himself passing out of the entertainment district, sort of to nowhere. At the top of a hill he stopped, and gazed. Out on the dim edges of view he glimpsed the end of the dome at the islands narrower part. Beyond there, just a few moments away was an unincorporated area. Maybe he'd go there one day.... And just walk around... Another thought to savor.

On his/her way back to his temporary domicile Starvax chose to take a route which carried him past his job in the governmental area, the civic center of Unity City #33, Lovely Hillview By The Bay. It was a 2 block square area of some 5 central headquarters vital to the running of the city, built around a green grassy mall. Towering among them was a great shining building, the main one, Central Hall, which had command of all other departments of governmental administration. Coming down its marble steps to the esplanade was a governmental official resplendent in a dark blue Unity uniform with gold placard proclaiming her high officialdom. She was speaking to a colleague; "you see all these trucks out there, they're covering it..." then her words were drowned out by the din of converging pedestrians. The young heshe turned, sure enough there across in the green grassy mall a fleet of some dozen media trucks outfitted with their tipple media cams, solar antenna's, satellite beamers, were waiting in anticipation, for something.

The Transman decided to take the speedwalk home; he was confused, and despite his youth felt tired as an old man. Life was grim, as he was practically friendless, and without a family. An adoptee assembly line product of Utopian humanitarianism. Nothing good nor great was coming of his life! Even those sporadic instant-erase messages sweetly planted in his wordhole hadn't been forthcoming, in fact none in the last... 10 days! Starvax faced these facts with disappointment. 'I haven't heard from my study group for awhile... Darf! I'll go back to my unit, crawl into my pod and sleep.'

When he got to his unit, found, quite aggravatingly there was a blank message on his wordhole. With no indication as to whom had called. As lonely as he was for friends! It was time for the 18th hour news. Beginning to strip off his clothes & put on a lounge jumpsuit, as usual, a wave of his hand switched on the media. Immediately a loud commotion issued out of it.

Starvax gazed horror struck at the Telly. Its 5 foot high, 7 foot wide screen stretched over the wall now vibrated with a fast action shot of a mass of people running! You could hear their voices! "AFTER THEM, THIS WAY!" Screams. They dispersed in all directions. "IT'S THE POLICE! IT'S THE POLICE!!" Then a close up of captive faces moments later, overlaid with the voices of two announcers: "Citizens! There's been a raid of subversives in vax 33! Beautiful Hillside By The Bay!"

The final pictorial broadcast proved to be a horrible development. As the Satellite re-play cameras did their close up along a string of streaked & dirty faces of the now handcuffed saboteurs being held in custody by squad of soldier(ettes)—with 2 scowling cyborg reinforcements standing by -- there was Dr. Anderson! His-her heart leapt to his throat. *"Mable! Is she there? Did they catch her in this too?"* The ferocious presence of these monstrous guards pronounced the fatal seriousness of their acts. Just then, as the announcers frantically yelled out the transpiring plots, unraveling these events of fate, each one punctuating their blow-by-blow description with labels like 'spies', 'alien agents', 'conspirators' it occurred to Starvax about his new found home, those secret classes! They now might be lost to him, those pleasant breaks throughout the mundane weeks! His heart sunk even lower. Hadn't wanted to admit how fully he'd come to rely on them, as if they were social events.

The announcers droned "CITIZENS LOOK AT THIS EXCLUSIVE REPORT LATER IN THE NEXT 24 HOUR BLOCK, FIND OUT WHERE THE BODY OF THE TRAITOR ANDERSON WILL BE PUT ON DISPLAY! LIVE OR DEAD! A SPY TO UTOPIA!" One, an androg, with a smiling, slick media face, turned to his-her co-anchor, another androg, querying, for the benefit of their audience; "What do you think Spencer? A Public Execution? How do you call it?" To which the co-announcer replied; "Well, Emerson, it sure points to that, doesn't it!" Amid fanfare and cheers of crowds of gathering bystanders the handcuffed traitors were being led away, to be removed, off to some undisclosed prison.

Stumbling into the pants of his lounging jumpsuit one leg then the other, he simultaneously summoned a drone by word command: "Unit 3043! Expect an express delivery and bring it up here fast! Post Haste!" Quickly on his cellphone he wired the television station, Media Central; sent out a frantic order for his own personal disc copy of that news episode "Send me a disk of this latest newscast, the 1800 hours Spencer & Emerson show. You can just cut to the arrest of the captured traitors report! I'm citizen star.1vax, 856 Sacramento Street, Unit 3043!" Shortly about 50 minutes later came a drone's heavy hand at the door.

Shoved the silver 2" inch diameter disc into his multi-media player. S/he played the episode over and over, on slow, then stop/go, studying it frame by frame, and yes, he did recognize a few of his comrades, but no sight of the blond, that Mable! Had she been caught? Had she even been with Anderson's group? Intently perused the short clip for his entire evening, so that by artificial dawn in Unity time he was red eyed, and weary. The worry of not knowing settled into his bones.

For the next 24 hour block Starvax moped around his job; did minimal work, dragged back to his unit, dining listlessly on the free Utopian dinner, so heavy hearted he even allowed the drone to choose his menu, a fact for which he was only distantly sorry while chewing grimly. Tasty food. That was just a minor concern. 'It might be the end of my study groups altogether. No more Anderson... and she was the best teacher.' But with the dim glimmer of faith—a word he did not understand, since no one in Utopia ever spoke that kind of language, but was a concept he had just recently become acquainted with by the old prophets writings--- that night Starvax curled into his warm heated pod, turned on the overhead light inside and continued, despite their arrest, to read his study books:

The 30-Day Ordinance, circa 2035.
Suddenly all over pre-Utopia in the nation still called Am-Erica upon which we now sit, there was put out into city streets the dark effluvium of grimy apartments, disgorged out of rat/roach infested, narrow walled rooms, people, squatting atop their belongings in a pile outside on the streets waiting for city sweepers to remove them to new domiciles. For those with insufficient monies, the abject poor, there was no place to go. So some 40 million were soon living in caravans moving every 30 days from city to city take advantage of local health care, charity food distributions, clothes; being in a strange limbo of economic exile, both protected of sorts, and denied, by the Federal 30 Day Ordinance--- which mandated that cities must keep indigent visitors inside the limits of their jurisdictions and not expel them, but must do so only for a limit of 30 days, after this, if picked up by police off their streets without a

job AND lodgings they could be forced---by martial law, at gunpoint-- to leave, unless, the 3rd alternative, they were hospitalized. As long as the patient was in a hospital bed they could stay. Without a doctor's diagnosis of acute illness, and vital care, whenever they were healed, they must leave. Or, the last option was death. Those economic travelers who were better off, -- veterans of wars on soldier pension, those who received social security benefits, or pension from private industry from which they had retired after a lifetime of work, or those with small family inheritance stipends were somewhat financed, but if their money was insufficient to purchase a shared house, condominium, or even free standing individual house with no common walls shared with stranger's, they must stay forever on the move like vagabonds, like gypsy's. *Give an account of what strategies for survival you think these ancient people used regarding the 30-Day Ordinance. Be prepared to share them with class.*

This historical summery had been Dr. Andersons last papers.

Chapter 7.

Night, by artificial means fell over vax 33. Under its great dome. Still hued with a smattering of flickering lights. The city still hummed of course, being a 24 hour international port of commerce and central intelligence, rivaled in the latter only by vax 1., --formerly Washington, DC, which was nicknamed by those who knew truly who controlled it--- Pentagon City.

Above the dome real earth was immersed in total darkness, the moon had waned, only dimly colored by silverpoints of starlight. At the western wall of the great dome, which divides the vax there in, from unincorporated areas outside, something was going on. A small cadre of figures in black wet suits had slipped over the retaining wall, and forded the water in the cement trench which ran like a moat along the outer, and inner perimeter of the dome, which separates from chaos the civilization we now know as the most modern, and progressed on earth, 4th planet from the sun, located at the edge of galaxy Milky Way. All the checkpoints in and out of the vax were here along the circumference of this circular edge set up at practically every 4th street, the rest being dead ends. Some of these means of access points actually ended after a few short cement blocks. Leading to nowhere. Indicative of some future blueprints of expansion. 5 figures had breached the inner west wall and having subdued a number of unsuspecting soldiers had gained access to the bottom level metal vaults in which is the mechanism, memory banks and sophisticated computers which control much of the electrical currents directed from the island nuclear power plant—located in a military patrolled unincorporated area—which flows into vax #33, and also runs the functions of one half of the dome itself! It must have been an inside job, because outer access codes were known, the correct route down into the heart of the vault was known, the maneuvers of the soldiers were known, which facilitated their progress. The cadre went immediately underground and entered the first stretch of short maize-like corridors, running to the right, then to the left without pause, right, right, left, ---heading directly towards the heart of operations. They had only moments for the automatic alarm would have gone out and the standard guard of dull soldier(ettes) would soon be reinforced by a precision team of tactical squad military personnel with their cyborg backups. Running down the last short corridor the dark clad team entered the control vault that now stood wide-open, where robots stationed permanently at their jobs were methodically going about raising and lowering levers, pushing buttons. Robots humanly replicated from the waist up—having arms wired for motor skills connected to a 'head', which held a brain programmed with limited functions. They were screwed into their seats on movable dollies. They had no lower limbs at all. These handicapped robots were easily knocked out of the way. Soon gloved hands laid bare the whole instrument panel which controlled light, air quality, raising/lowering of shade jells for sun/clouds adaptation etc. There the operations of the whole west side of the dome lay naked, exposed! One hundred titanium metal boxes, each containing identical yellow, red, blue, green, purple, orange, black, & white wires. Box after box, about 5,000 sets of wires per each box which fed into 50 switches which shut off/on 500 machine mass produced-identical transformers coils, then additional coils of wires looping in identical twists to magnetic posts; row after row of them. Black gloved hands went flying over this keyboard yanking out colored wires by the roots and twisting each switch with abrupt jerks, as if beheading a row of puppet queens & kings of revolution times!

Now functions of the whole western wall were giving way! Section by section all electricity running along the conduit from the nuclear power plant which flowed into that corresponding sector of the city was immediately cut off, kicking back into its reserves for hospital use, police & fire only. Vax #33 had lost control of it's whole western wall!

Suddenly a sweeping roll of darkness, total darkness blanked out half the city.

Back inside his comfortable unit, Sarvax glumly was chewing tasteless drone-chosen food. 'I shoulda' known better. Darf drone...' He grossed, when suddenly outside half his view of the city fell instantaneously into darkness. S/he cringed! Overturning the trey of paper plates & cups!

"It's the end of the world!" He was sure of it! Certain! *"It's D-Day!"* Death-day had come! *"Like those old prophets spoke about!"* Struck blind, he knelt to the floor, and groped his way hurriedly into the bedroom. The air was already cooling due to the unexpected loss of power. He crawled over the floor in the total darkness as fast as he could towards his sleeping pod.

Starvax crawled into his pod as fast as he could, jerking his pajamas in after him with one hand. His clothes soon went flying out. He cuddled into the womb–like bed &, cried. Sappy tears. Cried. Blowing his nose as one plays a horn. 'My mom and dad made me. They cared for me. They worried over me. They protected me. *Now I'm gonna die!*' Curled in the fetal position Starvax had this vague recall, that didn't come often. He rubbed his hands together trying to keep warm in the bewildering loss of temperature. This thought how his parents must have worried over him as an infant, sick and bawling, held him with their big rough hands when his were tiny hands, and he was a tiny being suffering from illness in the wilds with no medicine. Starvax cried! Like a girl! Like a baby child! Tears ran down his cheeks. He cried and cried. He felt the human race was hopeless! *'They really did blow themselves up in that 3rd World War! It's not a lie! And they're gonna to blow this city up next!'* This city! His city! He cried harder. He felt like he was devolving. Climbing back down the ladder, swimming in the oily murk at bottom of the evolutionary chain.

Chapter 7.

By the next day, power was restored. The fake sun had come back on. The Telly screamed off of the wall: AGENT SABOTEUR LOOSE IN UNITY VAX #33! AGENTS OF ENEMY ALIENS CAPTURED! COMMIT SUICIDE UPON THEIR APPREHENSION BY MILITARY MARSHALS! FEAR THAT MORE HUMAN COLLABORATORS WITH TREACHEROUS EXTRATERRESTRIALS ARE LOOSE IN UTOPIA!

After the televised capture of resistance fighters followed so swiftly by the wanton mayhem of saboteurs, vax #33 was put under siege guard. That very day, soldiers had been mobilized. They guarded each transit exit/entrance; each speedwalk outlet, each street, and the horrible cyborgs were everywhere! It had been rumored there was a fleet of 3,000 of them just waiting in storage; super-intelligent cyborgs hewn out of metal, bolts, wires, microchips equipped with all the latest scientific apparatus available to the scientists of Utopia. And in newer & newer models, each new batch more progressed then the one before it. Greatly improved since when the monsters had first begun to appear back in early pre-Utopian days, --the darling invention of crime enforcement. Citizens were frightened then, money had to be secretly allotted to the creation of them, and their cyborg race had grown substantially.

There was 2 hideous cyborgs! Two of them! Their large machine heads, sinuous alien long arms were frightening to the average human. And to make it worse, these two cyborgs seemed to be *laughing!* Having a chat together! —Most disgusting. The sight made him almost puke.

"Can they do that? Talk to each other?" Said a passerby to a companion, flying past him on the speedwalk.

An errant cybog had been known to tear a human apart. Easily capable of it. Their sheer physicality was overwhelming, 10 times stronger then the most powerful super-large male citizen. Because of the unreliable mechanical workings of the earlier models--- rumors told horror stories galore about out-of-control cyborgs--- it was never considered wise to have too many of them on the streets at once, but now, today, as they rode past on the speedwalk, every block or so gigantic hulking, a cyborg presence could be seen towering over the tallest humans, a hideous 'friendly' smile on the metal masks which were their 'faces'.

Utopias 33rd vax was mustering up all its military forces—in its streets and by-ways. Day saw such sights as soldierettes drilling in a formation of several thousand in the grassy park overflowing into the esplanade in front of Central Hall, across from the Bureau of World Statistics & Information where he worked. So it was possible to unhook from his pod and go over to the windows and look down at them—all thru the 8 hour block. It was a show of the Unity's power—designed to keep decent citizens feeling secure, and the few aberrant ones, ones with strange ideas, in line.

For every evil, citizens could see the punishment of The Unity speeding forth with emergency military might, going quickly to its cure.

Starvax felt uneasy. He felt confined. Simmering anger. For the first time he was seeing stuff. Stuff that made him nervous. Stuff, which hit too near home. The corpse of the lady Doctor who was a good teacher, broken, bloody all over his Telly wall. For an instant like a child again, he thought; *'I've never seen a night so dark! What a Dark night it was! Midnight Dark!'*

Almost immediately after the blackout, his luck broke. Returning back from the mandatory job, entered his unit, his hand waved with an automatic gesture switching on the Telly, brushing aside it's news blasting au current at a shrill pitch; WESTSIDE DOME SLAUGHTER! SOLDIERS PERISH IN A BLOODY POOL! 5 ALIEN CONSPIRATORS CUT DOWN BY ATOMIC FIRE! Saw a cryptic message pop into his wordhole, disappearing like invisible ink once he'd activated his password. **Nothing to wear to the playparty 'Bossa Nova Teacher?' Oh you! Well you can always wear your pink underwear!**

Starvax rushed thru the pages of the study manual at his desk pod, and found the code, appropriate to the statistics on the daily weather fluxuations inside the dome. Switched to the world weather channel on the Telly and downloaded the Climate Report. A simple mathematical calculation, and there was the next location.

For 3 more restless 24-hour blocks he studied his readings:

> The people will *not* take a political stance. So the price is their freedom & human rights. Thus other people have to do their fighting for them—and these heroes must be prepared to loose their lives.

So. He wasn't free. Now he knew. He wasn't crazy at all! It was the way The Unity had been set up! IT wasn't free! And somehow he'd known that from the start! Each study group made this picture emerge clearer and clearer. It had always bothered him. *Stuff.* Like…. 'If I just decided not to go to the Depot and plug into my screen one day I could be thrown out into the streets of Utopia with nothing but 3 blue uniforms and some underwear!' For a crime against the Unity was not working. *Failing to report consecutively to assigned job without an official excuse.* The work shy.

'If there was freedom I could stay in my sleeping pod anytime I wanted, and just crawl out of it when I felt like it! And checking in with my retina code and stuff, every other darf block! And… and…. All that darf that happened to me when I first got started at the Depot!'

No one no manipulating citizen could ever put anyone on a list again! And get them thrown out of a comfortable job! He'd see to it!

He had never seen a night so dark. *'Midnight Dark...'* And this gave him an idea. Citizen Starvax came up with a tiny plan. — As a means of sabotage. A needle-prick in the fabric of such complete totalitarianism to be sure. Midnight Dark. That's how he'd check himself in at the building roster in the next study group! A smile crossed his thin face, the first in many days. Then a laugh broke out! A laugh of victory!

***

The 3rd 24-hour block saw the young he-she walking briskly down a speedwalk---traveling out of the city once more.

Starvax promptly showed his hand, smiled facetiously into the lens, a faint half hearted beep sensor indicating s/he'd passed thru the security scanner, entered a checkpoint, and was now free to pass out.

They were back in the same multiplex construction, built semi-underground, but in a new cubical, a different wing on a subterranean floor.

He checked into the roster robot with a new fake name to match his fake occupation, MidnightDark400.vax.

Starvax had ominous thoughts. *'Who will be missing & who will be there?'*

The submerged buildings outer walkways were set on parameter between embankments of reinforced earth held back by iron & steel reinforcing beams & tensel-strength metal sheets making a wall; could see inside the windows. Gazing down into the meeting place from outside s/he saw someone arranging chairs inside, a man in grey pants, dark shirt, but view of his head was cut off so he couldn't tell who it was.

Today's study group was noticeably smaller in size. The cubical was too spacious for the small amount of comrades, which made the place seem unusually large. And their voices seemed to echo.

He noticed the tall man—he'd found out was called Kevin3,400.vax; who had given himself the last name of Buckminister. Kevin Buckminister, and the two women, all friends of Mable. Making a small gesture he waved, and a wan smile cracked his yellowish face. They nodded, not friendly. Later, he noticed, the trio move away suspiciously and all the remainder of the class did not acknowledge his presence, and after, did not speak to him.

It was unfortunate that more comrades hadn't had nerve enough to attend this particular session, because the class--- sadly minus Dr. Anderson--- discussed a most interesting topic—Drones.

Valdez: Hierarchy of intelligence. Chauvinism of the IQ. Wisdom of the ancients tells us, by our readings, and speaking with old timers, that intelligence does not by itself make for a superior humanbeing---and to think otherwise is a lie perpetuated by The Unity, the current dictatorship under which we citizens now are governed. Can any one here tell us— briefly (Valdez shot a dark look from under his craggy eyebrows) —why superior intelligence is not the ultimate best attribute, over anything less?

Several hands shot up out of the small group of comrades.

The answer came from a short, stocky woman: "Because some of the worlds foremost leaders of past times were noted for intelligence.... But they proved... well, time proved them to be evil. And what they left in the world behind them was destruction."

Valdez: (Excited) Yes yes, would you care to give us an example?

Short woman: Yeah: uh... The Hitler guy.... Uh... the guys who invented slavery .... Uh... the pharaohs of Egypt who made their slaves build pyramids for them, for their tombs, 'cause they were such self-ego maniacs....

Valdez: (Still directing his questions to the class) A lot of pharaohs did that. Who was the penultimate evil and who was just ordinary evil?

Stillness lasted only seconds.

Short woman: Uh well, the first pharaoh who invented the idea was probably the worse.... The penultimate. (The comrade anticipated Valdez next question) ... Maybe because... because all others just imitated him as a matter of course.... They didn't institute that idea from the beginning.

Valdez: Good! Excellent! This brings us to the topic of drones. Lower intelligence beings. *But human beings nevertheless.*

An uneasy sigh went around the room.

Valdez: We feel that... Maybe for many years past, under the early dispensations of society, those humans we now refer to as drones were simply just babies born with lower intelligence and some as well with

106

complicating mental illness. Society didn't know what to do with them. In the advanced industrialized societies like the previous empire, Am-Erica, they faced jail, institutions, & death. They were the homeless. The badly failed of society. New breakthroughs in medicines and psychotropic meds could stabilize the lower level citizens, so they'd not drool or loose track of what they were doing, yet, still not raise their intelligence significantly. The precursor to these knowledge's all came about around the end of the last century early 1990's all that medical and pharmaceutical technology we studied previously, and scientific information has evolved since. Now, today combined with our current means of reproduction--- SPOVA— (Another laugh titters like a wave across the room) what has happened? Valdez answers his own question) Yes. We know in advanced what humans are going to be born with defects. Yet, not all of them are aborted. Remember now, *Drones are human!* (Class makes another bodily shift, restlessly.) So Drudges or Drones, whatever you prefer, are naturally occurring low intelligence citizens—and the Unity knows about this, according their observations of chromosomes alignments, etcetera, even before they were born... but allows them to be born inside the wombs of SPOVA anyway... Why?

(A hand shoots up): To serve the Unity.

Valdez: Yes.

(A comrade speaks): Is that fair?

The short comrade: Its ... (The woman paused puzzled, for she'd never thought of the concept before now.) It's barbaric. It's... as bad as the pharaohs who made slaves. As the Hitler's with their concentration camp murders...

Star1.vax left the meeting satisfied, and unsatisfied. Her/his viewpoint about Drones (whom he'd never thought about previously) was now drastically altered. However the explanations to the class about the arrests were much too brief for him. And both Gojenko and Valdez had stated flatly that any discussion about it was taboo. Valdez had only said: "Comrades it's sad but we can trust nobody. Not even some of you here in this room."

S/he walked towards the antiquated transport to go back. Back to Utopia. Blue/white lights of the dome glimmered in distance. His thoughts were heavy.

Anderson being a high placed saboteur had been executed on the spot. Or so the media proclaimed. Her body presented to the public soon after. A 'trial' wasn't necessary –for alien spies-- under a legal format set down by the Unity. The delay of a 24-hour block before showing a facial close-up of the doctor could just mean one thing—torture. What had the good comrade undergone during those 24 hours? One last declaration of the newscasters repeated in his mind. *'So Dr. Anderson had been under observation already? Before their action?'*

Chapter 8.

There were numerous ways in and out of Vax 33. —Ones which did not lead to dead ends, or radiation poisoned wanderings thru uncharted areas, but to principal & minor mini-domed islands around the vax which serviced its needs, and its main artery being the straight through connecting #33 to other vaxs all across the continent in a gigantic web.

Daily convoys left along the superhighway out of the vax while others came in. Traveling in radiation shielded vehicles.

It was a modern, sleek, metal & and glass-clear tensel strength super highway built by Unity engineers which ran in 8 lanes, 4 going in, 4 going out. A clean diagonal straight continuum, with tributaries which fed out of itself into the various islands aside from its greater destinations, a near-by vax being 300 miles away. It was upon this highway the service vehicles went to overhaul & repair the nuclear power plant; it ran past a series of agricultural domes, which weren't human habitats, but glorified green house spanning multitudes of acreage.

And there was still another route. The fastest, safest, and more air-quality control way in or out of one vax to another was underground via the tunnels.

Starvax had been in the tunnels numerous times. But only to be riding for fun, having nowhere to go. He'd hop on the bullet train and journey out to the closest vax. In this case, a location once known as Angel City, which, at speeds of up to 750 miles per hour, could be covered in under 2 hours, counting stops. Then would turn right around and ride back! He loved the travel. A long long tunnel towards a brilliant dot right at the end of seeing, which stretches perspective out in a far reach. Dim bulbs shine every 15 feet on its straight a-ways track to tunnels end approach rapidly. Slowly the dot grows nearer, so you feel you are approaching destiny.

Once inside the Dome, underground, the bullet train stops, the tunnel siphons itself off into a myriad of tunnelettes composing the subway whose exits & entrances match up with the underground roots of the city's subterranea; its matrix of shops, services, mole-life luxury dwellings, and at some point this subway train stops being modern and somewhere under the bowels of the vax connects with that old, antiquated system, revamped and saved by the modern empire Utopia to form the long labyrinth winding and twisting 50 floors underground where the air was never contaminated. This first built in early part of the 20th century and continued by the fallen dynasty after the end of the nuclear war. And inhabited by earth survivors during the nuclear holocaust. They knew they had to go underground to survive. After the great firestorms they constructed cities beneath the earth. But then, the scientific advancements had brought tensel strength. The great domes proliferated by Unity all over the planet, and nuclear power being harnessed to work for humanity and not against citizens could return to ground level once again, lit by a new artificial sun.

Abundant forests had sprung up over the last 30 years despite the radiation. Strange twisted trees but trees, nevertheless, --producing more oxygen for earths atmosphere so, even tho these new forests were out in wild areas, they were the hope of earth, and Unity kept watchful eyes over them. Robots equipped with infrared biosensors, crawl 4 legged, around like insects to hunt, find and extinguish forest fires. They can withstand temperatures to 3,000 degrees Fahrenheit.

Further down greenhouse domes. No living gasses of humans or animals to process out, they only filtered out the noxious radiation, processed this into useable oxygen by their very product, plants. And on, out next, agricultural domes. Micro-mini robot fruit pickers ant size went chugging up and down vines liberating fruits which dropped into a moving trey which accompanied them kept pace below on the ground. Then the livestock domes, with various range feeding beasts to provide luxury meat as an occasional treat to the pallets of the citizenry of Utopia.

Also there were, amid the wasteland, various sites where the Utopian city dumped its garbage & other resources which could not fit under the human living dome. But which humans sorely depend on.

Slowly the Unity was filtering radioactivity out of the earth's atmosphere, but only a small fraction of it, so far. It was a laborious laboratory process, every time they took in air from outside into any of its domes.

Many citizens he knew and those who he'd overheard their conversations in the Depot lunchroom traveled in and out of the vax regularly to see family members in other parts of the known universe under different domes upon the grid of tunnels and highways, but no one, absolutely no one Starvax knew of—neighbors in his building, co workers, nor passerby's overheard upon the speedwalks & elevators & trains, *nobody* ever dreamed of going out into the unincorporated regions, for any reason at all, outside of a guided convoy processing rapidly along the superhighway to another vax, in a hurry....

So, one day shortly after the last meeting, on his 24 hour free block, the young Starvax carrying a small sack of food & drinking liquids, took to the speedwalk, went out of the dome, then continued to walk on over the antiquated speedwalk for a while, (a route he now recognized) stepped off and promptly disappeared down into a gully.

Many times he'd contemplated what he was now doing, but for years had been completely at a loss of how to go about this, or what direction to take, but after the study groups, seeing his way half planned already, and being outside the dome for the maybe only the third time, (outside of the bullet train) since he'd been taken into it as a child, and viewing the broken and shattered terrene close up, an idea had occurred to him to take that path already carved out—two centuries ago—the antique railroad line, which he'd glimpsed, rusted and crooked way down in the gully, sided by sloping earth covered by grass, broken bottles & bricks. And realized that he would be able to travel out, simply by walking along its path inside the unincorporated area for quite a distance. *'I'll just go walking...'*

So he did what an itching inside had summoned him to do for so long! Followed the old railroad tracks, which curved away into distance. Splintered boards on the side from collapsed ancient buildings. Moss had eaten the ancient ties to rot between the rusted rails and wood decayed, which wound between the demolished old city. Its rusted gutters, beams and pipes laying where they'd fallen in yellow grass which grew up then had perished because of radiation—but slowly, slowly, more grew back to find some alien poison sucking the green chlorophyll out of it which its vainly cells kept attempted to produce in photosynthesis, but then, even more had continued to grow.

Rotten boards sun-stripped of color, gone gray. Metal railroad line curved sections of track cut across acres upon acres. Soon found he was going quite fast this way, traveling thru these wilds, which towered around him. This rusted rail line had fallen into great disrepair even before World War

110

III. Was weed choked, here & there decaying boxes of dumped refuse of yesteryear. Boards fire-burnt or buckled up, and rock slides from bombed buildings covering parts of the path, but the rail line did provide an access route between all the bombed out hollow shells of buildings long ago deserted, of what had been dense housing, constructed in built-up blocks of the old city and its suburbs.

He got to a point in his walking—about 2 miles, in which, looking back, he could still see the great dome, blue/white shimmery bubble seated artistically on the earths surface. He stopped took out of his sack a piece of cloth he'd brought for the purpose placed this over a bolder which he feared might be glowing with radioactive rads. And fastidiously sat down.

Gazed about in wonder…Those strange animals, which flew wild in the air—birds-- could be seen out here—it was one of the first amazing things he'd noticed. He'd heard some citizens had obtained licenses to keep the creatures in cages inside their units, animal licenses, but only those citizens permanently domiciled could obtain these. Looking up into the air he saw a flock of them! A wonder! But the first wonder by far being the clear view of sky, limitless!

Sat and had thoughts. Starvax sorted thru it once again... *'Those other comrades were out on an action of some kind... where do the actions originate?'* No one ever spoke of this in the class---for instance asking for volunteers by a show of hands who wanted to go on an action... or something.... All they learned was... history. Illegal history. *'Where do you go to sign up for an action? Do I have enough nerve to?'* And what kind of action had Anderson and her cadre been on before they got captured? And… those missing from the study group. At first he thought he'd recognized some of them in the frame by frame perusal he'd done with the tiny disc, but had some of those comrades also been volunteers for the death action at the wall of the dome? *'Killed themselves before they could give information...?'* Had Anderson been tortured first? He hated to think about that! At first for her sake, but later in the interval that passed, came this creeping thought that since the death photos didn't come to broadcast until a day later, that she might have been tortured too, not just executed. And if so, what names did she release? Had she released a description of him under duress? *'Did Dr. Anderson ever actually know my name? Maybe she knew my name! Does the group know that I work for the Unity, in the Depot? Darf!'* But of all things haunting him, these being airier, complex, confused headache producing worries; was the one deep in the pit of his stomach, his longing for love and caring and that combined with, from his groin, the urgency of sexual need.... *'Where is that Mable! Mable473.vax!'*

111

Then, Starvax come to the true reason he was there…'*Out here, back where I come from….*' & then, a sad & poignant thought--- one which had haunted him a long time. For far too long… *'Where is my mother?'*

Starvax drank an enzyme booster energy drink and munched his crispy veggie/tofu substitution beef & mayo sandwich thoughtfully.

When he'd rested and eaten he decided to walk a little further, and later was glad he'd done so because as he cut across a little cranny hidden from view via the rails access among a cluster of broken down walls he made a discovery. A faded graffiti sign! A proclamation of the first primitive resistance against that ancient empire Am-Erica.

ANARCHY!

Wow! One of those protest signs drawn by real people back then! Comrades like us who defied their barbaric system! A colorful scrawl which had not been removed by the Unity during their frequent forays in to the wilderness, supposedly 'to hunt down aliens', which was televised, fed to the citizens of today's modern empire who really didn't understand the true purpose of them.

ANARCHY! SMASH THE MACHINE!

He stood, stunned. Jaw agape, and just stared at it.
Evidence—plain, for citizens to see for themselves!
Not removed by the secret police. How much more of this was there?

He'd take a picture—but cameras had been outlawed under the Unity unless he had media coverage and worked for the state owned Media Central.

By the time he returned a crescent moon rode high in the starry black cloud heavenly ocean above the perpetually tranquil faux-sky of Unity's 33rd dome. Wearily he crossed thru the entrance over the water channel flashing his hand and looking squarely, honestly, into the retina recorder, then wearily stepped aboard a modern state of the art speedwalk going back.

When he got near his temporary domicile a cyborg towered near the entrance to the compound; —in a gut level reaction Starvax ducked out of sight immediately; and hurrying down the street, turned a corner and there paced nervously beside some 24 hour non-stop shops. Idly wondered 'would I have done this before Dr. Anderson's murder?'

112

When he returned the cyborg was barreling down the street of empire on sidewalk-shaking stomps flashing its horrific smile at all good citizens & with a booming voice punctuating their souls with a deafening, "GOOD DAY CITIZENS!" Tho it wasn't day anymore—a fact which made people even more wary of it. Its broad blue back amazingly wide; wide as the side of a bus. Starvax winced.

Relentlessly the Red Jordan Arobateau Reading Society continued to meet. At the next one Starvax and his comrades held a treat in their hands! An article rescued from the greedy hands of the private sector, and liberated for community! That day Gojenko brought it in: "I've got something special, (upholding a green tattered book) an original! Not a reprint fashioned to *look* like the old ones but a real copy! Full of Prophet Red's misprints, which costs thousands of Unity dollars—it's so rare. Now Comrades, this book, and so many others like it are usually only to be found in the homes of the very very wealthy, which means, some of the most powerful leaders in the Unity, tho illegal, now think about that!"

As young Starvax's turn came to handle the green book and see it for himself he contemplated how the late Prophet had stripped himself of every resource s/he had -- to the bone--selling off his books, music discs, eating up each ounce of fat on his body until his ribs showed in order to continue on and write these pages---this green fading torn cover, self printed and manufactured which he now held in his hands!

There it was! Words of the prophet him-herself with all its misprints, ill-spelling and poor grammar! And shady sexual innuendos, which made him, blush!

In her-his minds eye, viewed Red walking the antiquated streets of the past empire, eyes searching sidewalks so as to find dropped coins/dollars, wherever he went; how it seemed the street had been scoured clean of each last penny! Pawffhhhh…! So, he had only said 'rejoice my soul for I am freed of my earthly encumbrances!' However, a pragmatist, he didn't laugh too loud.

He sold aluminum cans at the recycling center which $, he must promptly pop into the gorging mouth of KKK. (The printing center.) 'Sell all CD records & DVD's in my house; it would have been nice to have classical music to paint too-- but have done this because I want to tell it to you! And you and you and you! Here is my words: AGGGGHHHHHHHHHH HHHHHHHHHHHHHHHHHHHHHHHHHHHHHHHHHHHHH HHHHHHHHHHHHHHHHHHHHHHHHHHHHHHHHHHHHHHHHHHHHHHHHH

HHHHHHHHHHHHHHHghghhghhhhhhhhhhhhhhhhhhhhhhhhhhhhhhhhhhhhh
hhhhhhhhhhhhhhhhhhhhhhhhhhhhhhhhhhhhhhhhhhhhhhhhhhhhhhhhhhhhhhhh
hhhhhhhhhhhhhhhh! Whoops! That costs10 cents at the Korporate Killer!

Under the solar lights in the quiet classroom not disturbed by the gentle
voices of his comrades, Starvax handled the green book gingerly. His
sturdy, small yellow tinted hands thumbing carefully thru the time-
oxygenated pages. Thought back to the life/times of Red Jordan Arobateau
of how it was the custom of his days when he walked the streets of the now-
fallen empire, hungry—a voracious wolf searching for abandon stuff he
could use –his cheap shopping he called it. And how it was for s/he himself,
Starvax, in great comfort today. Securely housed (tho impermanently so,
and ever--shifted around at the convenience of the Utopia Housing
Authority). …Red's big complaint, his mantra, 'to reduce another human
being to the point of despair because they can't afford to pay RENT.' So
this is the world his ancestors had bequeathed him!

A society, which he hated! A world, which had no beginning and was
clouded in mystery. Its evil appearing once that cloud was snatched off!
Yes, s/he had a free domicile, but no information, no books, nor ability to
speak freely in public. Starvax had never known hunger. 'Hunger? What is
it! Something terrible! People eat… rats... Primitive people. My own
people.'

On his second time out, Starvax dressed more warmly, having ascertained
thru Unity weather reports that outside in the unincorporated area it was
foggy. Boots instead of shoes. A thermal parka, which held heat well. He
carried a large lunch and more to drink. His pack was quite heavy. Also,
disposable sani-wipes for elimination. Now, being familiar with this wild
region he was able to walk much more confidently choosing again the
antiquated railroad line, but after a few miles, out of curiosity, veered off in
a new direction. One that led towards the top of a hill. Now he had to fight
his way, picking his steps carefully among debris of the huge ruins which
lay everywhere, the materials of apartment buildings, stores, corporate
business, all collapsed grid-like in a surreal photo of destruction, long since
settled, for two decades barely disturbed but by the radiation and natures
forces, so it was wild indeed, like it had always been reported and such a
totally unfamiliar experience to him. No longer anything like paved roads,
those smooth ones of Utopia but found himself stumbling over tree
branches, climbing over twisted girders of buildings once uprooted by the
inferno of war, getting slippery footing on blocks of masonry, jumping over
torn apart raw gashes in earth for the first time, and always aware of the
Geiger counter ticking in his flesh. Starvax was rewarded for his effort. At
top of the hill came to a wonderful thing—had been walking—then steppe3d

into the rubble of something which had once, been a very great and grand construction! Tall strangely shaped building partially destroyed but much remained, up to 8th story high, but not at all the usual oblong creations which housed people once or banked monies, or information, or machines full of data; nor the longer low ones which held machinery, factories, they had been called; but more of a ceremonial place of some sorts, maybe a palace. Gazed up thru the top left side to where it's ceiling and upper section of its wall were gone, so it was open to the wind and sky, the universe wide. There down under his boots the flooring seemed to be very strong---stone… was it marble?

Everything inside this place was big! Starvax was simply amazed. Brushed the floor in front of him with the toe of his shoe, gold emerged; gold plate set into stone. A gold design ten feet long 4 wide. Intertwined was letters from the Greek alphabet, alpha, & omega. The first and the last. Symbolic of what? His footfalls gave sonorous echoes languid in the place. —He conjectured, 'this is a palace where they did their chants, or holy songs were sung all for this religion! It might be an ancient Cathedral!' This spiritual religion, which had such power over peoples lives! He walked further.

So here the people'd come to do their strange prayers. A palace where they felt comfort. Got spiritual nourishment for hard times. Hazily concepts occurred to Starvax that he never would have understood until those class readings.

Sound of the wind echoes thru the vast place…. Suddenly a noise! Something was being dropped on his head! Falling down on him, light, eerie- a ghosts touch! He jumps to hide. Squats down beside one of the overturned wooden benches. He is frightened; somebody is throwing something at him from out of the heavens! Transman Starvax ducks for cover! Looks up thru the open half of the ancient cathedral, there fly's one of those animals--- the strange mammals that fly--- birds---now he saw them, flying from rafter to rafter! ---There was a flock of them soaring on their wings above—and shedding feathers which floated on air! Feathers, spiraling slowly down! It was nothing. What had fallen on him—a handful of feathers!

Groped his way over broken long wooden seats--- primitive benches of some kind. Shattered windows multi-colored in the ceiling archways of the vast place. No matter that their beauty they hadn't been enough to stand against this horrible holocaust. Here was something else. A kind of plaque! Just a section. He scraped aside debris to read, 'so that man may proceed thru the dark lit by torchlight to a better place.' I'm doing that now Starvax said to himself.

Later that night upon returning to his unit, showered long under hot steaming water. Cold of the wilds had seeped into his bones. He wondered how people could have lived outside in that freezing weather. And killing summer hot. He thought of his parents. Some kind of tribe from which he'd probably come.

> 'They will go down, down, down to the bottom
> riding on the coattails of drugs, alcohol abuse,
> violence, & other self-life murders.'

--From those old days, about outsider people the Prophet had spoken of. This came to him when the drone shuffled up. Starvax secretly looked at its piggish eyes, its puffed face, and downcast expression. He thought to his study guide about the mentally ill or genetically damaged humans of past times. How, untreated, and often friendless and alone they lived lives beyond desperate. Beings who'd gave up but were still walking alive inside the confines of one of few places police/society tolerates them; where they can shuffle back and forth between 4 square blocks in the epicenter of the Tenderloin or the straight thru 2 blocks which is all which remains of skid row. And now, how, cleaned up mentally thru use of the psychotropic drugs, they were able to function in society, but, been genetically engineered to remain stupid, all the while, Unity realizing this from the very beginning!

The stupid drone inquired in its tin voice; "Is that all you need for now Mr. Star1.vax?" Starvax dismissed him nervously by a gesture pushing him away. For a moment he felt guilty. As if he'd been talking to a real humanbeing!

While sitting there with the manual on his lap, Starvax began to dream and think. He put it aside on the arm of his chair and let the comfy pod chair recline. Began to drowse. After awhile a knock came at his door. It didn't sound like the drone.

2 burly soldiers were at his door.

"POLICE CITIZEN STAR1.VAX! OPEN YOUR DOOR!"

He opened it. They stood before him in blue Unity uniforms, each with a proper identification tag & gold badge with serial numbers, baring the sun symbol of Utopia.

"We've come to ask about why you crossed into the incorporated area 6 times in the past 30 day block." Stated the first soldier.

"Why did you?" Asked the second.

"What are you doing out there?" Said the first. "Why do you go out there? You work at Depot 33! —Right down in the Civic Center." He pointed due southeast with a gloved finger. "Not out *outside!* What's out there in the wilds?"

Tousle-head, half asleep, dressed in his lounging jumpsuit, young Starvax stood, shocked, in the unit doorway as if straining to comprehend the words of a foreign language.

The two uniformed soldiers stared at him dully, waiting.

Both were as low key and disinterested as their low-level serial badge numbers. It was a routine call evidently. He was not too worried, although in the back of his mind it was bothersome, as he heard himself invent some feeble excuse, which one duely recorded on an electronic palm pad. And the other one didn't speak. Finally the soldier looked up from the palm pad and asked a shocking question.

"Are you still a transsexual?"

For the first time a shred, just a hint of interest reflected a glimmer in those dull eyes, bringing them to life.

"Nothing has changed." Said this flatly. "Yes."

To which the solider made no indication of having caught the sarcasm, in fact barely hearing—or were they simply trained to notice, to record everything, each response, each detail of a citizens life they could pick up in a few seconds of an encounter, those under suspicion anyway... while at the same time betraying little of themselves?

After closing the unit door with some misgivings, Starvax just stood there thinking, listening to the soldier's footfalls going down the compound corridor. Of course they had tracked him on the speedwalks as a matter of daily transport, just like multimillions of other citizens passing by. 'I should have thought about that possibility.... That the Unity could be keeping track of any citizen who travels outside the dome....'

It worried him; nagging in the back of his mind.... It was bothersome that for the first time there was a blotch, tho barely perceivable, -- but still a marker on that otherwise completely spotless record of his security clearance.

After they left Starvax was shaky, knees felt week; finally left the door to walk back to his pod chair but as he turned he saw a worse development. Horrified! There sat his copy of bound papers—Manual of Ancient History 1. **Red Jordan Arobateau Reading Society.** Laying there on the pod chair arm where anyone could see! He'd been too lax!

Never anticipated this! Them coming to his door!

It was at that point Starvax interrupted the routine pursuits of his free-time, stopped to sit on edge of the chair, took his erase-wand & the manual, and drew its tip over the title 'Ancient History 1' which emblazoned the front cover. Every letter of print disappeared under the slow, steady movement of the wand. When he was done it was just a book with a darkened face.

***

Made sure the shades were drawn way down tight—so as not to reflect any silhouettes on the shade which might have frightened the citizens of empire, s/he was so paranoid, & upset. Sighed; "Oh Mable… Oh Mable… Mable I'm fucking you!" And began to strip off his lounge suit.

Guiltily looking down at his secret pleasure. Slowly, with a studied motion, he pulled his dick out of his under shorts, flopping it over them, free, fleshy pink/brown. Stroked the head, ecstatic, while squeezing his balls. The same as any bio man's—except it couldn't make babies—sperms to be examined, then altered in the petrie dishes of SPOVA.

As he began to stroke himself was fantasying how he would slide his beautiful new penis into Mable and fuck her good! But his session was marred by the jarring recall of what had just transpired. Unity's police forces at the door of his domicile! Too close for comfort! THAT had never happened before! Just daily being clocked in the streets like every citizen. And he though, as his breath grew harder, wan yellowish face reddening and the jerk of his hand grew faster; *'Will I wind up erasing everything from that book?'*

6.
The latest no copy policy of the new director has really hurt Transman. Who must spend precious coins on copies at KKK. (Korporate Kinkos Kopy center or some other shop.

The Arobateau treasury is in penury.

Up in the morning, hungry, no food in the pantry---forgot to go to food bank, so busy writing JOURNEY. My last will & testament of a struggling survivor in this cruel New Age of kapitalist feudalism, starving under rent control despite which landlords keep gouging out pieces of flesh, friends are Ellis-acted out of their homes; in general prices continue to rise, and old peoples pension (like mine) is substandard.
There's money everywhere--you just don't see it. People dying for lack of money, people dying with money.

Walk to the library (9 blocks) not a single sou on the streets! Nor any aluminum containers but 2 beer cans. Didn't take them. Can't go around smelling like a brewery the rest of the evening. Maybe will shake down some treats out of my group at Muddy Waters coffee shop tonight.

> 'Journeys are very perilous' said Quip, 'especially outside the coach. Wheels come off, Horses take fright, coachmen drive too fast, coaches overturn.'

> Charles Dickens from a novel, 1829.

Times are tough. Assuage myself with thoughts of politics;

> *Now the clamor of war responds not only in the high places, but also in the remote corners of the realm. The people are filled with dismay. Fear creeps into the towns and villages. No place is safe, neither the Bourg as refuge nor the open country as a way of escape. Men know not weather it is safer to flee or to stay.*

> Mana Vita Sancti Hugonis; circa 1600rds.

And spirituality:

> The Savior is poor dressed in poor clothes, and walks on foot or rides on the back of a slow old mule--the Savior is poor so that s/he can speak to the common wo/man.

> Red Jordan Arobateau from JOURNEY, 2006.

There's a new song out whose refrain is 'Lets go to prison' with a telling photo of a bar of soap on the shower room floor. Is it about arrests for activism? Students arrested for protesting our fascist government? Or is it a drug song, about being busted for sales of Heroin, or Crack Cocaine?' If society isn't pro-active, and just simply punishing, vindicating, criminalizing those persons problematic, its children are going to glorify the very worst aspects of it, they will eroticize it, incorporate it into their being; they will go down, down, down to the bottom riding on pains coattails via drugs, alcohol abuse, violence, & other self-life murders.

Drive with Non-Professor Turnip; we pass the rough part of town, TL, see many who dwell there not because of poverty, but because of drugs/alcohol/ insanity and giving up—being like sieves thru which all resources pass. They can hold nothing. Some great sorrow has broken them early.

There had a strange thought. That my gift was given to me so I would find the right path. I was so damaged as a child—to the breaking point. ---I remember that, starting at ten. In my fantasies of murder. Glorifying of the hypodermic needle. And me hating and envisioning the breaking down of all structure. But in my art, knew I had a tool—my art sustained me long enough thru this life, gave me a purpose, gave me power, and gave me hope for the future, so that it sustained me long enough to heal. For half a century I existed on this. I lived on art like nourishment—until I reached a point that enough of the sad stuff had slowly filtered out of my mind & soul. Yes I found the right path. Took the higher road.

Very soon I will close this JOURNEY & hand it over to the children of the near-future. I hope the citizens of that unknown dispensation which awaits, just beyond the mists of God's real time will get a copy, that at least one or two of these few photocopies I could afford to make (bound in yellow card stock) will survive thru that tumultuous JOURNEY which entails wearing-away of material stuff, atrophy of a stock of too few volumes sold or distributed from their first beginning.

Chapter 9.

Walking slower then most pedestrians along the crowded speed walk, which still returned him rapidly from his job, his-her mind moved molasses-like over the events of the last few months. *'So. I been detained and questioned by the Unity. Darf.'* Gazing lethargically into faces of the huge building fronts, which stood everywhere, swiftly passing. Here and there another huge structure was still being erected. People poured into vax #33 from other vaxes internationally, as it was a major center of influence. Unity was indeed a global society. A society without borders—it tracked every citizen, everywhere.

Huge skeletal iron & light tensel-strength frame of a skyscraper-to-be rolling up its blue/green skin made entirely of windows like a person pulls up their blue uniform from the ankles, the outer layer of windows had begun upon a construction on its bottom floors. Utopias latest show piece, the 600 floor tall Unity Showcase Citizens Memorial Building. Starvax gazed at the too-familiar scenery while traveling by. Then a vision popped-up of Red, the prophet from the old dispensation; thought of him---back in 1990's and early days of the new millennium, 2000, occupying his narrow sliver of life--which was just enough apparently for him to survive and do his art & no more, and while wishing he had more of it-- life abundant--- was thankful for what he had... This was JOURNEY stuff... After awhile it was quite apparent that it was a spiritual journey Red went on.. *'I'm not quite sure what that means. Spiritual. But he talks about it a lot.'* Transman Red loved animals. Often he'd go clucking and barking around his studio like a dog/hen. For all his miserable life you could not help but see he was having a pretty good time. *'A better life then I am now! Me! Here in the Modern Age!'* Thought of the Transman carrying his heavy sack of books, as s/he turned off the speedwalk and headed towards his compound, fancied he was similar to that prophet in some ways tho not in most. People were short in those days, Transman Red being barely over 5 feet tall while he himself was nearly 6 feet from excellent nutrition and the absence of any illness at all -- but for those first suffered during his childhood in the wilds; but maybe not as quite as robust because of that-- and this strange melancholia which haunted him, not like most of the citizens of the vastly new, improved empire of Utopia--under dictatorship of the Unity. Citizens who had permanent domiciles—on upper floors. Citizens endowed with families. Citizens with a mate! Aw darf! Darf ! DARF! Stavax pounded the palm of his left hand with the fist of his right. He was such a drone! Such a stupid, stupid drudge! Maybe he'd just go underground, become a mole, living in luxury, medicated and high out of his mind on prescription drugs and enjoy every minute of it and only work 20 hours at the mandatory job! He had no luck with women! And he wanted A Woman! Hence a family! The thing he wanted most! Finally told himself; *'I'll break down, go to the Registry. They'll get me somebody. Some kind of mate.'* They had mates even for a trannyboy such as himself. The Unity had thought of everything.

When s/he got to his unit something waited for him in his word hole:

>*Tough times don't last, tough people do. Trust no one.*

Which was a quote from the ancient days via prophet Red that he himself had appropriated from a men's room lavatory wall at the TS Free Clinic along side 'I have a big dick' and other profane graffiti, which he'd copied down.

Excited about his appointment with the group Transman Starvax scurried around his unit, found the now hidden study book, examined how it corresponded on the Telly internet weather forecast, and mathematically calculated the next meetings hour & place.

Late that 24-hour block saw Starvax cozy inside his sleeping pod, having burned the midnight nuclear candle by reading excerpts of the Prophets journal in his study book. S/he had a dream. An adult Presented little Starvax with a big box. His/her chubby child hands studiously played with it, larger hands helped open it. Crayons fell out. A box of them! 100! The tot chose a yellow one. "I want the yellow one! I want the yellow one!" Yellow like him. S/he drew squiggly pictures and was taught the alphabet. Became an avid reader. His 'mom' & 'pop', state-appointed counselors, were loving to little Starvax. He was seldom alone. It was a most humane way to grow into maturity. However, unlike the case would have been if he'd had real parents, young Starvax grew up not having a family after some point. —His 'parents' now busy at their jobs raising another batch of children; those few brought in from the wilds, and those ones orphaned by rare accident.

In 2045, Jun Kim Suns predecessor, the first Dictator of the new Unity of Utopia had ordered the vast repositories of documents, books, histories, papers and ephemera collected by the libraries & universities of the old, fallen Am-Erica, to be opened, and their contents burned. Some enterprising soldiers at the Bancroft Library spirited away nearly the entire collection of Red Jordan Arobateau. —Why? Already that name was becoming infamous in growing numbers of the discontent. Rare fragments of his work was being presented in underground 'reading circles' thus this windfall of original documents was a treasure trove of illegal monies. Soon sold off to the highest bidder the works escaped without being destroyed. Now it remained for those collectors to release what they had into the information systems of the new underground groups to perpetuate their secret knowledge. Many collectors of them did. Fiction, diaries, journals were not all that had been salvaged from the old world. History documents, ancient maps, statistics of record from the old cities & nations, some of it at least floated over that large canal that divided past world from present—that cut-off from information's free flow by the military knives of fascist totalitarianism which the Unity proved to be. To be brief, books, documents, scrolls, all ancient works of the past had been regulated to flames in all major libraries of the world both private and public. Outside of those stolen by corrupt soldiers and sold to black market collectors, and what had been in private collections all along, it was all gone. Information decreased by a good 95%. What remained was now illegal. As far as robotical memory stored in the huge computer banks of global accounts— they could be swiftly erased by separate teams of technicians working as one via the Internet globally from every geographical location in earth, and upon its two satellites, & all research stations and ships in space. Which saved an immense amount of soldier power, as had been necessary to use for the burnings. It was a good thing & expedient to not have all that literature & writings, and factual documents laying around from a past which didn't exist,--novels, political treatises, history etc., because now it no longer clogged up the computer super mini microchip memory banks thus they could be used for more vital purposes --- security. Keeping track of each individual citizen of the Unity. As simultaneously accompanying the banning came an all out effort to combat the rise of domestic and international terrorism.

Around 2046 Old Timers could recall no particular upset, just that it was sad to see the darkened glass fronts of so many bookstores among the still-blazing lit up row of other commerce where throngs of pedestrians went shopping---after the edicts went out. Closing them as there were no more books. What's the point. Having bookstores? They were obsolete! Bookstores, non-Unity movie theatres, newspaper publishers, and many others of the ancient artifices artificially obsolesced by post-modern doctrine of the Unity.

Star1.vax was in for a shock. Today, there, in front of the study group, was Mable! Along side of leaders Valdez and Gojenko. Smiling yet stern. Handsomely attired in her blue jumpsuit accessorized by femmy little stuff, which made him queasy in his stomach.

He blushed, gazing at Mablevax; 'if she only knew I've had her naked under me in bed all week... Oh darf! Double daft in hell! What will I do now?' He-she was so frustrated. And knew he'd have to make his move soon. There was only 3 hours to the class. 3 hours! To tell her how he felt! To ask her to go have an energy boosting drink with him. –To go on a date! He'd run up there in front of all the students and ask now. *Now!* Well, maybe right after class...

"I'll lead our group today." Mable473.vax declared.

The class of comrades had now increased back to nearer that of its original size, but not quite. The room, sub-terra, without windows, with water pipes & electrical conduits running across it's ceiling, in a new location inside the dome, was too small. So they were crowded together, shoulder to shoulder elbow to elbow. --- 'Just like a big family,' Starvax marveled. It was hard to judge how many comrades would have nerve enough to keep on attending---seeing the trouble it could bring.

Soon Starvax's mind wandered. S/he was lost in the sight of lovely Mable. She looked older then he remembered; mature. And just as pretty, beautiful even. A strange new wisdom seemed to glow from out of her being. *'Maybe she's been on an action!'* He thought. S/he awoke awhile later to the sound of the leaders questioning his classmates.

Mable: Are there any old people living in your unit? Anyone? You comrade, there in the 3rd row! Pointed to a young man who, being attentive, was already busy thinking of his answer.

"None." He responded.
Starvax raised his hand and spoke, saying he'd had seen an old timer: "There's this citizen who comes around our department at the Depot. She's in the Unity party. I think she tries to make her self look young but you can tell, she walks crooked, like she's ancient."

A small laugh flared up, and quietly died, in the embarrassment of political incorrectness. The educated class was self-governing.

Mable: So you don't, as a rule see old timers.

"None in my compound." Said Kevin Buckminster.

Mable: Do you really think about why that is Kevin?

He wasn't forthcoming. So she looked around. A blank stare greeted her from mostly young faces

Gojenko: Most old timers live underground.

Mable: With the moles?

Gojenko: Yes.

Mable: Is anyone here a mole? (Looking around class.)

Silence.

Valdez at first seemed very nervous about the topic, but finally came to the defense of the old timers in a most dramatic fashion.

Valdez: Look at my Hands! Look at this! He began to walk down the aisle of students, extending his hands for the first time so they could see. They were wrinkled, very bronzed as if having once been colored by the real outside sun.

Yes, some of us are old timers! Some of us were in the old world, and are still here now, keeping a low profile. Invisible. We are not warehoused 50 floors down below in luxury apartments, every need taken care of, until we die--- die with our lips shut! Yes, some of us are risking a... he paused.... A lot being here in this class. *'Was he going to say, risking their lives?'*

Never thought about it before, but Valdez sometimes caught himself saying 'Goddamn it." Or some other....epitaph. A curse. Swearing. Something the citizens of Utopia never, never did. Starvax hadn't made any association, until now. It dawned on him. *'Professor Valdez is old!'* Darf! Darf and double Darf! Hadn't thought of that.... That he might swearing because he was left over from the ancient times!

So! The Old Timers were held in storage—by their 'free choice' in luxury apartments deep underground, severely medicated—so they don't blurt out anything from the archives of their memory to contaminate the peaceful security of youthful citizens of Utopia!

"Moles are Old Timers!" Somebody was saying.

Mable: We believe that some old people are forcibly medicated—so they can't tell their tales. And many, probably the most stubborn, have been removed. But this empire is sinister. It has turns and twists you wouldn't imagine. Some of the old timers in fact, many of them are employed in top echelons of Unity leadership. In fact, maybe they are the Unity. They help build it.

The class seemed to draw back in a collective a gasp.

Valdez: Also note the absence of many of the darker colored races yes? Anybody?

Utopia is international and so Unity's populous, mixing of many different people, so it is claimed. But we believe, due to the predominance of lighter skinned and white citizens, that at once time, in the near past, a culling, or selection occurred. As it certainly does in the laboratories of SPOVA.

125

A darker skin comrade gave a retort too—in brutal Hindi language.

Murmurs of agreement from the vastly light to tan audience. Most of them were white; Starvax with his yellow-tan was a distinct minority.

Mable: Because back then the lower socio economic groupings; those cultural groups hopelessly mired in poverty, embroiled in criminal behavior generation after generation over and over, which showed no sign of being able to pull themselves up out of it...... Well it's believed that when the domes first went up in construction, that the darker--thus often poorer--people, they were left outside.

Valdez: Left outside to die. (Bitterly.)

Mable: Out there a few survived. ----They composite the strange 'tribes' we hear of today.

Awhile later they went over assigned materials, Starvax proudly raising his hand in the air, was subsequently called on and gave knowledgeable answers. Near the end of the meeting Gojenko made an offhand comment, which shed a lot of light on the purpose of these groups. He only said it once. Quickly, softly, so comrades who weren't in the room then, or not paying attention would have missed it. He quite simply intimated the purpose of these groups.

And now, still musing over this quaint remark as others around him began to pack up their manuals, fragments of papers and palm pads into surreptitious satchels designed for music recording pods, and other subterfuge, Starvax thought too, maybe the others, Anderson and her team, and who ever the mysterious hooded saboteurs who had cut off the power out of the whole vax had taken action of their own. Working as independent cells. Maybe the study group was not to plan actions, nor recruit a guerrilla army, but to lift the veil of their eyes so they might see. See what they hadn't been aware of, creeping out of the shadows poisoning Utopia.... and they could make their own decisions what to do next..

Mable. She'd done an excellent job.

At the end she had a surprise for class. "Well, like many of us comrades here, I've changed my name. I'm now *Madonna Mable Goldman.*"

The class applauded. Her three special friends cheered. Fists upraised in solidarity.

"Its after two liberated women of the past century—Madonna, a pop singer from the 1980's who believed in a woman's free right to choose sexual partners, and Emma Goldstein, the radical women who fought for workers rights in the garment industry & struggled for citizens working 12 to 16 hours a day 6 days a week, to have their jobs cut down to what we have here in Utopia, 8 hour days. 40-hour weeks. Madonna Mable Goldman. You may call me that during class, but out there, I'm still Mable473.vax."

As he left the classroom Transman Starvax pondered a statement: *'left outside the domes to die? The dome gates shut in their faces!?'*

But he was in for a worse shock then cultural enlightenment. Outside class heading up the cement hallway with overhanging water pipes, Madonna Mable Goldman stood with 3 friends, her arm encircling Kevin—that soldier-size Kevin! Kevin *Buckminister..*

'Oh so its that way.' Icily, pain dropped into his mind. Deciding to walk on past, ignoring them all. Those 3 who wouldn't speak to him when Mable wasn't around! Despite his wild thoughts of proposing she & him go to get an energy boosting drink together--- on kind of date!

Poor comrade Starvax trapped by sex, love, emotion & lured by fashion!— A citizen female in a feminized blue Utopia regulation jumpsuit accessorized by shoes on stilts, dangling stuff from her ears & exuding the scent of perfume!

Delighted to see Starvax however, Madonna Mable Goldman immediately transferred her focus of attention to him—withdrawing her arm from around Kevin.

Nose in the air, tall, elegant, the proud Star1.vax walked coolly past without speaking.

"Oh goddamn it to hell Starvax." Mable swore.

He looked around at her, stunned! It was as if someone had poured cold water on him!

"WHAT!"

"What?" She replied cutely. "Is something bothering you? Is it something I said? *In class maybe?"* Madonna Mable Goldman stood hands on her hips demanding a reply that would account for his silly rudeness.

"Oh.. No….uh, nothing." Chagrined, redfaced; Transman Starvax stood there fumbling his fingers in his jumpsuit pockets. At an uncharacteristic loss for words.

"Well don't just walk past me without speaking Comrade!"

"Oh… I… I didn't' *notice* you."

"Oh Yeah! Yeah! Like nobody notices me! Tell me the truth Starvax One! I swore! Is that unusual? Yes! For you it is! For a good citizen! But not for ME! I'm a BAD citizen! SO! Talk to me! Aren't you glad to see me?"

By then Starvax had gained his equilibrium. S/he had managed to give his usual acerbic reply but he realized immediately how very foolish he was in light of his wanting Mablevax Goldman, that very person who stood before her now in all the glory of femininity, sex & power; her pretty blue uniform decked out with accessories—bracelets, earrings, bracelets, perfumes & other adornments plus the cuff of her trousers rolled half way up showing the shapely calf of her legs and her shoes had high heels on them! So he did a very impromptu thing; he reached out and touched her hand with his.

"OH! Starvax! I can't believe you did that! Touched me without my permission!" Mable drew back a bit. She seemed genuinely surprised.

Before he knew what was happening, in a miraculous whirlwind he realized that he & she were walking together, slowly, casually, thru the fields of the incorporated area directly to the slow slow speedwalk.

Taking a risk of security breach they took the rapid transit together. Taking a risk in investment of feelings he/she attempted to reach out. But didn't know how. Tried to make small talk about his observations. Things like how he'd go ride the elevator of that special tall building to the observation deck, so near the top of the dome it seems you could reach right up and touch it! Tho it was still way above even that as he understood, and how each hundred floors gets increasingly cold, and colder, and then they were back inside the dome and must go their separate ways.

He had her personal number now, in his palm pad, & she had his.

Chapter 10.

Young citizen Star1.vax made another pilgrimage outside the dome. Regardless of the consequences. S/he had wanted to search for his mother way back from as long as he could remember, this person he only had shadowy memories of, along with so much cold, pain & discomfort and a perpetually empty belly—but irregardless he'd craved to find her, relentlessly. Some months ago he had fashioned a plan to begin to look— out here in the wilds. The method had been a vague restless casting of a net, with such a vast ocean to sift... but today he had a designation.

Outside the dome free air of planet earth was spectacular.

Once crossing thru the gates into the unprotected area, outside the dome, he mounted the ancient speedwalk, rode aways, then stepped off. Down into the gully he went. Disappearing from sight. Traveling the railroad tracks picking over the rotted ties, then, 3 miles out of the dome, veered out thru entanglements of twisted girders of fallen buildings & debris. His footfalls went surely to that special place up to the top of the hill, the old ruins.

As before, he found a comfortable nitch, spread a cloth out fastidiously, took a seat, but before he could unwrap his lunch, sheer awesomeness of the looming palace overwhelmed him—to the degree that tears which he almost never shed---came to his eyes. Setting down his tofu/tomato & faux cheese sandwich he let his mind wander, and his eyes drift. Over the backs of upturned long wooden benches; up to the high rafters where flying beasts winged & preened and squawked, over half-shattered but most beautiful many-hued stained glass windows now miraculously colored by the real sun which shone thru them from the west. 'Wow. What a beautiful palace this was designed to be!'

'I wonder what went on here? Some kind of ceremonies the ancients practiced that we read about? Whatever it is it must have been good, because its so big, and so many people could fit inside.' Indeed if all the long wooden benches were counted as seats, and these, plus hundreds & hundreds of broken chairs first fire ruined, then mildewed rotted, scattered & broken which lay about in two vast enclaves off the main large arched enclosure were filled, the count could have run into as many as ten thousand, at once.

He sat in a stone alcove to the side, where rock seats, ornate, with jewels set in marble, now almost obliterated by dust, smoke, and creeping green moss; had been carved out of the stony side of the palace along one wall. Under his feet a layer of damp ground, sediment of dirt which had filtered in from outside over the decades. Wind blew thru that open section where the towering rock wall had been exploded by fire and had fallen away. He sat here in awe just as the first time when on an adventure he'd discovered the place led here by that interesting rise in the earth that beckoning rock fortress on a hill…. He'd wanted to see what was at the top.

Soon his thoughts grew as big & as high as the palace itself; uplifted; tears, so rarely shed, ran down his face. He didn't know what was moving him but his voice blurted out loud: "I got to find my mother! I want Mable to be… my mate! I want a family! I want a real home, and a unit I own --- on a higher floor! I want… " Then his vocal appeal, dying on his lips, was perpetuated on by a great echo in which it boomed away thru the canyon of the deserted shell. S/he craved for something he couldn't understand. And what had made these words blurt out loud from his mouth? Maybe something about the place itself had elicited them.

Young Starvax sat back against the mossy stone, somewhat surprised. Swiftly, a vision passed before his eyes! Sitting up, he stared into the middle of the vast palace suddenly seeing a multitude of people, many on their knees, some bowing facing the east, others faced the west. Starvax blinked. He peered deeply into the mysterious air, which shimmered in front of him having a presence of its own, and thus saw it in greater detail. Saw this multitude of humans was dressed in all styles of clothes—robes, sandals, long flowing gowns with royal trains, suits & ties; from days of distant antiquity and of those just recently passed a century ago. Some wore skirts made of from leaves of strange plants. He saw some were seated in circles together banging drums; their half-naked bodies swaying from side to side. And a sound could be heard, all diverse, all from different locations, yet they were all singing together in the same key. All in a strange kind of harmony as they bowed down before a Being! A Being as big as the palace! A Being made out of spirit, yet visible! & each was calling out to this Being by different names. They all had different names for the Being, yet it was the same Being & all its names were correct.

S/he was amazed! The vision waned. As it did he wiped his small hand across his yellow brow. Starvax was sweating. Perspiration ran freely from under his armpits, the small of his back was drenched. Like he'd just been in a fever and now the fever had receded. The vision had departed too, on its own accord. He wiped the last veils of the vision away from his face and blinked.

Back under the dome the main street is bustling with its 24-hour inhabitants. Outside of it the sun sets fast in the western sky. Shadows now engulfed the tremendous palace. Starvax suddenly realized: *"It's going to get dark!"* Darker then he ever knew! *"There's no light to find my way back!"* And raced out of the vast structure, jumping over its uprooted benches and fallen blocks of stone, & raced as the wind along his path back towards that blue/green dome which lay shimmering, glimmering, faint-shining, with its perpetual bright and good weather.

That fiery red orange ball, the sun was just cutting down under the horizon. Now it had disappeared in a rouge mist, which powder-puffed the western sky. Panting for breath he ran, his thoughts wild. 'Maybe I was worshiping back there! Yes I was right! It must be an ancient cathedral!' He thought of multitudes of early peoples bowing to the east from where this sun arose. Like a small ant he raced along his rough trail amid majestic scenery, panoramic wind-swept around. Before him distant purple mountains rounded down by weathering of ages faded to deeper indigo. The dying sun enflames that whole quadrant of blue sky. Bluepink morphs into purple; and alongside the horizon laid out flat, the rising blue evening turning to black night still visible, wide and far amazing--- was the blue/green dome. Shimmering bubble of civilization in which 9 million citizens are trapped, living working, sleeping, questioning, dying, ---everywhere from 50 floors under the earth to 500 at its top. -- At empires heaven.

Panting s/he gained the railroad tracks. His feet falling into the now accustomed path rapidly. *'Good, I can find my way back even in the dark, using these rails.'* Then the sun was gone. It was still twilight here tho, he noticed, breathing harshly as he ran, light still filled the skies. Western sky's portion was warm & pink where as the other sections of the sky were cold blue grey white, with no warmth. 'The ancients of our human ancestry bowed to this same sun, worshiped it, preyed to it, named their deities after it....' There was this. A stirring to know some kind of god—which Starvax hadn't had any idea what that meant whatsoever but could see immediately that it, this god, could be mighty useful.

Once back inside under the dome, all turned gray, & steel shadowy. Filled with enormous buildings of such great height. Austere grid of blocks after block built-up with towering structures.

Chapter 10.

One day later in the week, not far from the chilling episode with soldiers barging into his unit door, citizen Starvax was returning home from an utterly boring mindless day at the Bureau of Statistics & Information.

S/he had seen a tall woman clearing the Peoples Square with large strides. Followed by a retinue of medics with white coats, as he'd filed out of the Bureau with teams of other workers. When he got to his compound a van

131

marked Unity Medical Alert, Health Department was parked in front of his building.

Hastily in his newfound paranoia Starvax departed for the upper floor.

Just settling into his pod chair when there came a knock on his unit door accompanied by a loud authoritarian voice. "OPEN YOUR DOOR CITIZEN STAR1.VAX! UNITY MEDICAL SERVICES!"

Greeted at the door by three representatives of the Health Department in white coats & identification badges. *'Oh No!'* He thought, suppressing a violent urge to lash out, to yell, or worse, a fist cuff, or, to run.

"We've come to take you down to Unity Health Services to check your radiation level."

Utopian Health Services. He was taken back to Civic Center Square. The large faux stone building of the central hospital, graceful as air, built of tensile-strength girders, and faced in glorious blue/green windows lifted off of a replica of the ancient government buildings of yesteryear, 15 stone steps, up to its grand heights of nearly 200 floors.

There above on hospital's front wall was the Great Edict. It was in many places, in many different designs, and in many sections of itself, --- this one carved into stone. It could be seen throughout the world. Since the first beginnings of Utopia.

The representatives dropped him off in front of the place, where a nurse and a burly attendant also in medic clothes waited his arrival.

There on the steps at the above the entrance he saw it. He hadn't been here for a while. Starvax stopped in his tracks. "I want to read some of our Edict for a moment." Both aids looked at him-her with suspicion. He gazed up at the Great Edict and read emblazoned words chiseled into the plaque.

Then the attendants seemed to smile with approval.

> Article IX. THE CONCENTRATION OF ANY ONE BODY OF CITIZENS BY RACE, GENDER, OR NATIONAL AFFILIATION TO THE EXCLUSION OF ANY OTHERS OF ANY OTHER GROUPS IS NOT ALLOWED! WE ARE ONE! THE WORLD IS ONE PEOPLE! UNITY NOW!

Some routine checks, blood draws, ultrasound probes and scans, finally the nurse led Starvax to an exam room. "Doctor Seltzer will be with you shortly." And exited.

When he peeked outside, the burly attendant sat, directly beside the doorway, leaning back against the tile wall.

In a few moments the Doctor came in. She was transsexual. Quite pretty, mature, in her mid 50's—by her manner this was apparent, tho she looked the Utopian standard, a perpetual 20's; curly blond hair. Tall. A nature's freak—just like him, but going the opposite way.

"Hum..." She mused examining the charts with the intensity of a clinician. "Bone marrow is... hum... Yes, alright... hum..." She finished scanning the documents. "Well, you'll live. It's not bad." Satisfied s/he looked up at him. Then got to the part which apparently did worry her.

"What are you doing out there?"

"I go walking..."

The doctor looked down at the chart. "According to the police report that's what you told them." S/he looked back up. "Walking? To where? Why?"

Dr. Seltzer peered at him-her more intently now: "Citizen why did you purchase disc 527726 from the Department of Media--- on 3/17/40, the day of the thwarted attempt at sabotage against the State of Utopia?"

Cold, sickening, a chill shot down his spine. How did they know that? --- Why had they checked him so thoroughly? They had been secretly scanning his travels. His purchases!

"I go walking... I... I like the news... that's all.... Uh..." He paused; s/he was probing him with steely grey blue eyes. He had to give her more. Wanted to open up to this sister transsexual. So Starvax confessed his worst secret: "I don't have anything else to do. I don't have a family. I only have two friends, one moved out of the vax 4 years ago. I don't have a much of anything.... to have fun..."

Dr. Seltzer cut him short, impatiently. "Yes, yes, we know you don't have a family." Then leaned back in her chair, eyes still fixed on him intent, but her mind whirring inside like a lepidopterist pins a bug down in an album for cold storage, searching for a label.

133

"Star1.vax, I think maybe we should make an appointment for you at the Registry. What do you think?"

He gulped and swallowed. *'The Registry of Romantic Affairs! Oh darf! DARF!* ***DARF ON TOP OF DARF!'*** His brain fairly yelled. But he concealed his true feelings.

"Oh! Do you think so?" He replied sweetly, a smile on pursed lips.

"Well *I did it.* And it worked perfectly for *me.*" Dr. Seltzer said defensively. "I have a lovely home, a very satisfactory spouse. It's a wonderful life. Yes, and we are quite happy…" S/he-she replied self-satisfied. And that was the end of the debate. Dr. Seltzer twirled her electronic pen down the side of her computer-pad, and out popped a duplicate for him. She handed it over with a gesture of largess.

"Show this to your head at the Depot, they'll give you time off. I've made you reservations for 3 appointments for this month. The Registry'll contact You. *Go Starvax, and be well.*"

Then, with a flounce of her white coat, she was out the door. Calling, "Before you go you must see the Social Worker, have a little talk with him."

'See the Social Worker, darf.' Again the aid accompanied him but now following from a distance over the straight white tile corridors of Utopian Health Services as he went to the designated office.

Inside the office of the Social Worker was a bio male with prim lips, slim, quite tall, seated behind a desk. He was attired in a white lab coat over street clothes upon which was pinned his Utopia badge. Almost thought he might be a Transman himself, but those tell-tale large hands and head, and great height meant that probably wasn't so. He motioned to a chair in front of his desk.

There it lay. He was opening the copy of Starvax's record. Doctor Seltzer had given it barely a thought—to a doctor it was minor.--- To a nosey social worker it was significant.

"Hummm…" He said officiously. "Radiation level up 100 micro millimeters, a fraction of a point greater then previously." Meaning then it had been at his last examination (mandatory for all citizens) 1 year previously. "Do you know why?" And began tapping his electronic pen somewhat impatiently.

134

"Yes. Tons of radioactive particles shot up into the air from the war."

"War?" The social worker repeated and now gazed at him intently.
"War?" He repeated once more, he had stopped his tapping.

'Darf! I've messed up!'

"Uh… the alien space monsters war on us! On OUR Unity!"

"Yes." The Social Worker nodded, brusque, too eager to return to Starvax first comment so thoughtlessly blurted out, which seemed to have stuck in his bureaucratic mind. He scanned back over the record for a second time. "Lets see…. You were SAVED when you were uh 3?"

"Yes."

"Did the people who raised you – out in the wilds-- did they ever talk to you about these things…? This *war* stuff?"

"I don't remember anything." Starvax lied. "My minds always been bonk. Always. Up until the time I was saved and put in kindergarten. The wonderful kindergarten! ---The wonderful UNITY kindergarten where I played with alphabet blocks and number wedges, and crayons and we sang songs."

The Social Worker beamed in approval. But added, critically, "Citizen Starvax, you have a fine mind, your brain's not bonk. We examined you thoroughly in the scanner earlier, and you haven't lost any significant IQ points from the 170 you were enhanced with after we first found you. Nature gave us help. You were already quite an intelligent child."

He paused a moment. Young Starvax sat hopelessly exhausted from his ordeal, and pissed. Wondering what was coming next.

The worker radiated concern. He leaned closer. "It's not safe out there, citizen. There's crime out there!" He paused to let his words sink in.

Young Starvax wasn't as afraid of the lower-rank social worker as he had been the doctor. He understood Utopian hierarchy. "It's my free time." He said somewhat belligerent.

"If you insist on returning out into the wilds, which you shouldn't, I insist you carry this tracking device."

The Social worker gave him an oblong box, black, small, about 3" by 1" with no visible dials or gadgetry.

"What do I do with it?"

"Keep it with you always! If you're in trouble we'll know! We can tell." He pointed at the device. "The soldiers will come to rescue you! ---It fits anywhere." He added, as the puzzled Transman turned the box over in the palm of his hand.

"I'm telling you again, Starvax, don't go back out there!"

"Does this go on my record?

"Of course citizen, but I wouldn't worry about it. Unless you plan on getting more... infractions."

"How long do you keep it on my record before it passes off?"

"40 years citizen."

"I'm sorry... about this."

"As you know we have billions of names to process, constantly. And, sometimes we're slow. Sometimes I think our Unity operates at drone speed. Ha, ha!" He thought that was funny.

The Social Worker was quite a poet. He leaned back and philosophized. "In here, under our dome, we citizens live in a terrarium of safety, where as they are living out there in the wilds, horribly."

When the ordeal ended, Starvax stumbled down into the tile hall, and foggily groped his way to the elevator. Only then did he realize the burly attendant had vanished. His mission accomplished.

The elevator half full of citizens descended to street level.

'Darf. Go to the Registry and they'll match me up with an appropriate wife. No more lonely nights. No more drone prepared dinners, alone. We'd have a wedding and a honeymoon in a luxury suite! A luxury suite way up on a high floor with a spectacular silver star dotted overview of this entire stupid vax!' He'd pull off his bride's wedding gown and he'd melt! He'd dissolve into a slimy pool of cum, pheromones, joy, happiness, and sweat, into the ancient Nirvana!

7.
192 steps up Mason Street from Pine to the hill's top on Broadway. 39 steps up to the grand, ornate Cathedral entrance, which is fine, thick old wood, with fixtures wrought in bronze.

It had been exactly a month. He headed up the hill. Another round full moon shone down! He approached the cement steps praying with vengeance!

(A step.) 'Oh Lord(ess) Have Mercy. Protect! Protect us!' (Friends, animals, innocents.)

(Another step.) 'Oh yeah, and protect me too.'

(Now aloud in a feverish plea!) "Save the animals God Almighty! Please! The pigeons in New York City! They're trapping and shipping the birds out to Jersey City to use as target practice!

> A bullet pierces the grey fluffy breast
> of the pigeon.
> May its soul ascend
> to the Great Mother
> of all homeless pigeons!
> May they live there in eternity
> in the house of our loving Creator,
> Amein.

Dear Children, Children of the future! I do not see how you can live your lives one more instant without turning those thoughts and feelings upwards to we know not what, but searching for the pure, the divine, the good and the saving One. Because we all run the race, and begin to know at some point we're going to drop out of that race—realizing this more strong and stronger as we go further and further. That it just remains a question of how long, how far we can travel, and upon what great impulse.

Every detail of our lives eclipses blocks of time---so its important not to dwell on anything but ones bare bones necessities. For me, the art to which I've been given and have expended on that, everything. Energy wise, time wise, all wise. It is my great impulse.

Wherever epochal dramas, journals, novels, poems…. one writes and presents to the world; written information, ink & quill-scribed bibles, Korans, torahs —the labors of monastic priests, --- stone tablets, papyrus scrolls; to modern day computer print-outs, time has a habit of taking out of context what it will; accentuating in bright lights what it may choose by popular demand, drowning the rest in obscurity. The paparazzi will appropriate its favorite messages. So the visionary runs the risk of their lofty passages being edited out & the other, common crap remaining, which ain't exactly what you'd meant to say! What will the future know about me? That Red was a spiritual person, a thinker? My guess he'll be noted for his excesses of eroticism. 'Certain Passages…' Thus labeled a sex crazed horny horn dog.

Now, for my last exhortation, closing this first volume of JOURNEY, (the Daily Diary); about theology. To remind you that regarding our Holy Bible-- just what it says, it means. – "In My house there are many mansions." All kinds of diverse persons and groups and beliefs are in the huge, universal mansion of Creator! Thus you all are going to be up there dancing in joy!

Maybe I will be known as a prophet by future generations!

Poet! Scavenger!

I have an enviable freedom because of being my own publisher. I don't have no editor, no reviewers, no critiques, no distributor… so no one tells me anything. Are the results better writing? Would I get writers block like so many famous artists who suddenly have a 'public' to account to? If so, it's a little late—since Red Jordan Press catalogues over-80 separate books!

Salvador Dali was a consummate artist plus he knew how to market himself. When you become proficient in your genre then you're free to wander the world self-defining into a character. This 'character' helps peddle your product. *'I will go wandering….'*

State of Empire 2006:
Pressure on the large continental land masses causes them to actually sink too, as well as the sea level rising due to natural, epochal variances, plus global warming—human created, this an unnatural cause. Island nations are Disappearing. Islanders see the water level rise further and further inland. They report having first noticed the sea level had risen a while back, slowly, but recently greatly, and now it's up to their back doorsteps. Leaders of Island Nations are greatly alarmed for their people and are asking nearby continental nations which are safe being on higher ground,

for sanctuary; some for thousand; others tens of thousands of their population. They shortly will be a people with no land.

Over the last 50 years land loss has accelerated to 50 miles per year. There is a slow collapse of the ecosystems of species of flora & fauna, that are now dying out at an alarming rate, predicting their likely extinction if some compassionate reversal of human behavior isn't forthcoming. The rising sea level gobbles up 2 acres of delta lands by the hour. Loss of all wetlands and swamps and marshes is a possibility. Soon coastlines may be submerged. Without wetlands the oceans are lapping at the foundation rock upon which the coastal cities are built, gnawing away at the landmass underneath which supports them. This predicts a land failure of many surrounding coastal regions, thus shrinking the landmass of continents, the complete eliminating whole cities, states and sea-level nations like Holland.
—Dear Children, let's hope this is not a prognosis for the future!

The human experience is full of traps. Traps springing! The economic variety, and also crime and failure; those cut down in wars by early death.
—Some traps are ones can foresee, some, one can't.

***

Little and poor and short he moved thru the night city streets relatively unscathed, because he looked mean enough to put up a fight and too poor to be worth anything.

He came Out of Chinatown, where blocks of Chinese novelty markets are advertising sales, -- due to perpetually closing--- as a lure to customers. Past where the homeless are hunkered down in Laech Wellessa (Ivy) street, 3 shopping carts deep along the curb. Empire, San Francisco of the open hands. *"I don't want no Heroin. I don't fuck with Heroin..."* His Journey to the transsexual clinic to get hormones. Beside the water cooler a roach scuttles across the tile floor narrowly missing his foot.

Signs of the resistance have sprouted up everywhere, for times have gotten rougher everywhere tout la monde.

Eternal Impeachment!

Hence a re-call on both divine and governmental levels. Impeach: To bring a public official before the proper tribunal on a charge of wrongdoing. Meaning the faux president of those stolen elections, (2004, 2000). The bribed Supreme Court which suspended recount of the votes of that unjust and tampered election, and the governor of the state who ordered the

Supreme Court to halt the recount. Meaning the Halliburton/& U$ Vice President cartel that went to war to make money and were loyal to that cause alone, --- even tho in so doing shortchanged the war effort by refusing to pay for adequate backup to keep total peace on the streets of Baghdad and its environs, thus, de facto murdered 400,000 Iraqi nationals, plus 3,500 U$ military service men & women—all on the sake of saving money! No money for communication systems between ground/air troops of our armed forces! No money for armor to plate the convoy vehicles bringing supplies in & out of Baghdad, no money to buy bulletproof vests for the infantry solders in the line of fire! (They had to buy their own if they wanted it.) I could go on and on! Yet 93 billion dollars every 3 months allotted to this war effort pick-pocketed out of the wallets & purses of American workers!

It would be foolish, foolish, foolish for me to idolize revolutionary warriors & preach actions which could cost you your future--- acts I myself probably will never do. This in the style of a Mafioso don who puts out a 'contract' or commissions 'hits' (murder) upon his enemies to lower rank soldiers. In my case a flaming firebrand who puts out a contract on the entire ruling class, plus current fascist government in power. Even our own Emma Goldman idolized in previous writings who paid a man to commit a revolutionary assassination she herself could not/would not attempt. But likewise it would be a great error for me to dam up or label 'unthinkable', or 'unwise' what may prove to be the only avenue of action which may well be left to citizens of the future weather that be far or near, who by the happenstance of fate in conflux with the progressively downward spiraling standard of living and digress of liberty & independence, may leave that future generation at the absolute nadir of existence, having had every last human right stripped away from them, and no recourse as to change their miserable condition, except by violent, desperate acts. This awful digress having started with, at the beginning, overlords who had set the tone by controlling industry, tho they don't labor in it—the means of production according to Karl Marx--- and set bare survival wages for a norm, offering no workers benefits; to the impossibility of ownership of housing, even a room of ones own by the manipulations of rich land-stealing moguls. All these enemies of the people who eat 3/4 of the pie themselves, hoarding the rest for their families alone-- digressing from that point, to the last, those petty bosses latest come along, underlings who rush in on the coattails of their masters at a later date, who proceed to snatch up every crumb, leaving for the people, a totally empty plate.

On the other hand, for reflection here's a quote from Dorothy Day, circa 1915:

"Life and struggle seem very tawdry in the twilight. This bleak countryside makes me feel that I should struggle for my soul instead of my political rights... I feel peculiarly small and lonely tonight."

So as far as what I'm preaching, leave it to yourselves, your conscious—and above all the times in which you live when reading these words—they will speak to you the correct path you must choose.

Red Jordan Arobateau
December 8, 2006
5:36 AM Pacific Standard Time
San Francisco, CA
USA

Chapter 11.

At that point h/se realized he couldn't go out to the unincorporated area again—without a good reason, a Unity Acceptable reason.

Then a big obstacle was thrown into his/her progress of days. The next meeting was again outside the dome.

This time he was summoned directly by Madonna Mable Goldman, and could not refuse!

He did not tell her, could not, about what had happened to him, over the audio wordhole, when she innocently mentioned one of those arcane quote, from which the class calculated their meetings. **"I'll dance at my party, or what good is it?"** A dead feeling inside. He'd been cut off from the group! DARF! Oh darf. And promptly sank into a pool of despair.

He turned his body, shifting his position in the pod chair, in front of the Telly. *'No I don't want to fall asleep here—I'll just have to get up to bathe and set out my uniform and go back to my sleeping pod and go back to sleep all over again...'* But he didn't even shift his weight again in the chair it was so cozy & nodded once. ---Eyes blinked open—then shut. Forcibly opened his eyelids but then they yielded a 2nd time & thus fell asleep while assuring himself he wouldn't.

Later Starvax bitterly reflected that he could barely close his eyes &: *'soldiers would be knocking on my door!'* And how he had: *'achieved this*

141

unit on the 30th floor; been here 3 years and nobody beside 2 friends, building maintenance and drones has ever entered before!' No doubt due to his vast unpopularity.

Thought about Red's times how happy he'd feel; nostalgic, savoring the air of home when he'd find himself in a neighborhood of brown/tan faces—after the largely white San Francisco predominant, but then, soon realize he was not accepted because few could identify him as a black, so he really had no race. Then thought about his own predicament being obviously in the minority because of his own uncertain beginnings, plus gender condition, here among the ordinary citizens of this new empire—but not being totally foreign either. 'That's my greatest problem! Having to disclose to any future mates my transsexual status. It's just a painful issue. I can't get a normal date, and now they're shipping me off to *The Registry*— that's the place people go who can't get dates by themselves and need help!' And how his last chance he'd hoped for, to meet a woman at the study classes was now aborted!

When Starvax came, drowsily to the surface of conscious out of his light nap, he awoke with a plan!

He had a brilliant idea…

Starvax had told his first best friend (who went off to vax #32 for better opportunity on the lower rungs of The Unity) 5 years past, upon meeting this very unique individual (having just bumped shoulders together at a mandatory Public Citizens Rally, and, each recognizing the other to be a kindred spirit had introduced themselves on the spot) something to the effect of how: "There stood the hardest man I've ever seen --- who is a dike, but also, in fashion, a fag; but not even that for he is sworn to a sexless life—of a nothing!"

Statvax's other best friend had no sex at all, one of a special minority who had themselves neutered. Univaks. They formed their own global federation—numbering in the million or so. Univak738,000.global.

Being summoned to his friends compound, Univak738,000.global now stood before Starvax in a clean blue jumpsuit and polished designer space boots 'built for traction upon any speedwalk in the modern age.' Citizen Starvax had been vague as to why he wanted to see him, not wanting to communicate the true reason via telescreen nor wordhole.

The two greeted with their customary hug, diminishing into a more formalized handshake, followed by a bored "Hol low Bud."

142

Univak saw his friend in his unit doorway, slim, tall, tho not as tall as himself, impeccably attired in a formal jumpsuit which seemed to call out for accessories—which he had-- a fancy matching shoulder bag which bulged but not so much as to be suspicious.

Univak. He too was tall. But unlike Starvax who was regular shaped, he was very angular, wide shoulder & a narrow pelvis. Would have been a bio male except he wasn't born one, and nor did he wish to be—either male nor female. He had somehow slipped thru Utopias monitoring systems and been allowed to be born a weird androgyne. –Those who are androgenetic. Given hormone therapy starting at the age of 7 when his physical disability started to prove life-threatening, he had since decided to go under the knife, and became a neuter.

"Want you to do me a favor, bud…"

"What?"

"I want us to go to the public screening on The Animals of Utopia Satellites. It's about The Unity saving wildlife. It tells stuff about the new satellite we're stacking; it's a great movie. I want you to sit there in a pod chair and hold something for me. I'll be right back."

"Hold something? Hold what bud? You'll right back? Where the darf yuh goin'?"

"This."

Starvax fished into his manly purse and produced a curious looking object. *'Here's this infernal black box they gave me. Darf! It's attached to me!'* Besides it was the heavy Study Guide for the Red Jordan Reading Society.—Titleless.

Univak had long legs and walked faster even then Starvax who could be fast. He was the tallest of the two even tho Starvax was a neat 6 feet. They moved thru the crowded streets together attracting no attention.

There were no cars, automobiles, busses, or trucks on the streets of Utopia due to the sad experience of the last dispensation and this was so globally. Before, all the world over, in its separate nation states—burning fossil fuel in combustion engines, burning trees for warmth, cooking, and to clear the land, plus carbon dioxide emissions from aerosol spray cans that propelled hairspray to style the hair of American & European women had contributed

143

to the near-annihilation of the human species. Had learned that painful lesson, but not before, in conjunction with natures own warming/cooling cycles, people had contributed to the current global state of super-temperatures which still had potential to destroyed the human race. Only in the hands of the rich-- very rich –did you see a steering wheel as they drove trepidatiously thru the miasma of pedestrians and speed walks. These being emission-free vehicles, the hydrogen powered clean air cars. And there were the omnipresent Unity services, governmental, military etc, for which, in emergency, every other thing stopped.

The two got on the speedwalk together, Univak primly stepped rhythmically in a direct line, never missing a beat, while Starvax dawdled, increasing then slowing his tempo dependant on if something s/he fancied might appear off to the side to which he might give a curious look.

The two went into a Utopia screening studio. This particular place, which Starvax had purposefully chosen, was unique as it was inside a vast auditorium one of whose separate arcades led to a grassy strip outside. One unguarded by one of those overwhelming abundance of scanners. It was there that a citizen might slip away without passing thru a detector which read the eyes and heat print of the individual person, filing it into the multi-million of transactions of citizen comings/goings Unity had to process daily. An anomaly, which had not yet been caught and remedied.

The two walked down the dark aisle, found two pod chairs, but instead of sitting next to his friend, Starvax just gave his tracking device to Univak. "I'll be back in awhile."

"How long?"

"At the end of the picture."

"2 hours?"

"Well. Maybe you better see the picture twice if I'm not back."

"4 hours! DARF!"

"Well, maybe just… three. Thanks bud."

"DARF!" Univak spat in his deep voice, but with a lowered tone out of politeness for other citizens situated in their pods nearby, wired for sound & virtual reality 3-D thick, already enjoying the film's beginnings. After a moment, turned, glanced with a dark glower at the departing back of his friend, and thought; 'hope this won't get me in trouble, whatever it is.'

As Starvax quickly jogged back up the aisle on long legs, the audience was crunching popcorn, and consuming caloric-free junk health/food treats amid rustlings of "Oh's!' and 'Ah's'. Another in a plethora the Unity's popular free movies had begun.

Back in his seat, disappearing behind a row of citizen's heads, Univak was casting a foreboding glance at the box sitting beside him under Starvax's hat, which he had left. Exiting the theatre, young Starvax's sense returned to his chagrin, with an icy blast of reality. S/he knew the scanners would come up with his image & retina print once he exited the dome at its seal portals! And again when he entered. And maybe they'd happen to catch him on the speedwalk too. So what difference did all this subterfuge make? 'I can beat the scanner at out at that new complex tho. He figured lamely. 'Kids are always trying to fool the scanners. I did as a child. It's fun.' But knew this wasn't a real plan by any means.

He hadn't been thinking... his only idea was, 'I gotta get out! Just got to get out of Utopia! 'It's even not about me wanting Mablevax so bad....Not even just to see her... There's more....'

'I gotta go back outside to the wilds! I got to!

His muse, his soul (that's what the old Transman would have called it) ... Whatever, compelled him. --- 'It's not just because of our study group either... its.... For my Freedom.'

The moon was cloudy like a sick eye with blurred vision ---A fuzzy moon.

Time had marched on, it was already late. The downtown fairyland of towering yellow-lit cubicles beehived inside skyscrapers over which this moon hung, dismally, had been dimmed-down to be mildly dark-- inside the dome in which was never night. Not in Utopia. Starvax stepped thru the metal portals with a small group of citizens. But when he passed thru, it was into total darkness punctuated by low wattage light hung in arches over the antiquated speedwalk which they moved on, dim, set every 20 feet. It seemed to take forever to go past on this squeaky contraption, but at least it still ran at a late hour to accommodate maintenance workers who were servicing the new constructed complexes for sanitation, and the never-ending struggle with safe-air filtering system. Around them lay a fine layer of radioactive dust laid out by the settling air of earth, which was

145

continually being processed globally, in a limited way, by Utopian technology, in the hopes to one day neutralize it.

The inner most fringe around the domes was dumped with human effluvium tossed out from inside when sanitation officials had their heads turned— rather then go the extra few miles and pay a costly dump-fee at the regulation sties, so a radius of the first half mile or so was a causal garbage heap; gullies piled high with rusted mattress springs, un biodegradable plastic containers, broken furnishings, piles of mildewed clothes, age old rot, from the past where, unprotected by any tensel-strength dome the bitter rains of raw weather had washed them. Further out where he had ventured, was more pristine.

Breathlessly he entered the room. Mable Goldman was waiting, a wand-shaped chalk printer in hand, having just written on the visual-reality board:

> Each generation must, out of relative obscurity
> discover its mission—fulfill it or betray it.
>
> Fritz Fanon, Wretched of the Earth.

And the class itching, agitated, was taking its seats with unsmiling faces.

Gojenko began on a very serious tone. A tone, which almost suggested he had been crying. "As you know comrades a lot has been happening on the news lately. Much of it, as you have been taught is pure fabrication, but sadly much is also true."

Valdez: (Interjecting) "We have lost comrades. Good friends." He accompanied his words by a gesture of his gnarled brown hands.

Gojenko: "Witness the absence of other members of our group. Time is short. We have tried to teach you many truths. We may be meeting less often while we regroup. And at odd hours, like this. Trying to slip under the radar so to speak. Remember, its up to each of you to keep the faith."

Starvax leaned back, and let his mind float away. That statement on the board staring down at the class bothered him, and he wasn't sure why. Would he be true to what he believed? What a difficult scary decision! Especially having only learned about these astonishing truths recently!

When they had a moment, Mable came up to him, walking assuredly; her round, womanly form in a pretty blue uniform, a determined glint in her eye; a woman of power.

146

"I decided I really like you comrade Starvax." She paused, her full lips pressed together a moment, her large eyes blinked. "And …. Well, to get to the point…. I want to have an affair."

'Oh darf. Did I hear her?' So easy! Words he'd hungered for so long now! For years! *'I won't have to go to the Registry at all! Wow! My future is sealed!'* He melted into a pool of love staring back at her. His hand, darker, unadorned, reached out and took her pale one with fancy rings. So again their hands touched. Skin to skin. Soft. Warm….

They arranged to meet; a 'love tryst' as comrade Madonna Mablevax put it sweetly, head in the air, like a conspirator in a romance espionage. At a signal she'd would choose. She'd notify him.

Then the class resumed. She ignored him the rest of it, and after walked back to the dome with Gojenko and Valdez, ostensibly to discuss radical business. She was moving up into higher echelons with powerful leaders.

Chapter 12.

Next week just as Starvax was relaxing after a tedious shift doing dull, meaningless work at the Depot; and was ensconced in his pod Telly-surfing, a message text flashed across its screen in big bold letters: ***'Citizen Starvax you're being called down to the office of the Central Investigator to be questioned. Someone will be up shortly to collect you. Don't leave your unit until they arrive!'***

Almost instantly they were there.

Out in the corridor were 3 uniformed soldiers. "It's routine. Don't sweat it." Counseled one in a friendly tone.

"Gather up your three best uniforms." Stated another.

Down the corridor heads and shoulders of other, proper, citizens were leaning out of their doors to gawk. As they led him away Starvax saw nearly the entire hallway of other units, full of citizens he'd barely known, their heads retreating back inside and their doors closed in finality. When they got to the ground floor one of the drones stood holding its mop and cleaning rags, staring impolitely with its piggish eyes; and the young man almost caught a glint of satisfaction on its stupid face.

147

At the curb was a small fleet of sleek new white cars painted white. Hybrids, emission-free; each on its side baring the Unity of Utopia shield, the sun symbol, and blue letters UNITY OF UTOPIA OFFICER. Inside one a Unity official armed with a camera, small but exceedingly complex; protruding with levers and measurement gauges for depth, & angle adjusters, whirring, focused at the entrance. She got out, continuing to photograph the outside, then began to walk slowly across the sidewalk up to the building and entered.

'She's gonna take pictures of my unit I bet. *Why*?'

He was driven to an imposing skyscraper, unmarked by any official title. It was nowhere near Unity's official Buildings which surrounded the civic center. They went up a very large elevator, which glided up so smoothly he had no idea how many floors they passed. Led down stark white hallways lined with soundless doors.

They entered one of them.

An anonymous room, more like an office then anything else, also unmarked, but for a small plaque resting on a desk embossed with gold letters: Office of Investigation.

On the desk sat his study manual.

The Investigator sat behind it in a chair; he had big wide shoulders like a retired soldier. And beside him stood Doctor Seltzer! Pert, Doctor Seltzer stared at him. Large, pretty, but aggrieved.

"DARF *Starvax*! Are we mad at *you*! She slammed a 12"-thick collection of documents down on the investigators desk. "To think I *trusted* him! And a he's little tranny too!"

Starvax lost it. He was so mad to see his manual—with it's obliterated face laying there. Blurted out stuff he didn't even understand! Stuff gleaned from those 3 short months of study groups!

"Don't you think citizens should have ideas of their own? To be free? Don't you see they want to think for themselves?" He had upset his cool.

"Now that's a horrible idea!" Doctor Seltzer snapped. "You know what that would mean! BRRRRR!" S/he shivered in exaggerated disgust. The she-male spread out her hands into incredulously long fingernails well poised and painted. "---What *that* would mean for the whole Unity? Her long body bent down over the desk, reaching over the Inspector, grabbed a stamp and stamped the manual's paper cover in red ink: 'SUSPECT THOUGHTS'. Then rapped it viciously with her knuckles. The Inspector summoned a drone that shuffled in officiously. The drone was the highest ranking drudge Starvax had ever seen, decked out in a fancy Unity uniform with a big gold badge, of which it seemed quite proud.

"Take this away! Get it out of my sight! It's been photographed, we'll add it to the burning pile."

She coughed waving a hankie and covered her face, as if the 'noxious manual' had exuded some poison from out of its binding.

The drone complied with quite a bit of bustling and unnecessary flourishes and pomp as it clumsily placed the manual into a garbage disposal sack. Then exited, bumbling back thru the door.

Dr. Seltzer perched her narrow rump in an elegant Unity suit on the edge of the Investigators desk. The Investigator glared at him.

"Who is Midnight Dark?"

"What does Bossa Nova mean?"

"Why did you go back? You checked into the robot, we have your eye scan, --but we caught it on a very low angle. Were you trying to duck the scanner? And your names not on the register! How could that be Starvax?"

"You went out into the wilds immediately after it was suggested to you that you do not. You defied the... suggestion.... given you."

The Investigator bent over the desk, almost shouting; "We gave you a tracker.... you didn't take it along!"

Together they pounded him.

"You went out with a Mable473.vax." Why are you in such a class? What do you do there? We looked at that study manual.." He pointed in the direction of the departed drone. "That's DAFT! Its fabrication! The work of aliens with a superior intelligence! We find them all the time Starvax! It's an alien plot to destroy our civilization! Did you know that! Did you stop to think those who would introduce you to this kind of darf might be aliens? Did it?"

149

"I never thought about that."

"Well, they are!"

'Oh darf.' That thought had never occurred to Starvax. S/he didn't know who to believe.

"You see! Too trusting! I'm telling you Starvax we find these manuals everywhere. We burn them. You should have brought it straight to Utopia headquarters and turned it in! You would have gotten a reward! You would have been heralded before the citizens!"

"You would have been on the telly—on the nightly news report!" interjected Dr. Seltzer.

"Now look what you've done! Put a big blotch on your perfect record! A Perfect citizen! *Ruined!* That's the reason the Unity is so surprised." The Inspector grumbled to himself... "We should have kept a closer watch on you. Being an *immigrant*." He mumbled irritably, to himself.

"Who else was in there, in that class?"

"I really couldn't say…"

"What are their names?"

"I don't know! I don't know! I don't talk to strangers much. I don't!"

"Well you seem to know this Mable473.vax!"

"Yes but just her."

"Names citizen! Names!" (now beginning to tap the surface of his word palm with a growing impatience.

"Really! I don't know anybody! I don't know anybody down at the Depot even! And I been there 5 years! Ask them! They'll tell you!"

"Yes we have inquired.".

"Ah. Then you see… You see I'm telling the truth."

"Were being very lenient with you citizen. But you must cooperate. We've been nice."

150

Then the Investigator did something unexpected. He rose up out of his chair, becoming quite a bit taller then it had seemed---tall as a cyborg but not as thick, and fairly bellowed at the top of his lungs so that blue/green veins on the side of his neck stood out in cords: "NAMES!"

"Well….yes.. I do know… only one. I'm telling the truth…." The Investigator was waiting! Was he about to jump over the table and attack? Making a deep sigh Starvax spoke. "Kevin. Kevin Buckminister." He replied bitterly.

He was sweaty & his thin body trembled. "And two others… the leaders.. Gojenko & Valdez."

The Investigator nodded grimly as if he already knew…he had resumed his seat, but now cast a fiery look from under his eyebrows, like a pot simmering; "No other leaders?"

"I really don't know anybody…just ask.."

"Yean yeah, yeah, the Investigator brushed that aside; "Who Else? WHO ELSE!" The floor shook between them.

"Dr. Anderson." The young wo/man felt his life fleeting out of him He slumped in his chair, a broken soul.

A short interval passed amid whisperings from the two, and shuffling of papers & clicking of machines, processing information.

For a moment he thought of the black box. Would they take that back? "That box you gave me. How does it work?" He queered listlessly.

The investigator and Dr. Seltzer cast a look at each other, but said nothing.

"It works by incriminating you…when you fail to take it along as suggested." He finally said.

The Investigator was stamping papers with his electronic wand, and summoning various screens on his telaportal. Machine whirring came out of the recording equipment as it spat out a document.

"Citizen Starvax you are under arrest of the Unity. You have forced us to have you removed. You will be placed underground for a period of 1 year. And another years probation."

"You will have orders not to appear on surface for 1 year. We'll move your job into your unit. You can go anywhere underground."

"You will be given every amenity Mr. Starvax." The heavy set man added on a kinder note.

"There's all kinds of shops and malls and cyber human interactive sports arcades. Its fun." Dr. Seltzer said naughtily.

"Gather up your uniforms."

"No disorderly conduct will be allowed." The Investigator added peering at him from under craggy eyebrows.

"Your infractions are small. They only involve being somewhere illegal, and possessing one illegal document. You didn't really do anything. We hope we can correct you."

"Thanks. I'll make up for it." He muttered.

"You certainly have." The Investigator responded triumphantly. Starvax blinked.

What did he mean?

Dr. Seltzer rattled off: "You're quite expensive young man! You cost us…. Lets see, in citizen hours, soldier hours, our investigators, our secret police…My Time…. hummm.. 150 blocks of time…. 24 hours to a block….uh 3,000 hours time… once we found the first anomaly at the gates, the portals to the outside, and…. Uh…. Then at the door robot checker…. We had to trace everything back citizen. Yes, you were expensive in labor hours!

So. It satisfied Unity just to dump him sub city. As Starvax was led away he heard himself babble, once more, " I'll make it up, you'll see!"

"You already have dear." Called the Doctor this time.

'*What does she mean by that?* '

Chapter 13.

He was placed in a unit underground at minus 23 floors (sub).

Looked, awestruck around at the luxury apartment.

There were no windows at 23 floors under earth's surface, only the one door leading to the inside corridor. However his new place was completely glass encircled by a magnificent terrarium, 5 feet deep behind 5 inch glass, not penetrable from the inside. Green/blue, ferns, Bonsai trees, plants of jungle descriptions, waterfalls which fed into streams, rerouted under the pebbly tank bed back up into new waterfalls further along. It ran from ceiling to floor. Shields of thick drapes could be pushed across it or opened at the wave of a hand on sonic ray at a certain angles.

'You will be given every amenity Mr. Starvax..' The inspectors voice echoed in his ear.

'Living in a terrarium where as they are living free albeit horribly.'
Already he felt the tug within him. To be complacent, comfortable, protected. Or to have liberty...

Several hours passed. Starvax sat alone in his opulent suite. Time in which he gradually lost his angst over the quandary of being underground, secure, in luxury—yet denied freedom by the Unity... Felt less, and less of this until he'd eventually begun to think more and more about the Registry; when came a knock, then a mild voice at his unit door. "Permission to enter sir."

There stood something he'd never seen before-- a black drone!

Its head was shaven.

Its body well-formed and strong, but the same obvious signs of mental retardation as any drone.

"I'm supposed to turn on your Telly, in case you don't have it on. They said you might be looking at your walls. Unity wants you to see something. It's nice." The drone waved an ebony hand in air, summoning the Telly to turn on—did all this in its black skin, blue ebony, to the wonder of Starvax; then shuffled out.

His eyes focused on the screen, the hourly news was about to come on…
'Aw darf, some more of my study group comrades have been caught I bet…'

There the unisex newscasters shouted uproariously--- "A victory! A citizen has been saved!"

"Oh!" Starvax peered interestedly at the screen, then to his horror he saw something bone-chilling!

"Its me! AW FUCKING DARF IN HELL! IT'S ME! They're pretending its *me!*"

'He' was being paraded across the screen between two medics in a fake-engineered photo, his face bruised, hair wild, and different clothes upon his body—now in tattered rags.

Androg Spencer was screaming into the ear of Androg Emerson while congratulatory pounding him on the back. "CITIZEN STAR1.VAX@33 SAVED FROM THE WILDS! *AGAIN! FOR THE SECOND TIME!"* Drumming up enthusiasm of the estimated 5 or 6 million citizens, two-thirds of vax 33, who were tuned on at that prime time…

There were the pictures of the front of his former building complex! And, now showing the inside, his former unit! That's what the Unity photographer had been doing with her fancy camera!

As he watched his doppelganger in Televised close ups, couldn't help but observe, as if he was a third person, a spectator, un-involved, taking detached view of that portrait on the enormous Telly screen, and thereupon began to critique it. 'Evidently I'm part the genome of some Asiatic race, it shows up so obviously…. right there…And, there….' But then so was much if not most of the citizens of Utopia. Part that, Asian, plus part European white, but he was some other component as well….

'OH DARF… darf.' Starvax exhaled. Sighing deeply; slumping back into his chair. The Unity had everything planned out!

Next the news was punctuated by a blaring Utopian commercial: *"We are going to need 65,000 new deep space technicians! We don't care where they come from! Join Unity Space Fleet today! Young citizens, are you over fifteen? Well come down to your Unity Recruitment office now!"*

Disgust etched itself into his expression. Slender young Transman Starvax returned his pod chair to its original position so he faced away from the now-silent Telly and continued to stare into those glass walls of his new apartment, which surrounded its every side. Eyes immersed in the terrarium so its true beauty sunk into his memory. So much was crammed into these spaces! Little floral tableaux here and there complete with delicate small bridges made of waterproof material—for there was real water; the terrariums were alive! Growing plants. Moss. And rushing waters. & it had a voice! ---Issuing waterfall sounds, rushing of winds, which caused palm fronds and leafs of the dwarf trees to shake. ---Even sounding up to gale strength! Delicate palms, spiky bushes, myriad of clover, and other grasses. A few simple flowers. Bushes baring red berries. All the building complexes terrariums were tended, so he was told, by some unseen gardener who came in on designated time blocks twice every month, which the occupant, or owner of the unit would be warned of in advance.

On the surface of the earth, under the dome, the moon sat outside the new city--- which was set within the wasteland & ruins of the old---above it all. Peeked from out of mystic billowing grey/white clouds. From here the moon glared as if viewing the planet thru a keyhole. But Starvax couldn't see this moon, buried deep, deep, inside the earth, entombed inside a luxurious vault as if he/she was some rare and precious gem down at the bottom of a mine.

As Starvax lay sleeping in a deep hibernation, but not dead, things transpired, little of which he knew.

Starvax's first night down below, s/he awoke after only a short while, and turned restlessly in sumptuous silk sheets on the king-size bed. Feverishly he recalled a remembrance. When he was a child he & his classmates at school were often taken on field trips. Once it was to a hospital, into one of its wards deep underground. Here the medical professionals, future clinicians, geneticists and social workers, were being trained. Their teachers had taken the children down to the 46th level. Down there, sub, in an antiseptic atmosphere of white tile corridors, autopsy rooms, computer banks storing newly recorded scientific data, it was explained to them how some human parents had been lost somehow, or were not around any longer, so any children they might be going to have who might be.... different then Unity Children are suppose to be... were allowed to come to term inside the organic bio-medical SPOVA wombs regardless of that very real possibility.

And there was one they visited—this study—Mark—was the name the research scientists had given him; which was written on the tag outside his unit. It was a comfortable, spacious unit on a locked ward. It was not

155

known to them but there were worse studies, which the children were forbidden to see.

'Take 'em down to 'the zoo'', was overheard by the perceptive little children more then once. This, evidently is what this specialized ward was crudely and insensitively labeled by the young trainees in white lab coats who bustled in and out of locked doors and hurrying down corridors with word palms in their pockets, Telly portals hooked to their head and stacks of video books, —they were Utopias future geneticists, social workers, doctors, scientists.

Their teachers didn't refer to this area as a zoo, so as not to confuse the children who had already been to a real animal zoo of Unity already, but in this fashion: "Today children we are visiting a very special research project, in a place where our future doctors come from!"

The children had been allowed to press their faces to the glass and look in on him thru the blotted out space "Children this man can't see you, but you can see him. He can't hear us at all so don't worry about disturbing him."

Saw this man, Mark, a mentally ill human, who was the study. He paced in his suite—it wasn't a cage but a wonderful series of rooms, and he was free to wander out of it, tho only down certain corridors, and into a private garden at one end. All the other access doors were kept locked, by which attendant's physicians, and psychiatrists came and went.

This disturbed man was surly and slovenly, his clothes regularly cleaned, he soon fouled, and he was always disheveled. He'd rub his hands together grimacing and chomping his jaws, muttering unintelligibly, and often would scream, scream at the top of his lungs, and went pacing back and forth throughout his suite, knocking over anything in his path. Mark was constantly visited by some team of professionals, or the other, who, being trained in the art of cajoling, persuasion, and keeping an cool-temper and countenance even when confronted with the face of madness, so as not to worsen the situation; along with their curriculum; would try to communicate to Mark, at the same time as they observed him, take their daily notes then leave. A sanitation team cared for the man's hygiene and the upkeep of the suite, which needed constant maintenance, as can be expected.

After tossing & turning fretfully some more, Starvax retreated out of the luxurious 'love suite' of his second bedroom, and went scurrying back to his regular sleep pod, and there finished the night in deep slumber. But later in the day while taking a break from his job, as Starvax sat in the pod chair again, relaxing, observing that lush green vibrant view, he had a flashback from last nights dream. A sobering thought came to him…. Tho Mark had no way of knowing it, he was a study. He was being observed… Now, down here underground, in his own situation, hadn't he, once, while greedily eye-feasting upon the lovely terrarium thought he'd caught the shadow of human being behind its outer wall? Maybe *he* was being observed too! Thru what he thought was such beautiful terrarium glass!

No matter weather fact or fiction the young man swiftly *felt* he was being observed! --- With growing horror, 'maybe they're watching me thru that glass. Or maybe not. Maybe it's the subterranean paranoia everybody talks about; the reason why they give anybody meds who asks!' Starvax shuddered. Veils of terror swept over him, one after another, each grew stronger, so his stomach actually cramped—hurriedly s/he pulled the thick expensive drapery closed! Starvax stumbled thru the suites 5 large rooms, yanking closed each curtain by hand---not waiting for the smooth gliding, but slower, and uniform mechanism to do the job. —Until all the glass walls were hidden from view and the luxury suite became an ordinary unit. Like any he'd ever had, with ordinary walls.

After a few days of getting orientated in his new surroundings and regime-- which now, faithfully included taking a pill he had been advised to use, "which neutralizes you to your new surroundings citizen---many people take them down sub, weather they've been 'reprimanded' by Unity or not."

Starvax faced those ordinary drapes covering his entire luxury suite, which had instantly lost part of its glamour. *'Oh well, up above ground I mostly kept the drapes shut anyhow.'*

He was taken to see something he'd avoided before, but now there was no escape. –Upon Unity orders. The public tours of Traitors Gallery. First hours of the block, one morning, putting work aside, he was whisked away on a tour with a convoy of other citizens, to see the body of Anderson. "Right here citizens is Traitor Anderson925.vax@1 who betrayed Utopia to aliens from outer space!"

The Gallery was a stadium size facility thru which thousands of citizens paraded on a 24-hour blocks, plus film crews from Unity Media. Today it employed a squad of industrious drones who were cleaning.

Featured was Dr. Anderson. Nearby were the 7 previously unrecognizable corpses, which had first been filmed on the Telly still hooded, clad in black wet suits; they now lay in full face, unmasked, rudely naked, and having been restored by the medical/scientific undertakers of the Unity to their original vibrancy. –Tho quite dead. Further on in this serious display comrade Starvax saw the body of a short woman who'd been in his class, and someone else he thought might be one of Kevin Buckministers friends, one of those two women who had been rude to him. He went up and paid particular respects to kind Dr. Anderson. She looked fine. Not a bruise nor contortion of pain which might suggest torture. The face had been straightened out. If any limbs, or digits of her hands or toes had been removed---torn off-- during torture, they had been perfectly restored by Utopias plastic surgeons.

In a news cast soon after came a follow up: "Citizen Star1.vax is making excellent progress in his rehabilitation. Full PT and RR before being returned to his unit in that *older* Sacramento Street high-rise we showed you earlier." To which Spencer—who played the stupider of the 2 univaks blurted "Oh Emerson! So you must mean physical therapy with rest & recreation!" Then Emerson turned to Spencer in order to see his/her reaction saying, "I bet something else Spencer, I bet Citizen Starvax won't go back to Sacramento Street at all but to a brand new owned luxury unit— high living – underground!"

"Wow! That's good news! Emerson!"

Gradually, reports of himself faded from the public conscious.

The Register called to set up a first meeting for Starvax's potential marriage dates. He thought: 'It might not have been a bad idea… a few months back….' Before meeting Mablevax. He was totally not interested.

The shock of his whole ordeal was wearing off—now he was taking a double-dose of the Unity prescribed 'happy pills'. Mood elevators, which calmed his nerves simultaneously. Once, a month later Starvax had an alarming thought, that perhaps citizens were mandated to live underground *'to make their conditions so difficult that they must take these drugs… Maybe it's a way Unity can put any troublesome people to sleep—without them realizing it.'* He had learned to question authority—once he'd been shown it's first flaws. Resigned, but not completely, he popped a single pill into his hand, then broke it in half, discarding the other; taking only one quarter of the required dose, but it was already having an effect; not caring so much whatever happened.

'Well they don't know everything.... Starvax contented himself by thinking. As s/he popped half the 'happy pill' into his mouth. 'They didn't know what Bossa Nova was…. Because they don't know history!'

Having been forbidden contact with his two friends Starvax now entertained himself with memories of them and recalled an episode when him and 'brother' John6,084.vax@32 had an uproarious time drone-watching.

'Citizens with a low intelligence see mindless daft they enjoy, but Unity long ago looked at them as wasting resources Thought that their population would be a drain on Utopian society. But then some of the Unity's great minds got a brilliant plan. An idea, why not put them to good use? They can sweep floors, empty the trash of empire. Do everything a normal brain citizen loathes. In exchange they have decent living arrangements secure underground; good food, medical care, recreation suitable for their intelligence levels—everything they could want---plus being commended for service to the Unity! An Annual Awards Dinner & Commemorative Pageant was given for the drones every year. A grandiose celebration which heralds all their special purposes in Utopia, for which it is grateful. He and Johnvax had seen one such commemorate service.

Names of fallen drones were read while the gathering, of some thousand stood in somber attention, with a moments silence—for drones did die young. Never accounting for more then a possible 20 good years of service before their enfeebled and challenged bodies gave way.

Then a series of gala programming followed, including award winning literary compositions by the highest brained drones; this years title being: "My purpose to serve Utopia." Stuff meant for a 2nd grade child. How he had laughed with John6,684. And later, repeated the funny story to Univac738, 000.global. His other friend, so they laughed together: HA! HA! HA! HA! HA! HA! HA! HA!"

Starvax had realized at some point he really hated most drones, just as he was wary of soldier(ettes). This, even before he'd been found by the study group. Because of their close cooperation with Unity. He saw time and time again how throughally those poor drones fawned over Unity officials and how closely they obeyed Unity. Zealously. Maybe because their lives depended on total obedience. Drones & soldiers, who had been given the power to enforce these ridiculous and killing laws of the Unity. However the real question lay within their own conscious. In their innermost heart of hearts what did they think about it all!

One day shortly after his arrival, found in his word hole: 'welcome to floor 23 Star1.vax! You are invited to a community meeting tomorrow night at our local Unity Community Center, its 2 seconds down the underground speedwalk, past the mall! Ask your drone for a map.'

Starvax, mean-spirited attended this meeting, just to be on the safe side. In case he was being watched. He didn't regret it, since it was most informative. But not by the trite drivel which was being spoon-fed to them in spiels after spiel by a succession of Utopian underlings, but by observing up close his new neighbors. One impression about the meeting was that at least half of those in attendance were ancient! You can tall by the way they move their bodies, that they're aged. One elder man shuffling along—face still smooth and young as any 30 year old, which was ridiculous—made a telling comment, when another, young citizen complained at having to pass thru the scanner twice in a 2 minute succession at as many checkpoints, and having to step off the speedwalk unnecessarily, because of a stupid soldierette. "The government use to want to strip you naked to scan you at the check points, that's the old way we did it. This way, the Unity way is better." The oldster testified. Then gave a dark look, adding: "It's better in that way at least."

To which another apparently older woman laughed in a croaking creak—which was another way you could guess a citizen was secretly old—and spoke: "And this way." She pointed jerkily to one side of the lavish community room, where sat several large & ample banquet tables piled high with platters of food. To which the old man replied to her: "But the old days.. Those were the happy times." Stavax stared somberly at the old man, and finished his sentence for him. *'Before what? Before the Unity cast it's death nets catching us up out of our free land?'*

And another time he just overheard the tail end of a conversation between two old timers and one had been saying; "after while Unity will have everything. Things sure changed since they nationalized all the jobs and private housing."

Wandering around through all the winding corridors, malls and public arcades down sub he encountered more old timers in one place then he ever had seen above ground. *'It's like the study groups said, there're warehousing them down here... below ground.. where not a lot of other citizens will ever see them....'* Or talk to them. And hear what strange stuff they have to say. Stuff which was slowly passing out of the public conscious, just like a past news broadcast fades.

Three cheers for The Unity. They had liberated humanbeings from their torn-apart hell war & failed social structure and turned it into a paradise.

160

Day after day, citizen Starvax hooked into his new homebound work program, completing files and fielding calls for the Depot Of The Unity Central Bureau Clearing House of World Statistics & Information. Yakking away to a non-stop procession of citizen's calls, just like he always had. Plugged into his familiar screen showing beautiful views. For the very first time in his 5 year history at the Depot, it occurred to him, *'maybe they're watching me thru this screen! Maybe they've been looking in at me—any time they chose—since I've been working here! Maybe they're observing everybody! To make sure nobody does anything wrong!'* However these ugly thoughts lessened as the blocks sub marched on & on in timeless weather and stasis of interrupted space.

His paranoia had subsided due to the work of happy pills, and, sometime curious, and missing the wonderful view, he did crack the terrarium shades open, but it just depressed him, reminding him that he was deep underground, and that's probably why they were there, to compensate; and his view of the city was gone.

Nightly he masturbated to videos of other people's sex, substituting his Mable's face, remembering her soft touch.

One thing the Unity hadn't taken into consideration was Starvax's brilliant 170 IQ. Tho he'd never used one particular gift much before, he found it quite simple to reconstruct from memory much of the old study guide, which had been taken from him. Starvax began this as a secret project. Building his manual back again from first remembered fragments, which like islands then built bridges to others upon others and soon began coming together in its entirety. Disconnecting his Telly portal, he used the manual disc recorder to produce this work, print it out, then emptied the files before reuniting it back to Telly Central which was probably wired for observation by the Unity and might come under scrutiny at any time. Keeping only a single hard copy for his own use. And tucked this snugly under his sleeping pod.

He hated the thought that he might have to erase emotional-packed contents of his precious work-study guide if he ever had too. He pulled it out at least several times per day.

This way the time moved, first one block, then another, until the season had halfway come around measured by revolutions of a shining sun in the sky, which no longer was above.

Went to community meetings and often strolled about the gigantic 5 story high mall containing many funshops which serviced the local floors, and

161

visited other malls elsewhere sub. 'I'm just not allowed to surface.' Which in fact meant he could go just about anywhere underground, but not pop his head up into the artificial day. Therefore, unless he really was being watched thru those terrarium walls like a fish in an aquarium, he was under only a loose scrutiny.

Unity Holidays came and went—with Jun Kim Sun the 2nd Dictator of Unity dressed up as a jovial Santa Claus with a red suit, white beard----a rolly polly physique greatly contributing to his believability.

In the center of the mall was a huge tree—which extended up to the 20th floor, the X-mas. X-mas ornaments hung over it, big. And gigantic red reindeer collars 25 feet long with bells silver bells 3 feet in diameter stationed here/there like statues. Again he'd overheard a comment, from two citizens standing viewing the X-mas, who he hadn't noticed, believing them to be normal 30 year-old appearing humans as everyone more or less seemed, until hearing them speak, and instantly knew they must be, under all the cosmetic surgery very old. One began: "They use to build huge Christmas trees up ground in that place before they named it Peoples Square yuh know, with fake ornaments too big for a child to hold—big gold balls, too big for a child; tho any child might want one but a poor child could never afford. That child was me." *These Christmas trees grew higher and higher and thus more out of reach of every modern person.*" The prophet Red had written that in his journal! Starvax was amazed at some of the conversations he overheard from the Old Timers.

What was odd too, was the occasional citizen who recognized his photos from news broadcasts, who would stareat him; this sometimes accompanied by a point and giggle of younger citizens. But few spoke. All this was by now cultural, part of the superficial dealings citizens have with each other. He had many small adventures subterranean. All of them contained. Pre determined by the created framework of Utopian policy. Starvax went out during every 24-hour block for at least 3 hours, making the rounds of floors, and malls. It was only upon hearing these colorful nostalgic reminiscences which gave him a unexpected glimpse into something fascinating—the world as it once had been--- did the world open up into something more infinite. Mysterious. Some eternal question, which s/he must ask. After eavesdropping on the two oldtimers beside the X-mas, going back to his suite, immediately Starvax burrowed under the sleeping pod, even before changing into his comfy lounge jumpsuit, to find the restored manual. 'It's amazing to hear real people say stuff that's sounds familiar, because old Prophet Red also wrote about it! -- And what they called Christmas, is really X-mas.' Apparently this idea of 'Christmas' had once begun as a religion, and before that, predating the religion, it had been a pagan

162

tradition. But it all grew more and more overblown & had become a symbol of their mighty impossible world spinning faster, faster, becoming more difficult to navigate--until more & more inhabitants spun off from its center—those great great great descendents of the ancients who put up the first tree and worshipped it from the beginning-- and these moved on seeking something. Pilgrims again, searching for what?

'Yet, those were the happy times....According to that old timer.' *Before The Unity of Utopia cast a death web over the land?*

'My building back on Sacramento Street still had a private owner.' S/he knew many parts of Utopia were still controlled by the rich. But they were being chipped more & more away by encroaching Unity. Once established they would never let go. And for the poor, of the early part of the century it had been a good deal in many respects.

'Unity will have everything.' What did that mean?

'One thing that bothered me is they have reduced my testosterone shot—and the darf pharmacists wouldn't deliver more. They tell me its my new recommended amount.'

Citizen Starvax wasn't a normal man in the normal biological sense of the word, Mother Nature didn't design him to be-- just some strange accident, or 'specialty' of nature—which the Unity was debating weather or not to stamp out. To toss out of its 'acceptable grids'-- patterns for the geneticist to approve or disapprove any given fertilized ovum to be brought to term inside Spova wombs. Not being a normal man who produces great amounts of testosterone in his testicles, Starvax relied on the method of interjecting the similar dose directly into his body, into the muscle tissue of his upper hip.

This lowered dose was enough to keep masculinizing him, but noted he'd lost the stronger drive he'd had on the former amount. He missed that energy level. Noticed recently that he was more concerned with being comfortable then searching in wild places. Even his wanderings sub had grown more contained, and more often s/he was content to sit, a pod-potato snug in front of the telly.

He had much time for contemplation down sub, for tho quite entertaining, most of the diversions were all the same. One mall looked like all the others. One funshop was the same variation of a common theme. And he worked to further his manual by reconstructing from memory all that he had learned in what they'd spoken about those many wonderful meetings.

163

Also s/he had dreams.. *Strings of dewdrops hung in the air like bright sparkling jewels,* nothing like he'd ever seen under Utopias dome...

The light fell in crooked patterns to parquet the cave floor.... It had been so, when he was a very small child. Light, pure and strong.. S/he had been free once, only didn't know it then... *'It's a beautiful place, where birds hung in the rafters. Birds, proffering themselves to the morning sun. Their airy blue or green fluffy bodies twirling among the vines.*

Pre-Unity of Utopia, around the year 2035 a new innovation which was a mild form of socialism ingratiated itself to the more radical vax's then known as cities, along the west & east coasts and several vax's Midwest inside the old Am-Erican continent. Which decreed by eminent domain that private (not public) ownership of houses exceeding that of one in which the owner & family themselves resided, was illegal & this excess must be converted to public stock which then would be deeded to individuals as self-owned units. Large houses were subdivided into smaller units. Hotel rooms were expanded by one half and became small units, and all units were complete with the basic necessity of bathroom, kitchen, and sleeping areas. Those renters in them at the time would be moved out temporarily for a period not to exceed 3 years, and would have first rights of occupancy, which equals ownership, or of refusal of their former unit; & all accrued monies they had previously spent on rent and other fees to a landlord, or property management company was now to be used *retroactively* as a down deposit for that unit which they would then continue to pay off at a new set, affordable monthly mortgage plus condominium dues. Property tax was abolished. These funds went in part to the former owner, a portion went to the vast Homeowners Association—part of city government (which later combined itself into the Unity.) This city owned Association paid for all renovations, new deeds for the millions of little private owners, upkeep of the outer portion of the structures, etc. On this plan, by this means, Transman Red got his permanent dwelling—thus preventing something so feared-----that he'd die alone and abused in a cold heartless public nursing facility for the poor. That ugly fate did not come to pass—he was saved! Saved by socialism! By 2040, 5 years later this transition was complete, leaving the housing stock of the cities in the hands of ¾ small private property owners cozily ensconced in their own units, the previous landlords shit out of luck! And ¼ public projects, which were slowly being converted to private ownership as well.

Exceptions were those reserved for the severely mental ill, the extremely troublesome not fit to live among more civilized persons, or former felons on parole, drug rehabilitation and other irregulars.

T Red was so happy now on his tiny Social Security pension, which went to pay for his own unit! Where-in he was safe! By law any privately owned unit was no longer allowed for any reason whatsoever to be attached for any purpose, financial or otherwise. No taxes were due upon it. No more legal collections for gambling debts. Usuries of any kind. Nor use of this unit as collateral for bank or investment loans. No construction liens. Nor city repair assessments. The citizen was secure!

This, and much more, while slowly blocks of time passed on an ever-moving star clock, s/he transposed; radical ideas from his mind into the new manual. S/he wandered for hours underground, thinking….

Many things were surprising, sub, tho rumor should have prepared him for most of it. The homeless of yesteryear who their class had read about, those long ago humanbeings ragged, disheveled, unkempt, tucked into any niche or windowsill, or bus stop bench they could find, hiding themselves away into nooks & crannies of the old city, some peaceful, others violent and drug crazy criminal, were not part of Utopian society. Starting back around 2030 those a-socials had been picked up off the city streets & jailed.. The worst of them, those monsters who had hollered their insults at men, intimidated women, and scared children, had been removed permanently. Some of the better composed ones were medicated, and even by those primitive pre-Utopia therapies were able to be rehabilitated. Starvax secretly believed that some of them could still be seen down here today! Old Timers crouched in the 24-hour movie theatres with sullen expressions on their plastic surgery enhanced faces. In the first beginning years of the new dictatorship, when they were still young some a-socials were set out into outer space to work the maintenance docks. Cooking, cleaning, drudge toil at the ends of the space shuttle flights on both the developed planets, earth's two satellites, and numerous space stations. Just as in the days of the wild wild West, where 1800'rds woodsmen, trappers and scouts went ahead paving the way for the more conventional pioneer families. These individualists, many of them half-crazy, to service the rough territory of the new frontier-- outer space.

Starvax worked a mild 20 hour shift. He walked. Thought. Remembered, and reconstructed a doctrine unlike any he'd ever been exposed to in 30 years inside the domes. Increasingly he withdrew into self. A lot of moles did that. And watched the TV channels of empire.

Recently the news was punctuated by blaring commercials from the Unity; "we are going to need 65,000 new technicians, dockhands and space hogs, we don't care where they come from! ENLIST NOW CITIZENS!"

This was all over the news 24 hours on-constant, for several months. It was only later the actual reason for the sudden surge in employment emerged, and that only in incremental text flashes. At first media had it that "a solar explosion of such violence sent dangerous radiations waves thru space. The crews of the space stations and satellites were told to stay inside the facilities until it passed, and now they were being returned to earth for 7 years to de-radiate, so new fresh workers were needed pronto!"

The real truth finally came to light months later, where Starvax sat glued to the Telly in mild blue fonk. It seemed that there had been a accident on one of the older space satellites. Now the evidence could not be suppressed. Because pieces of the old satellite kept being washed ashore into some space bay or the other on the Moon, Mars; on the satellites Astros and Nebula and parts were steadily being gathered by space ships in random hauls as they tooled their way back and forth transporting goods, materials and human workers. So finally there it was. Component of a gigantic, exploded space station here and there in a jigsaw puzzle multi-millions of miles apart, sitting in top security storage in different places, put back together, in virtual reality at least, by using computer cyber imaging. One section then the next, plus all that was melted into isotopes, re-imaged, they fitted back into the familiar big white shield shaped edifice 5 stories tall that had once spun leisurely in outer space 30,000 miles west of Astros. Most prestigious of it's kind when construction had been begun, Pre-Utopia, 2027.

Then 9 months since Starvax had begun his mild spirit probation, underground. Soon it would be a year.

> Because in summer temperature outside zoomed to unbearable 140% or even later in mid summer 160% at which point most people died. Diseases long dormant in the formerly colder climates—like malaria, swamp fever, encephalitis, now ran rampant all over the globe, slowing progress and dwindling those populations, which remained. Fire scorched…

'Now what was that again…. Fires… from where? Lightening which struck from the sky? Sky outside domes?'

> While in winter, snow drifts some 40 feet deep…… So the old people's generation had learned ways how to survive these climates.

Yet, At the greatest, lifespan for them must be no more then 50 or 60 before diseases killed them, or as they slowly lost ability to withstand these temperatures. They hunted wild beasts for food, just like the ancient cavemen 20,000 years before. And lived deep inside the caves; going outside for food & to hunt berries & dig roots before snow grew too deep and covered the ground. Or before scorching heat from the sun became too intense. In spring and fall the temperatures fell upon the Northern continents of earth to cool it to a mere 105% and in these milder seasons they could survive in the in ancient buildings. This was pre-Utopia when all the world lived outside any domes. And about then the early Unity began, on the continent known as Am-Erica with the strength of a new invention by scientists working in already blueprinted, pre-fabricated underground bunkers, tensil-strengh. Thus creating its domes, and a safe haven to begin civilization once more.

He marveled about the past, and worried about his future. *And he wondered if he'd ever find his mother.....*

Once, a newscast showed the inevitable, another capture of an outer space alien. Then, they showed something almost unheard of, a ordinary soldierette with a gun! (They were unneeded by now.) A regulation 3 effect ray gun, whose typical settings being stunner/striker/killer. She was guarding the lab where the examination was being performed.

"SEE THE MONSTER BROUGHT IN FROM DEEP OUTER SPACE! SCIENTISTS EXAMINING IT RIGHT NOW!"

When he saw that his gut got queasy. It made him so upset! Turned away with a nauseated feeling, which didn't make sense at first. Not sure why.. but ran right back to one of the bathrooms of his luxury suite, grabbed the pill bottle & took 2 of them. That aliens face. As a child he'd seen that same look on captive animals in the zoo.

To add to his problems. Twice in a row he'd rescheduled the Registry of Romantic Affairs and was running out of excuses!

His full name was Star1.vax@33. The numeral signifying the city where he was born (in his case, taken in) and where all his permanent records were stored—even if he moved to another vax like his friend John6,684.vax had done upon first coming up from vax 32, Angel City, to work for the Unity here in Lovely Hillside By The Bay. With instantaneous statistical information at the tips of the fingers of officialdom, it wasn't necessary to ever change the vestigial resting place of the original documents. Johnvax had returned to Angel City for advancement. The only way to climb vertically in Utopia was to cooperate with The Unity. Main advantages for cooperation was to rise up in its ranks, as his friend Johnvax, who now lived in a nice home above the 200th floor—and owned it ---not just a temporary stay, to be shifted about from one unit to the next at whim. Also, you could travel to space. A common phenomenon, comings and goings from earth to either of its 2 satellites by vacationers as well as scientists, to Astra and Nebula, which Unity was busy adding on to with settlement buildings and lay only a 30 day voyage across the solar system; or to its stations on the Moon, and Mars. *'I'd always wanted to go to space, to live awhile, a few years at least. Maybe on Nebula. Mores happening there, stuff to do. I always wanted to live in above the 200th floor too.'*

Secretly Starvax toyed with the idea of cooperation, and advancement. But not long. For he had more pressing issues.

> Libraries, museums, in which great, irreplaceable artifacts had been gathered over decades; carrying away all the treasures and the U$ Military of the dynasty pre-Unity? Where was their military defense? Its soldiers, secret police? They were protecting the Ministry of Oil! Protecting gas exhaust pipes! While the seat of the world's culture went up in flame!

He daydreamed that soon he'd hear from his old group, somehow, just as they'd first found him. Or some other subgroup of comrades of the Red Jordan Arobateau Reading Society, which had proliferated underground over all over Utopia. In fact he hoped they were proliferating right now! Even as he lay dying—23 floors underground!

One evening around the 16th hour of the 4th block he was dismayed to hear the voice of Doctor Seltzer on his audio:

"Why haven't you been to the appointments at the Registry we set you?"

"Uh... Oh.... I was sick."

"*Sick?* With what pray tell? What is there to be sick with? Well, we have a cure for it, whatever it is! Did you go in to a medical clinic?"

"Ah, yeah, I was just on my way.. tomorrow."

There was a pause of irritation from the other end.

"*Starvax,* we can get you a robotical sex doll if you like…" she said nastily.

"Gee… the thought is tempting… I'd thought about that myself."

Actually it made him think of hideous cyborgs; their artificial maniacal grins. The sex dolls had prerecorded voices that hissed sexily, saying smut. Wet orifices, and flesh like appendages…

"It can only do what you tell it to do, Starvax… *How do you like that?*"

"I'll have to think about it some more."

"Since you don't seem eager to get a girl--- or a *boy*—thru the Registry!"

"I'll be at the next appointment."

Nearly a year and a month had passed, his probation was working out fine. A perfect citizen. Just has he had been before… but not quite. A deep gulf now divided his mind from the mind of the total Unity. Soon his friends would be able to come visit. Another 6 months and he could go back up ground on escorted convoys.

S/he TV-watched avidly now, ensconced with a happy pill for internal security, the cozy sleeping pod to warm him outside, watching news of the world thru Unity Media, the only channel available—tho it broke down into 400 different channels each was exclusively Media prescribed lore. He waited for news of any more revolutionaries, but none came. '*That's a good thing, because if we don't hear about them, it means they're carrying on without being detected.*' Although twisting reality for political means was expected by even the dumbest citizens, the Telly was truthful with regular stuff. In the spotlight on the Spencer & Anderson News Hour there stood a new tensel-strength construction, 800 floors 5,000 feet high. Skeleton of a new building before she pulled up her skirts of blue/green windows and outer skin, the Unity Showcase Citizens Memorial soon to be providing sanctuary for more émigrés to vax 33 from all global and inter- terrestrial ports—the bustling vax which lay so many floors of crushing weight above his head.

> Dwelling outside Unity's Great Domes might mean living to be just 50 or 60 before radiation isotopes inside the human body finally overwhelms its cellular mass and the individual died an agonizing death.

He dreamed of ways he could smuggle his friends up before the 2nd year was done. He dreamed of ways to find Mable. He wanted to go back out to the wilds, no matter what the cost! It was so beautiful out, free, from under the dome!

Things were all in a jumble! Starvax felt like a coward, but he knew it was risky if he ever somehow found Mable to even bring her back here with him. So his luxurious bed –built for two citizens—was in vain. As she wasn't on the building register as his friend. Only Univak4,000 and John6,684 were, having been listed automatically by Unity, which was aware of everything. Further, the robot would not recognize Mable even under an alias. Apparently from what he now knew—having never run into this problem before in his 30 years, mild years, as the diligent guest to his host, Utopia which had taken him in---- he knew now that the wheels of low level security moved slowly, but they did move. If the tired security of Utopia moved too fast, fatefully Mablevax, even under an alias, would come up on one of the other of its gigantic sub lists from eye scan and body image alone, and within a few hours. They would be caught in the very moment of lovemaking! It was inevitable. This system could not be outwitted! In all instances at all checkpoints there was recognition. A voice. Retina image scanning. Body type. The microchip transmitters had already been planted into their cells flesh since birth (Starvax at the age of 3). These means & records of detection could not be avoided.

He had reassumed communication with his friends during the increasing ennui. But later, after not hearing from him for a month, Johnvax called on his audio: "Hi buddy. How's doin'?" Sounding jovial, excited, which, because of not being happy, just added to Starvax's blues.

"Guess what I got!" He said in that little teasing way of his, which wasn't malicious, but aggravating.

'Aw darf! He's got somebody in his lovebed. Aw! Am I gonna puke or what! If he does I'm gonna die!' -----Uh... what John?"

"A DOG!"

"Dog?" Young Starvax relaxed but still was pissed, in that he also wanted a dog. Had wanted one for years. And, a cat.

"Oh dude, that's great!" Heard flat words fall from his mouth, then, "I want a cat brother. *And* a dog."

"I'll get a cat too buddy. I could have an elephant up here in my place, *on floor 265!* HA HA!"

One evening as Starvax just finished adding to his remembered fragments of the precious manual, late in the 22 hour of 5th block (by now it was summer of 2057) his audio summoned him frantically to the Telly, and there a mysterious text message flashed across his wordhole. "Wow! It's Mable! Mablevax!" Somehow she'd been able to communicate with him.

'I'm coming to get you.' Is what the text read, then dissolved into a blue miasma of aqua peacefulness.

'When?' He yelled frantically into the text.

'There's no time like the present!' Then that text too faded.

Moments later, a soft tap came on his door! Unbelievable, there she stood, in front of him! She got there so fast! On sensible shoes. In a thick thermal coat. She carried a medium size ladies cosmos pack. A faux 'rain' hat pulled down low over her eyes like a spy.

"You must have been in the building!" He was in shock! "AH! AH! MABLE!"

"Yes, I was." Starvax..." She pushed herself hastily inside and took command of shutting the door.

"Look at my nice place! Come in and sit with me! I got so much stuff here! This is a deluxe suite! Yuh ever seen anything this nice Mable? I got aquarium walls, their fabulous.... Wait..." He headed happily towards the perpetually closed drapes to show her.

"Yes, I've seen these places. Plenty of them... Starvax...do you want to go with me? Get away from here I mean?"

"Get away?"

"Leave this place!" She stood, hands on hips, boring into his eyes with hers, serious.

He looked at her, stunned. His lower lip dropped. But he had only had to think a few seconds. "Yes." Came his reply.

"Are you sure… comrade?"

"Yes. I'm sure. I want outta here so bad, I can't even tell you Mable! I've tried not to think about escaping for a year. I can't stand it much more. I want to be with you! I've been dreaming about you every night."

"Well then. Go with me. Get some heavy space boots Starvax… Bring a sack of whatever you need… just a few things. Only the most important stuff. We have to leave now! We don't have any time! I might have been spotted by one of the scanners in your hall."

For a moment he stood, astonished, but then swept her up in his arms. Felt her warm body, her soft breasts, appreciated her arms holding him tight, her thighs pressed to his.

"Star! We've got to go now!" Gently she pushed him away.

While racing down the hall young Starvax's head itemized what s/he needed. *I'm really gonna get out of here! Gonna be with Mable. She'll be my woman… I'm not stayen' prisoner of darf Unity no more!'*

In a spacious closet he snatched down a hardy blue jumpsuit designed for wear/tear & stepped into it. He knelt down, creeping in on all 4's and under the clutter grabbed his best space shoes—meant for hard travel, substituting them for the lounge slippers on his feet. Inside also he grabbed a small pack, (less noticeable to Unity scrutiny). Ran down the hall to the first bathroom, and carefully procured his emergency mini vials of testosterone self-administering rub on jell.

Speeded past his love room without time for a last glance, but a split-seconds thought of it popped into his mind ---its untouched luxury; super king sized bed; how many nights he'd crawled into his sleeping pod down the hall alone and snapped off the light to a medicated sleep, oblivious to his true longings. Starvax shut the love room door inside his mind. *'I'll probably never have a place so nice again. So what! Now I got a woman of my own!'* —But what a price!

Across the kitchen, he dashed into the pantry, shook loose some 24-hour energy bars to take along.

At the last moment he raced back into the bedroom, dove under the cozy sleeping pod to procure the manual, & shoved it into the sack. *'I'm ready.'*

He was making the decision of a lifetime.

Hand in hand the two raced to the elevator bank at the corridor's end and waited, catching their breath, for a red flashing light to appear over one of the sets of polished metal doors. There the pretty blond explained her sudden appearance. "I've got friends who smuggled me into your compound-- down sub. Can't explain to you. And don't ask who! Anyway, the less you know, the better. In case... something happens to us..."

When the elevator came Mable got on before him. A panel of light sensors designating levels was to her left, she glanced at it, —several were lit—and then turned away without selecting any. There were only a few other citizens, who appeared to be cosmetically young but in reality, old. They disembarked first. The elevator was headed towards sub-50. Which he assumed was the last level. The last passenger, a drone in a Unity maintenance uniform exited next, upon this, Mable immediately turned and pressed one in a trio of brown buttons—the old fashion kind which protruded, furthest to the end of the panel, that one must touch to activate. "--No one even knows what these are for. Huh." The pretty femme gave a sad little laugh.

Metal walls enclosed them. As they rode down deeper into the earth Mable relaxed a moment. She continued in a low voice. "I've been thinking about you too Star."

In the few seconds the ride took. Star took hold of Mables shoulders, pressed her against the metal wall, his mouth sought hers. Her hot mouth opened to his. He tasted her, the fullness of her lips; his hands slowly began to run over her big round breasts---and she let him. His thighs ground into hers.

Elevator doors slid smoothly open onto an extraordinary view. It was one of those things that sometimes accidentally appears behind the pretty plastic backdrop of Utopia, which is grim, utilitarian, and not pretty which only drones see, and the very lowest laboring classes of ex-citizens, its rehabilitated prisoners. Startled Starvax hung back half inside the metal elevators threshold afraid to venture out. Grey outer walls a full 3 floors tall, some 40 feet high at the compounds 4 ends, which stretched out at great distances, taking up nearly half a city block square. This space was cris-crossed with gargantuan reinforcing beams vertically & horizontally. There were no rooms, just one vast rough area, littered with spare utility train cars, maintenance equipment, and busy teams of drones at labor. This was the buildings whole bottom. Loading docks located at its southern side. Across it's ceiling and four walls were water ducts of various dimensions great &

small. Numerous sewage drainpipes and major panels of electric current conduits. Slowly they exited the elevator. The young man trepiditously, at the sight of yet another unfamiliar territory opening to his Utopian standardized eyes. Noises echoed in the vast stadium-size cavity enhancing sound. Crash of a freight car coming into a receiving port as one of the loading docks opened, a freight train was pulling up to it, and tons of bagged refuse from the housing units & malls above were going to be deposited inside its cars. Grimly drones went about their work, loading tons of bagged garbage, preliminarily reduced, sorted and compacted into large containers, which would now be shipped out to an island in the unincorporated area, the waste station to be processed, its subsequent bulk shot into space to add itself as fresh terra firma for Astros, Nebula, and the satellites.

Went to one side, near the loading docks, about 600 feet away. Mable walked at a fast clip on her ladylike but sensible shoes leading them there. 'What's taking her so long? Aren't we gonna escape or what?' Starvax suddenly got paranoid when a strange figure approached them, it was a drone! Instantly Starvax was apprehensive, knowing them to be the lackeys of empire.

Drone carried a pair of space boots dangling over one deformed arm which it offered to Mable, then handed her a large backpack, which it partially opened; the drone indicated inside; it was full of foodstuffs... cans... a flashlight... supplies. "H... he... res...here's wha...what you a....asked for... C... comrade."

Enfeebled arm patted him Starvax on the back. 'G....g...." It was trying to say something! Distastefully he bent his ear closer. "G...ood sp...speed Starvax!" The drone sputtered. Then shuffled away.

"How does it know who I am?"

"Haven't you seen? You've been all over the news!"

"Ah darf!"

They began walking, swiftly towards one of the docks.

"All drones aren't bad—They're not all Unity's lackeys. That one, Jane, she hates Utopia just as much as me---and as you're starting too..." Mable told Starvax patiently as one would explain to a child.

Starvax stared dumbly ahead. *'Well...Didn't even think about it. Yeah... Just might be many drones who hate their position in life because of the exploitation—.'* Mable was saying; "some have been removed out of their great dislike for Unity & how it treats them."

His brain having processed this information, he asked; "Well how do you know which ones you can trust?"

Mablevax replied in a soft voice, "How do you think we got you Starvax? I'm connected to some very powerful people, in some very high places. Recruitment for our group found you, like we discovered Jane... like we gathered everybody in your class. We have very powerful people among the Resistance, some top Unity party people are secretly Comrades! So we have access to citizen's files, to drone lists; it's at our fingertips. Its easy to scan thru them and see... which among the people has a possibility... for change...For... dissatisfaction with the way things are... That's how I know so much. That's why I've been places. Places you'd never believe even when I tell you."

The young man was impressed, excited, nervous, but with growing fear; he followed at Mables heels, in his heart he couldn't wait to get out... He knew where he wanted to be, that special place out in the uncharted areas.

Vax 33 was an 'island' not literally, only, in like all vaxes, it was a dome separated from the mainland –the unincorporated territories which predominated earth-- by a wall of steel & tensel strength steel & glass-like imitation tensel strength which allowed for its gigantic height and width. The bedrock into which it was set was actually a peninsula, ---ocean on 2 sides, a bay on the 3rd, but the 4th side was land. Land, which connected to the whole rest of the mass of the (formerly Am-Erican) continent. So, in theory, it would be possible to flee out of the vax into the wilds, and, if a direction was charted first south, then, once past that large body of water the bay, they headed east, one could get lost in a very vast wilderness of uncharted territory, 3,000 miles of it, by skirting other vax's & their islands, a free territory without end, until the opposite coast, in the east, where the ocean then would be reached.

It was to this ground they were now headed.

The pretty blond woman in her spiffy blue Unity jumpsuit clattered along, the heels of her shoes staccato added to the noisy clanging of the workers; she approached one loading dock not being used and they walked thru into an iron & cement tunnel that had railroad tracks leading out into the darkness. At this point they climbed off the dock and began to walk along a narrow ledge overlooking the tracks beside a damp wall above which was a low curvature of ceiling. At some 300 yards distance a twisted figure

175

suddenly emerged out of the wall, waving a signal flag—it was Jane! Who then disappeared away down the tracks; the two hurried to an enclave there wherein was a very old rusted iron door whose hinges and locked seemed oiled and recently handled.

Starvax opened it. They gazed upon a netherworld no longer used.

'This must be one of those old tunnels I've heard about."

Madonna Mablevax replied, looked at him like a parent patiently watches a child waiting to see how much it can be taught at one sitting; "we have information. We got a hold of blueprints of the old cities subway lines---dating back a century---which had the original designs and found this tunnel that use to carry citizens in commuter trains from the old city San Francisco to their homes in the suburbs."

Unity's new Express train, where its rapid transit (sub) first left out of vax #33 must take a sharp 80 degree angle turn then goes creeping steadily thru the grey cement sided tunnel at only 40 miles per hour. Little ahead but few feet is visible but the grey cement reinforced tunnel walls, as the train, 220 feet underground slowly navigates the angle—just steel conduit and dim lights--- then enters the straightaway that goes out with no variance of a split inch to the next destination, vax 32, Angel City, the former city of the Los Angeles. So would this antiquated tunnel, prototype to the modern express, first built over 100 years ago carry them, at least a very short portion of that route—enough to take them out behind the parameter of the dome!

Not far from them under the tomblike earth, silver rails of the Express curved steadily soon Unity's train will zip past 350 miles per hour, entering the straight away over what it must travel for 750 miles without a stop half mile underground, silently on electro magnetic cushion of speed; unlike the old commuter train its iron wheels clanking, echoing, spinning foreword.... But now, all is silent, but for the footfalls of these two humans. The rails went dead a century ago. This spur line no longer used, like the appendix in the human physique. No longer necessary, but still present.

"If we can just get out from under the dome and Utopias security scanners; if we can make it to the uninhabited area…"

"We'll make it comrade! What's to stop us!" Mable huffed.

"They might have found out I'm gone. That nosey drone in my compound knows everything!"

"Don't be negative! They wouldn't be able to find us even when we've come up missing on their scanners! You're not carrying any black boxes are you?"

"Darf No!"

Madonna Mable Goldman knew a lot. The decrepit old tunnel stirred with their footfalls, echoing.

As they walked, after an hour, with some effort of breath, Citizen Starvax queried: "What I can't figure out is … this outer space alien stuff we're forever hearing on TV, are those aliens real—or is Unity inventing them?"

He saw in his minds eye a brown wizened creature, hairless, big sad eyes peering out of the wall-dimension Telly into his luxury living room. A creature who's expression was of silently accepting its fate; which had made him feel like crying, but he couldn't.

"It's done to get hype. Hype is the glue of Unity. It frightens people, keeps them interested in the daily world, reminds them Unity is protecting them. It keeps people herded together following a leader without thinking for themselves like sheep. Following a dictator, that idiot Kim Sun."

"Have you ever seen a sheep? An actual sheep?"

"Not really. Have you?"

"Yes at the zoo."

"No one is allowed inside the Agra dunes—without special clearance, but I been there." Mable said, almost boastfully, taking big breaths to match her steps. "I just didn't get to see the sheep. But as far as actual aliens----extraterrestrials I mean, the resistance isn't sure if they exist... or not. They just might."

Starvax hoisted Mable's backpack on his shoulders, it was heavy with water & nutrients; she pointed the flashlight ahead, lighting their way. At first some light leaked in from the parallel tunnel, and noise still echoed behind them. They could hear the distant clang as freight trains slammed into the loading docks carrying fresh fruits and vegetables from the island Agra-domes outside the vax to stock the malls, supermarkets and restaurants in his luxury compound and others in the underground city; but at some point in the curve of the structure the paths grew separated. In a while the tunnel

177

was entirely quiet but for the disturbances of their own feet over the packed earth & gravel alongside the rusted iron rails.

The old railroad bed was hard traveling; rough under his space boots, and then the tunnel took a decidedly upward slant, steep and exhausting but Starvax had an idea.

"I know what to do—." And he turned around, continued walking foreword, but now facing backwards… judging his steps by focusing on the curved tunnel ceiling. Promptly Mable followed his lead, holding the flashlight beam which jotted, & jogged against the cobwebbed & mossy wall. The incline was not so painful on their legs this way. They soon found this made time go by swiftly, and not so difficult. They did not finally turn around until the distance they'd already come from had grown although the goal was not still in sight being clouded in darkness.

Starvax felt they had barely made a dent in the distance, but Mable was engrossed in something. Was she counting their footsteps to measure the miles?

Strings of dewdrops hung in the air like bright sparkling jewels so much finer then those artificial which gems which are sold under Utopias dome…

The light fell in crooked patterns to parquet the floor of the great palace. People gathered here for reasons of mystery. It had been so since the beginning & would be so at the end of time.

The people had such freedom in those days, only they didn't know it then.

'I know an even better place then that old heaven the Prophets spoke of.' He thought. 'Once we get up ground I'll lead her to the old ruins. And there, right there I'll take her with masterful touch.' He would inserted the full length of himself into her special vagina woman-place, something he'd rarely done with any live citizen who was not a sex doll. The little weapon she carried between her legs, waiting for him as she had now promised.

Where birds hung in the rafters.
Birds, offering themselves to the morning sun.
Their blue or green fluffy bodies twirling among the vines.

"I know a place we can go!" Starvax spoke his thoughts aloud, finally, but Mable didn't ask where, her flashlight shining the path, mouth in a tight little line, she strode valiantly along.

Chapter 14.

At 18:00 hours ten cyborgs exited the dome, after the ex-citizen Starvax turned up missing, and the alien spy Mable473.vax~1 was scanned multiple times in the building of where formerly perfect Utopian Civil Servant Star1.vax~33 had been housed sub, on probation to the Unity. The soldier(ettes) exited the dome at 18:15 hours. The cyborgs were superior models, per instruction of The Unity's Security Forces High Command. These new models impervious to the ill affects of the poisoned atmosphere of the wilds could gain speeds, running, fast as a land creature on 4 legs. Much faster then any human could.

A sportscast, had been broadcasting on numerous of Utopias 300 plus channels, in a full of fury of bionic super males in a warlike clash against rival teem, but the great escape and hunt was now superseding the game in favor of the chase. Soon the drama spread to other vaxs especially in vax 32, ---City of the Angles, to which it was rumored the two might be headed! CITIZENS BE ON THE LOOKOUT FOR ESCAPED PRISONER STARVAX AND ALIEN SPY MABLEVAX WHOM UNITY SUSPECTS ARE IN COLLUSION DESTROY UTOPIA! THEY MAY BE HEADED TO THE CITY OF THE ANGLES!

200 feet below surface now, the two resistance comrades walked, hurrying foreword. It was only after they had gained good ground, having covered about 3 miles did Mable say what she'd been doing. "Count the doors comrade, here's one we're coming to, you'll see."

"We're counting? To measure how far we've come?"

"Security exit gate 41, that's ours."

"We'll be outside the dome!"

"Yes!"

Every 500 yards was a rusted exit gate rusted over. Water leaking down thru infinitesimal cracks in cement & soil, separated by 100 years, obliterated by green moss which grew even in this nearly lightless netherworld would, behind which, once the gate was opened, spiral iron stairs turned, up, upwards.

Hours went by. They had by Mable's reckoning, about 3 miles left to cover now. The 29th gate had been passed, foreboding, crusty and almost missed it because of great long vine strands & moss which grew around, clutching to the modicum of pure sunlight which managed to filter in thru the cracks 5 levels above their heads. Their pace slowed from growing tiredness, but they didn't stop. Pausing only to extract two energy bars from the drone-prepared backpack. The two were gulping down water from numerous bottles. And they talked.

"You wouldn't believer Utopias upper echelon's Starvax! The very top-notch brass, yuh know," Mable cast him a coy sidewise glance to see his reaction. "They give private parties. Big ones. Spectacular. Luxury! And I saw it all! Every citizen is expected to attend. Government engineers, the usual ones—the very rich, owners of buildings like the one you use to live in Starvax--- inventors who got the original patens for tensel strength, scientists the Unity can't do without.... Every week there was a party, they all had to attend or they be put in jail! Unity officials played golf with the rich snots, and went to polo games, and Unity's team always wins! Always Starvax! Or everybody goes to jail! Dictator Kim Sun has it his way or no way! He's always there cheering—because his sons, he has like 7 sons or something, they're all on the Unity team! Ha ha!"

Comrade Madonna Mable Goldman told young Starvax many things she'd learned from being in the Resistance underground, which had put her to work as a spy infiltrating the Unity's top command.

Just before the great fall of earth, during the dispensation directly proceeding The Unity of Utopia, a great financial & banking collapse was eminent. The world teetered upon the brink of total hopeless disaster—a complete collapse of its major player Am-Erica hence impacting those large powers directly under it, the Euros, Chin-Ah, Indy-Ah, hence the spreading effects of dissolution upon all the smaller and tiny nations on earth.

In times like these some less severe, the people turned to point their fingers at the Jews. A small, ancient sect of people who 'controlled the world banking by some secret cartel' which never could be proved. This was a spurious charge---natural needing a scapegoat they'd pick on one historically familiar. Instead of try to save themselves the leaders turned pointing the finger at each other fuming and fussing as conditions rapidly plummeted. Thus wasting time when change was overdue! The drastic measures necessary to set the nations aright weren't employed—out of the greed of the very rich, and the total stupidity of comparatively small politicians who were stodgy, hanging on to their measure of freedom & personal revenue and refused to change. When that greatest of all nations Am-Erica went down, Chin-ah went down, followed by Indy-Ah, it became like the dark ages of Europe, 1200 AD.

The dim lit, echoing musty old tunnel was now straightaway, level, and extended forever. They walked. Counting rusted iron gates every part of a mile.

Comrade Starvax was so excited! He was going to be free! He wanted to tell Comrade Mable all his hopes and dreams!

Their breath had gone sour as they trudged along, Starvax shifting the weight of the backpack increasingly so it was more to the left on his sturdy shoulders, then back to the right.

Starvax was in a delirium! He had a woman, maybe they would become a family and raise children. As a non-biological male he could be an excellent parent—even if not being able to be the actual male contributor to the genome.

Of course citizens would breed---in Utopia, but the offspring's were not necessarily from their parents--- couples could choose each other in romantic fashion, but the Unity controlled genetic lines & planned all babies according to the availability of donor lines & correct future societal breeding patterns; they guarded the strollers and baby playpens of the future in Utopias formal egg/sperm banks (SPOVA) so all new couples of whatever configuration by gender or race or age went to SPOVA to select their child which would be then hatched synthetically in the incubator house, to which they could attend 24 hours daily, singing & cooing to the infant while seated in cozy pods beside their specific womb.—Then upon hatching the first mass grouping of infants would be induced and inoculated by the Unity. Subsequently followed by early training, the head start training, then kindergarten, grammar school, high school then further into higher education and on into the professorship and master degrees. So all arrangements of citizens homes who wished to rear children went to SPOVA to select a child which was suitable to their temperaments and in keeping with what breeds lines were ready, well monitored to avoid accidental inbreeding, genetic defects, etc., however sometimes mistakes did happen, as had been the case of his friend John Univak Global...

The couple was approaching the 41 gate. There it was! Unlike the others, the vines of stringy moss wet decay been clipped back directly around the rusted iron gate, and it was slightly open, letting in a gust of cold air! Pulling open the iron door they stared in wonder.

A spiral staircase was outside in a shaft of light. Up top some 5 stories of winding turns, over debris strewn stairs, daylight! The cover gate had been taken from their hinges & removed!

Clank, clank, clank of their weary footsteps, they emerged into the free world.

The polluted air of earth.

S/he reached his hand towards the earth—he touched the soil.

What a view-- what a magnificent view; grey blue totally airy blue grey with puffy clouds, the real world. 'My earth! My inheritance!' Handed over to them by the prophet Red and his generation who'd fought as bravely as they were able. Who'd gone on peace marches tho not believing everything the leaders who led them said; who lay down in demonstrations, tho they might have gotten up and left when the cops gave their final warning—to avoid arrest; attending rallies till late in the evening, and going stoically to support the victims in court cases against rapists; holding their candles against the wind in silent vigil early mornings for political dissidents on the dock– they kept the fires of the Resistance burning! They kept the spirit of the people alive!

His eyes gazed now onto the wide sweeping world panorama few citizens of Utopia will ever see—just the medicated soldiers(ettes) who, the powers in control allow to go there, knowing that remaining unmoved, they will return… Gazing at that world of so much —but not seeing. The truth brims over in human hearts once people realize it. And they don't give it up. And find that they must fight for it. Starvax stretched his being in the new air. Felt the good earth, reached towards the highest heavens begun by some infinite Creator. It's one world, her-his world.

Plants of many varieties grew lush green, and the sound of crows CAW CAW! Flying, cutting thru air on beautiful wings.

Starvax saw they were in the vicinity of the route off the old railroad lines he'd once followed, and now, as they were cutting straight across the hilly regions, he hoped that special palace, the old cathedral would come in sight!

"Lets stop there just a moment, before we go on…"

Comrade Madonna Mable held a small compass which she'd extracted from her sack, she was puzzling, figuring the direction due east.

But Starvax knew where he must go… he was heading back to the old ruins… "Mable I have to show you something first."

"Star, is it on our way?"

"I gotta show you Mable… We gotta stop and sleep anyway. Or we'll die!"

"I know! My feet are killing me."

"Follow me!"

"STAR! IS IT ON OUR WAY?"

"Darf!"

"Aren't you afraid we'll get caught! You've worked at that darf depot too long! You've been an upstanding security AAA citizen so long it's made you daft! You trust the Unity too much. Starvax! Haven't we taught you anything? Oh goddamn it Starvax!" Mable put her little hand over her mouth.

About this time Starvax realized he was depending on Mable to get him out.

Grim, he began to trudge along ahead of her. He had just thought somehow once they were free---outside the dome they'd make tracks to anyplace he chose… and maybe he'd find his lost tribe who he had come from…. He'd mentioned before in confidence to Mable that was his pressing goal.

"Don't be daft Star! We've gotta press due East!"

"We gotta go back to that palace Mable! We gotta rest somewhere. We gotta eat. And night is falling."

Hand in hand they flew past all the landmarks that were familiar to Starvax but were a wonder to Madonna Mable Goldman. A bridge collapsed but impassible but for a few rusted beams, which could hold the weight of only a very small animal, they couldn't walk over it he told her, but could pick their way over stones in the river bed of the nearly dried up due to the hot late winter of earths new jungle temperature.

Between the ancient, tall, but ruined buildings he looked up and could see blue/white real sky immediately above them, clearing. Space. Little chance of ever seeing this in the forest of more dense, 3 times taller new tensel strength buildings of advancing Utopia.

It was such beauty his heart wanted to cry with joy. Tears!

On the rise of hills they'd gaze back at the dome. occasionally looking at it for a landmark. As they grew further away, hilly rises in the land, and enormous chunks of uprooted concrete began to block it entirely from view.

They went by a route thru a different city, where buildings had once also grown big, towering. These now-fractured skyscrapers broken into pieces. To their left was the neighborhoods of a more humble level, trudging hand in hand into the giants, approaching the middle of what had been the great city, and soon there they'd find that old palace, that special place he'd seen his revelations.

Behind them lay the dome, far, glimmering in austere beauty. They both knew it's cold warmth, knew that it was a giant funland of everything one might want or need --for a price & they did not want to pay that price anymore—which had become more awful then it seemed.

The big structures pleased Mable, who turned her head this way and that in awe. "Start watching for any aircraft overhead Comrade! If we stay under the buildings, and rocks we won't be sensed.... They still send off radioactive emissions. Unity won't pick us up, we just can't be out in the open.."

Marching until every tendon in their bodies ached, but could not help but gaze around them at the fallen skyscrapers of which evidently had been a enormous city... And to think there were thousands of such cities all over earths face—no longer habitable....

"So tell me what the resistance thinks happened to this old empire?" Said Starvax, exhaling a deep breath, as they moved on.

"We think its possible that a cartel of scientists from the U$ military, some top international financiers & industrialists got together and engineered a psuedo destruction of earth in order to gain power."

They both had read the study manuals, which depicted living conditions in the old cities, whose pieces and chunks now crunched under their space boot heels.

They had let it fall apart maliciously, to make people desperate, then anything could happen...

184

Crime was everywhere—desperate street homeless now gone crazy on drugs, that forgotten underclass pushed aside, numbering into multi-millions, had escalated their narcotics habits. Whereas before they'd simply smashed out car windows and invaded public spaces to sleep and urinate, now they smashed out living room glass, breaking down doors invading private homes, burglarized them when residents weren't there, murdering them if they were. Drug lords feuded with rival gangs. In a short span of time society made the leap from 100 murders per year—considered an atrocity in the early turn of the century 2000-- to nearly a hundred murders per week and the numbers continued to climb.

The old world already had had a foretaste of what could happen.... Back in the last century, the later 1990's, it had seen collapse of the social order under the Soviet Union; Bosnia Hertzagnovia, in former Czechoslovak. The Sudan in Africa. They had seen it after any natural disaster when law keepers temporarily recede and all criminal violence, banditry and thuggery crawls out of the woodwork seizing opportunity.

Western, and middle Europe began to disintegrate—the East already in more primitive circumstances didn't have as far to fall into mayhem. Africa was already sunk in a mire of unimaginable despair. Nuclear war broke out between several warring nations at once. Subsequent radiation clouds drifted randomly over the earth in killing waves. Global warming was growing to killer proportions, resulting in an a second environmental holocaust on top of the first. But future minded people had already begun our outposts in space. And scientists in secret bunkers had developed the new laboratory process, which would be the backbone of the future. Tensel-strength steel, glass and other building materials. Then Unity came, marching in their clean uniforms, seizing control of what was left of the fallen nations capitals, straightening out the mess, executing criminals, and bringing citizens to law.

By that time, deep into a world wide holocaust in which no nation was spared, and every one of them had fallen apart, it cost pennies to maintain forces in a world wide domain, using an unlimited supply of soldiers both male/female because of wage, price leverage, and perks of permanent housing inside the safety zones—the new domes—which rapidly went up. All natural resources and all food supplies came under the jurisdiction of the first Dictator to be used immediately, so with ease the combined forces pulled itself together in unity into the beginning of Utopia, out of a volcanic molten meltdown.

After the Armageddon, hell fire sinking the planet in chaos, the choice was easy. Permission to enter any dome was at the price of becoming a citizen.

A citizen could no longer vote, they obeyed. And had a good life. They no longer thought for themselves nor pre-destined most of their own future; they followed instructions given them from above. They choose security.

Chapter 15.

At 18:50 hours Unity's terrain crawlers were mobilized to begin combing the dense overgrown & ruined areas of the old world due south of vax 33, starting in a ten mile length, imagining the traitors would not have gained much further on foot. It wasn't until later that this width of searching was spread out into a radius encompassing the whole landmass surrounding the vax, abandoning its futile route which had first spread out, only due south.

At 19:00 super scanner equipped helicopters flew out of Unity heliports to begin surveillance over the radioactive poisoned ground below. Their mission was to sweep Arial maps from above, imaging the escaping traitors with infrared sensors.

For some reason which wasn't clear and once discovered never made public, a rather strange order of top priority was issued from somewhere, either out of military top command, or initiated from the Unity Party's inner circle, so the search was directed to the southern most quadrant going towards vax 32 whose destination is 750 miles away, upon which it was suggested that the traitors may be traveling.

White-painted heavy terrine vehicles armed with squads of 20 soldiers and 1 cyborg each crossed over the lugubrious opening dome portals out of vax 33 military base and onto the screen of the TV viewing public at prime time. The cyborgs were older model. One after another the convoy's vehicles rolled off on a southernmost map, headed towards vax 32, out over into the unincorporated area, their huge tires able to lay flat almost any obstacle, and to climb steep rocky slopes, ford the polluted rivers of the old world—the hunt was on!

The cyborgs, which accompanied each heavy terrene crawler, were ill equipped to handle rough ground. There was some suspense as out of one particular crawler a cyborg was flung overboard due to the bouncing & jostling. The cyborg gained it's footing, teetered on a rocky place, then heavily collapsed. —It was difficult to pick up the 1,200-pound giants whenever they fell. It took the whole team of 12 soldier(ettes) pushing and tugging to set the monster back up on its metal legs once more, and was most disconcerting to see. The older cyborgs didn't do much good in chases---only in enforcement after the criminal had been captured; being not as swift as the newer models who would soon be in hot pursuit of the traitors, 108 miles away and closing in.

Tonight every screen of 9 million Lovely Hillview Beside the Bay inhabitants was tuned to the chase.

Spencer: After they're caught they'll be tried and sentenced in a secret court. What do you say Emerson?

Emerson: Of course they will be tried in a court and then they will be put to death, so citizens have 2 fewer worries then they did previously! These traitors will be removed—permanently!

Spencer: (Smiling) Permanently!

***

Above them towering twisted buildings overgrown by moss and grasses originally displaced some 300 years ago by human-made brick, mortar & iron, had conquered the city once more, growing in heavy green webs across the twisted skeletal designs more fantastical then all the wonderland which was Utopia. Trees in odd formations squatted low to the ground, due to the radiation which had blasted them, but had made a comeback within the fatal air of post apocalypse earth.

Starvax and Mable sweated with exertion, their spaceboots had switched into automatic release of the amount they'd charged them in their long hike, and now eased travel considerably, providing an increasing boost to each step. They neared the place where Star wanted to go.

"I have my manual." He said proudly. --"Let me read to you from it when we get there... after we're rested."

"Goddamn it Star! You seem to think we've got all the time in the world!"

'Daft Mable!' the young man thought, irritated, but did not speak.

Just being free from under the dome was so exhilarating he'd given no thought to the rest of it... having always worked and always had a roof, a pod, a plate which was full.... For it really hadn't occurred to Starvax (not having had much time to think nor plan, when comrade Mable appeared at his doorway, luscious vision in a blue jumpsuit and sensible shoes, woman who he wanted) -- that the Unity would actually come after them---- Starvax thinking it was only what he did or didn't do inside the dome which put in peril his citizenship. The idea that they might want to get him back, just to destroy him hadn't even entered his mind.

Starvax was still smarting from Mable swearing at him that unknown curse from antiquity. He replied finally, "allright then Mable, what are we gonna do next? We gotta rest. We can't see in the dark. Our space boots will be fully charged when we set out… later.. maybe in the morning."

"We're not on the right course…. We need to progress east…" Mable had marked her compass due east; the course they were on was off by a mile. "There's going to be a drop off waiting for us. The comrades have left food and water for our journey."

They walked on fast, faster, and no longer spoke.

Space shoes weren't exactly designed for running away from cyborgs, nor were they intended for outer space—but taken from real space shoe design, and adapted ideally for traversing the city streets of Utopia which no longer had private vehicles. They earned their wearer energy, dependant upon the miles they walked in them from the beginning of each travel, so, after a great amount of walking---when on the last legs of their journey so to speak—they were able to cover quite more a distance with little effort.

Now it was just a matter of maybe an hour before they'd arrive at his special resting place. The area looked familiar. The sun was beginning to set ahead. --- 'that red/orange ball, the real sun, is east---so we couldn't be too far off… I want to take her there, to my palace…'

Walking was easier now with the space boots having attained their first cycle of energy, but they would have to stop soon. The sun was gone, it's last light quickly leaving the sky. "We're almost there. I recognize this place… its so built up and tall, it was the inner city, before … the war."

They talked about Utopia tossing their words breathlessly back and forth; the crunch of debris under their feet, still surprised by the wildness of this grotesque city surrounding them, so breathtaking in its brokenness.

The new order, the ruling party of Utopia which now controlled the world— was if anything more corrupt then the old divided nationalistic empires & wealth-based cartels which had recently passed away—in that it was a whole unity completely dominant on earth, from which there was no other nation nor power left which might offer escape nor an island of refuge.

Over their time together Mable told him more. This newly arisen empire, Utopia, under its 1st dictator picked & chose who it accepted within its domes--- (that was the generation before theirs which began in 2030) & that became apparent after the initially huge influx of citizens when Utopia was being born. This pre-sorting was done strictly & by a fixed grid of demographics, choosing all of the light skinned races of a clean non-criminal background; only accepting a fraction those of its dubious elements to be used for experimentation both voluntary and involuntary, and for exploration into deep space, or as ground workers on the newly colonizing Astros, then later Nebula her sister which followed. It accepted only some of those individuals from darker races of outstanding or redeeming value. Much fewer of & none of their criminal element whatsoever for any reason, except for experimentation which was not told to the new inductees, nor was it voluntarily. A significant majority of citizens of the new Utopia were female. This was balanced somewhat as the top echelon, the ruling party or Top Command, was predominantly male—tho not exclusively so.

That real sun was setting fast as they neared landmarks familiar to Starvax, and climbed the remaing rocky way up the hill effortlessly on the power of their space boots, now fully kicked in. Finally, at days end, Starvax's great palace towered above them..

"Wow. It's impressive." She linked her arm thru his.

Big winged seagulls snowy white, orange feet curled under their downy bellies flapped past; a flock low flying, over hung a moment examining them for food—then with loud shrieks, EERAK! EERAK! flew on their way.

On the once-magnificent anti-chamber of the cathedral someone long ago had painted a big A, inside a circle; around the circle was written: 'Sooner or later every empire must fall.' With a small peace sign in its lower hemisphere.

Near darkness birds began fussing in the trees settling into the bushes each with its tiny, ferocious 'CHIRP!' rustling among the leaves already invisible in dusk. Last suns light illuminated the old cathedral sufficient for Mable to drink in the view as, exhausted, they stood wavering on their space shoes— which by now were holding their bodies up-- and surveyed the grand old ruins; stained glass windows red green blue violet orange yellow, some intact, most shattered, streaked by carbon deposits from storms, the war and generations of dead time. Stepping over the pews and shattered shards of beams from the partially collapsed ceiling they went thru the great hall of the palace until they came to a section of cement niches, choosing one of many built into the walls designed originally for meditations or genuflections of supplicants who came there; this was overlaid with ceramic stone set with facsimiles of Mother-of-Pearl, gold gilt, turquoise & rubies. Here they began to bed down. They gathered leaves and laid them down, then threw Mables long thermal coat over. Starvax selected some sections of lumber, put these criss cross against the niche, then from out of the backpack produced a large flat package, shook it out into a large piece of synthetic fabric, silver coated which was rainproof and heat holding. Laid it over the lumber in a makeshift tent. Once hunkered down inside, their bottles of water set out of the pack, and their few remaining nutriment bars. Last, Starvax opened the heat pack, which was a solar cell storage, and activated it. Soon a warm glow invaded the compact perimeter of their tent. Cold drafts swept across the hilltop invading the old cathedral but they were snug. Flashlight lit the interior of their domain.

They stripped off their clothes. Venus-like, Mable's round womanly physique, pink flesh colored/pale. Starvax was naked & lean. Starvax strange off-white color—yellowish, full lips & strange hair made Mable wonder what race of people he'd come from in the wilds, but she held the question in her mind to ask later; she had so many things to say! More important was this animal intimacy.

Starvax was exhausted every muscle in is body ached each tendon stretched to its limit. Exhausted but due to having injected himself with a double dose of his testosterone, the masculinizing hormone added fuel to his erotic flame.

 Together alone! At last!

Out of shock of brown wispy pubic hair his wonderful apparatus hung. Fully formed penis 6" in length, a meaty, thick diameter, and it was growing with anticipation.

Mable fondled his cock between her small hands. Star was pleased. Embarrassed, a grin his face. He gulped air.

"Wow! How neat!" She exclaimed.

"The Unity gave it to me after my genetic evaluation —they saw I was going to be transsexual."

"Oh! How wonderful!" She fondled his manhood.

He reached his hand towards her, he touched her human body, ---he touched her heart. The heart, the soil of humanity...

She touched his full lips, his strange hair with the painted nails of her fingertips.

'What racial background are you Starvax? Who was your family?' She wanted to say, but she would wait, since he had moved himself to press against her; he was loving her, kissing her ears, arms; his hands slowly moving, finding their way over her body, soon he had positioned himself atop over her, held his turgid organ, softly probing her hot pungent hole; pushing into her with slow, rhythmical thrusts, so delicious she had to close her eyes and enjoy, surrender. Feel...

***

After they had made love they lay holding each other and talked.

And it was dark. Midnight dark....

They turned on the flashlights steady solar energized beam, low.

This tall, slender stature man lay beside her, nude. Voluptuous, Eve on an oyster shell in a garden of Eden, pretty Mable ran her fingers over his chin. A fine beard had begun to grow on Starvax's usually clean-shaven 'good citizen' face after 24 hours in the wilds with no electric shaver. After intimacy it was easier to be comrades...

"How do you know about Unity and stuff you been to, like the Agra Dome?"

"I know the top people in Unity. I know the key players. One in particular. Renault."

"Wow! How did you infiltrate them? Thru those comrades in the resistance?"

"I was his mistress."

"Awf! Darf!"

"I thought I'd tell you after... Star. Just to make sure you didn't change your mind.... About being with me."

191

"You were with one of the top people of the Unity? Darf! Mable! Well then why do you want me! I'm bonk! I'm daft! I…"

"You're everything he isn't…." Mable said simply, touching his cheek with her forefinger. "Renault lives surrounding himself with the finest. He is rich, from a billionaire family…and his father was a brilliant scientist on top of that… Renault is, or at least he was, a scientist too. He and his father and their company s invented some components, which went to create tensel strength…. He owns patens on it. He owns patens on the whole structure of Utopia. He owns stuff… he's one of Utopias founding members.. although there's not suppose to be such a thing, and the Unity is stealing all the patens and bank holdings and property by nationalizing everything, and we're all suppose to be equal, ha, equal under the Unity. Yes, Renault lives the finest lifestyle. He has he finest women…. the finest men…. the best of everything and he has a piece of every body. He's so jaded he doesn't care about anything. He's the top, the very top… so effete… Renault don't care what the resistance does as long as they don't spoil his play party… He's so spoiled, he's useless. He's always high on narcotics, he gets the best medications, only the best. He'd wouldn't care if Unity falls tomorrow as long as he can keep up his meds and his pleasure palace… and his mistresses."

As the night grew cold they talked politics, snuggling in the solar packs blasts of warmth, and that generated by their own bodies, under the lightweight but thermal covering.

Both agreed that an inordinate amount of old timers were housed sub. Star told her he hadn't understood what a 'mole' truly was until he'd lived there awhile.

"They know too much."

"But they don't say anything."

"They know better. They're afraid of what Unity can do to them. Remember, some of them lived thru different empires before. In the east, the old Soviet, in the middle east under the tyranny of religious nations, in North Korea under the strictest regime. Under the warlords who sprang up inside Am-Erica after it fell. They learned to keep their mouths shut."

"They all had the Christmas at some point in their lives.. They had the big green tree with huge gaudy gold ornaments. They all know about it. They tell each other tree stories."

"Yes. The Tree Christmas."

"They mostly stay together, the oldsters."

"Yeah, that's natural, they talk among themselves, so who cares! They aren't considered a threat.. its just oldsters like Valdez .." Mable gave a dark look from under her eyebrows, which was scary under the dim light in the tent. "Valdez. He came up from being a mole, started our study group and began to educate young Utopians."

"Where did all the people who couldn't get into the dome go?"

"Something like 80% died the first months, of exposure… maybe several billion people worldwide. But some, and their descendents are still out there in the uncharted quadrants."

"Like my family?"

"Maybe, yes."

"Unity shut them out… To die out there! In the 160-degree heat, and the sub-zero cold with snow! And the pollution eating them away, radioactive acid killing them every day! Darf, Mable! … So a lot of citizens were left outside the domes?"

"Not citizens comrade. Had they been citizens they would by no means be left outside….. I'll tell you who was left outside.. beside many of the dark skin, and the obvious criminals, they left the a-socials, the work shy… the religious zealous… the communists and radicals… like us…. But if Unity knew they were valuable, highly educated they weren't denied entrance easily. They were taken in and resocialized… A lot of old lefties are around….from the radical years of the old world. They keep their mouths shut, they know better then to stir up trouble…. The resistance is counting on them to step in, if Utopia ever starts to … fall apart… And… we….us… the youth… we plan to shake it until it does!"

Chapter 16.

By block two, 2:00 hours, a lone Unity Top Command vehicle had entered the chase. Sleek blue-black stealth colors with the ability of 100% camouflage. It was solar & nuclear powered with anti gravitational mobility, so it soon overtook the slower-moving terrain crawlers, and then hovered at the front of command about 5 feet above surface level. Inside,

193

were top Unity superiors, both military brass and suits from the private sector.

This rare side of Unity Top Command spiked even higher, the torrent of interest, which was now spreading globally from out of the relatively small vax 33 from where it had first begun. Nearly 4 billion of earths multitudes all over the planet and it's space stations & satellites were aware of the chase. Telly viewing soared. The eminent pursuit of former refugee Star1.vax, and Mable473.vax, alien collaborator, traitorous spy had escalated from global to galactic.

By now the odd mistake had been uncovered; that false diversion south, but it would take several hours until new reinforcements would be readied before the extra circumference around the entire vax could be searched, whereupon the moment they began to, immediately traces of the traitors had been picked up—going in the opposite direction!

This boded the couple more time…

Empire moved as swiftly as possible, every square mile must be sifted and for greater distance just in case the escaping traitors had had a vehicle waiting at their disposal—which they didn't.

More vehicles, now, those with the protective white shield joined the fray, Unity Media came along armed with high-tech cameras; they knew how to really play up this odyssey! With medics following along the trail 'just in case' in their white puffy radiation free germ-sanitized jump suits the ensuing caravan was a circus complete & traveling at a good clip, considering the rough terrain, 25 miles per hour. Throughally, inexorably they approach the zero hour.. the capture…the hour of our death…

White covered shielded trucks, media, news people in radiation proof suits were moving jerkily across the scene in every living room and viewing pod.

"Clues have been found!" A newscaster upheld a pair of sensible shoes to those, which comrade Mable had thoughtlessly discarded in the tunnel of the abandon subway line nearby the sub basement of Starvax's deluxe suite.

***

The towering sky above, once black, now simmered with a hint of blue in the slowly steady lightening sky, turning night into a fresh beginning... day was coming, unstoppable.

It was nearly time to start out; their space boots fully charged were ready for this next day's journey. Enabling them to march twice the length as ordinary.

First light broke thru the far high rafters of the roofless Cathedral.

It was such beauty her-his heart wanted to cry with joy.

S/he would never again feel like getting up in the morning, not like here, -- back there in those awful homogenized day its false 'daybreaks' and 'sunsets'—what a laugh.

During the night they hadn't realized in their comfort but at real dawn, here was the evidence; 3 almost empty water bottles, and wrappings of nutrient bars... *'There's going to be a station of food somewhere along the way.... Mable knows where...'* Starvax said to assure himself. He did not mention to her that these last bottles of water and nutrient bars were ones they looking at.

"Let's go."

"Wait a minute." Comrade Mable pushed a tiny lipstick, pink-red, up inside a cylindrical object applied it to her lips; made wonderful bow with color around her mouth. Starvax observed, wonderstruck, at these feminine doings.

With its citizens so pampered by Utopia how could they ever change? ' *'tho they knew change was right...'*

***

So they marched due east in space boots, determined, headed off towards the first cache of supplies planted in secret by the resistance. Still a good hundred miles away from their pursuers.

Nearly noon they came to the spot Mables mathematical calculations coordinated to the precision of her compass had led them.

A raw sun scowled high up in the sky, lighting broken scenery with brilliance so there was no doubt what had transpired. In a departure from green/brown foliage overgrowing crumbled 1980's edifices, in anomaly, lay Utopian made products with torn glittery modern wrappings.

Their stuff lay in shreds, scattered over the hot jungle hot radiation polluted earth floor. Easily opening/closing containers had been mauled. Claws marks on ripped-open tinsel wrapped nutriment bars. Wild animals had stolen their cache of supplies. They hadn't touched the water.

Starvax pounced on the stuff, on all fours, frantically searching the ground.

"If its animals wouldn't know about water bottles.. if its humans… and they didn't take it… it must mean they have the or own water supply somewhere.. and lots of it…." Starvax offered, but he looked glum.

"OH NO! STARVAX! THEY DIDN'T! THEY COULDN'T HAVE GOT OUR FOOD!" Mable just stood silent for an awful moment. Then bent down to kneel, prayer like, on the ground holding painfully onto a scrap of nutrient bar, and combed her pretty painted nail fingers roughly thru dirt, leaves, and twigs, searching for scraps of food amid the disaster of wrapping foil, pieces of tin containers and ripped apart preserve-foam; clutching each thing she found; scooping up between her fingers each shard, each broken bit, to hoard it desperately in the palm of her hand, but cut herself on a jagged sliver of metal which made her scream, release both hands, throwing the mess as far from her as she could so it all fell away into thin air —in a gesture dangerously near madness. Then Mable collapsed. Just sat on the soil, moaning, rocking back/forth. Starvax came and put his arm around her trembling shoulders, wisely saying nothing. In awhile, she was able to compose herself.

"Well. Maybe it's both." Mable said after finally. "Maybe wild animals found our cache, tore it apart, then humans came along and stole what was left." Mable bent closer, nose above the soil, to examine any clues, footprints or paw prints, like a detective.

But her voice was thin and wavering. Confidence was drained out of her.

She toyed absently minded with the few un-shredded water containers.

'Maybe it's the tribe who lives out here—maybe I'll get to see them. — Maybe some of them are my family.'

"Aw Starvax I'm so sorry…" Suddenly it was apparent that Mable had been holding back a lot of fear. That she knew little more about the wilds, about any escape plan or survival then he was now painfully obvious to her lover, Starvax, as she stood, uncertain, nibbling at the last mineral bar like a little girl.

196

"So you're sure Unity will be looking for us?"

"Yes Starvax! They'll try to find us. Be sure of that!"

"I don't know why... I'm just gone... you'd think its enough that they just not let us back into the dome--like they did to those billions of people they left outside all their darf domes in the beginning of Utopia."

"They'll be looking..."

"I don't know any top secrets! They're... their idiots to want me!"

"They don't care about that."

"They don't know everything."

"They do know... everything. They can find out everything... Everything but what a citizen is secretly thinking...like stuff a lot of the oldsters know, but will never say. Like a lot of us comrades who work right under their noses... And regular citizens who will never tell what truths they've discovered not even on the day they die. It's not like in one of those daft science fiction movies... There the authorities read your mind and do know everything."

"They never found out that John—Univak Global, my friend-- held that black box for me at the theatre when I went outside... He never got in trouble for it... Unity just gave John a promotion... he lives on the 236th floor in Angel City with his *dog*." Starvax commented dryly.

"Unity wouldn't have given him all that if they knew." Mable agreed. Then Mable stares at the horizon, like an intuition has passed before her eyes. Her eyebrows furrow. "They'll be looking for us, Star. They might be out there right now... right over those hills...and coming... fast."

She pauses, strangely, in a manner, which alarms Starvax even further. And continues in that little voice; "You don't want to go back do you? You could always say I kidnapped you... that I had a 3-effect ray gun but threw it away..... I'll back you up Starvax. I'll help you ... I'll lie for you. I'm good at it."

"I don't want them to catch us. I don't want to go back to Utopia."

"This is all my fault. Our fault. The resistance. Because we found you. We taught you. But it's not too late for you Star."

"No! I thought about it seriously, but darf no.".

Silently they picked up what remnants they could. Water bottles, invaluable; as they had not yet had time to search for some source, like an old well, or antiquated container which might have captured rain. They now had another heat holding tent pack, flat, square, weight only 3 ounces.

'Hum wild animals wouldn't bother these water containers, and the tent because thy give off no scent of food... and humans... humans who've lived in the wilds for 2 generations.. They might not understand what this tent pack is for...' To Starvax there was hope! S/he was finding that there were answers at their fingertips... Maybe there was a way they could survive in the wilds... but his comrade believed they hadn't a moment to spare in this place and must keep moving. An imperative. So to continue to travel was their goal.

But after another hours walking, fast on their charged space boots Mable continued to be drained of hope... Even tho by now since they'd left the dome they'd covered around 120 miles. "I'm worried & you're not walking fast enough! You're *wandering!"*

Wandering haphazardly, poking the soil in front of him with the branch of a fallen tree hunting crazily for water. He flung away the stick, and adjusted his backpack with a flounce, its renewable solar heat pack dangling outside catching the fierce fiery sunrays.

"If Renault was here he'd ... " Mable suddenly silenced herself.

'He'd know what to do!' the words screamed into Starvax's mind in a burning hurt.

Immediately they were at cross-purposes. The idea in back of his mind had grown. "If we stop, we can look around for a source of water. We can begin foraging for food.... I want to live right here! I want to find my family... I want to see the people who inhabit this marvelous place."

"Your family lived here 30 years ago Star! We gotta keep going...." She was adamant.

Starvax reconciled to the fact that they were running but wasn't sure where. It had made sense to run to get outside the dome. But what had been his victory to Mable had simply been the beginning of a long journey.

***

Having traveled with the armed posse which was tracking after the two, the stealth car pulled out of lead position which it had attained easily, catching up to the rest a day ago by sheer force of its nuclear/solar dynamo and by being unhindered by land surface. It had drifted into the forefront of operations, then hovered there for the last 24-hour block. Finally the stealth car had outstripped the land terrain vehicles by an increasing amount of time, and soon went out of sight. It caught the escaping duo in its radarscope at 18 hours—4 hours ahead of the rest of the convoy. It came, soundlessly into their area and in its constantly sweeping radar scan finally picked up Starvax and Mable, just minutes over the next ridge.

Fanciest vehicle he'd ever seen not on tires, but above-ground on anti-gravity reverse magnetism, glided quite rapidly unimpeded by boulders, ditches, rises or obstacles & appeared before the others. Starvax shrieked in fear.

There was no roar of powerful engine, no vibration of spinning tires… completely silent. A stealth mobile.

"Oh I've messed up bad." Mable fell into his arms. Her lower lip trembled. She who was so strong. Comrade Mable was crying. Collapsing in a heap on the ground. Tugging at herself.

"HERE! Take these Star!"

What was she doing? Removing her space boots?

Mable was pulling off one of her space boots! Take it!" She offered, tossing it to him.

"HERE! Take them Star!"

She tossed him the other, which fell with a light thump in front of him. "HERE! RUN STAR!"

Run like the wind!

Starvax grabbed the boots and his pack; raced towards an embankment!

Three, four men were racing over the uneven ground towards Mable. "Darf goddamn it just hate that Unity is getting all this fucking publicity!" He could hear Mable swear in the distance—then last parting words, a hideous

199

screech burst out of her red painted lips "STAR! STAR! STAR! The rest muffled by a mans hand, black gloved, clamping over her mouth.

She struggled to yell again, but suddenly as the first mans hand clamped over her face, another, Military brass, had joined them, injecting a vial of chemicals into her neck. She was silenced fast. He and the suited man yanked Mable's unconscious body off into the stealth car.

Mable and Star were being separated by Unity High Command. When their unmarked stealth vehicle appeared, at first they focused on securing Mable, but ignored him, drugging & dragging her away, but then, as the car was prepared to leave, without hesitation last man left to get inside turned, pointed with his 3-effect ray gun set to 'killer', aimed at Starvax, but the nimble young man was gone!

The Unity goon turned to look, just in a split-seconds time enough to see a pale yellow hand disappear over the side of the embankment. Starax was escaping!

Quizzically the 4th suit peered back into the vehicle, looking towards what appeared to be the leader. Inside a man beckoned him to step back into the vehicle with a snap. Was it worth it to chase that peon Starvax?---- No. Because the newspersons of Unity Media would be along shortly & it might be embarrassing, photos they might snap of the high command expending such extravagant resources in running after such a low criminal, and for what?

Breathlessly he bounded off in massive arches. The last sight Starvax had seen of the Unity goons, one in a 3 piece grey suit had a ray gun in his hand, set to kill.. *I always thought civilians were suppose to be unarmed!'*

He was jumping wildly on his space shoes, gobbling up precious energy meant for hours, within minutes!

"Man gone! Midnight Dark! Bossa Nova Teacher. He just vanished over the side of that hill, can't see just now. Catch him!" Radioed the suit. A big 3 of Utopia's upper crust, inside their top ranking military car sped off silently. Disappeared.

Chapter 17.

Trails of hanging moss draped over boulders, rotted frame lumber and rusted iron of former house units dissolving in raw weather.

At distance s/he could see the wide blue sea—and on a wild impulse decided to head there. Its great beauty and majesty compelling. Tho s/he sensed that was a dangerous move because it would offer no way out on one side.

Starvax wasn't thinking clearly. Jumbled. Using strategy one moment countered by the next with misjudgment and stupidity.

Sitting on a rock he paused a moment; unlaced his weary space boots, and lashed on Mable's fully charged pair in exchange; putting his own back in the satchel. Needing to put as much space between him and the enemy as he could.

Run like the wind Starvax, run like the wind!

Exhausted, but mechanically renewed, with mighty bounds he leapt in 10-foot arcs further & further away from the scene of Mable's capture, as quickly as possible.

***

Hours fled by, his feet pummeled along. He did not stop pumping his legs up & down propelling himself over the rough overgrown soil towards his goal. At some point while heading towards the great water the ground seemed finally to decline. Nearing dark, Starvax stopped in a low point between hills where the sea was no longer in sight, a formidable grove of trees ahead. And collapsed there. Crouched on the earth, breathing difficulty from the long dash for freedom, worried, in great agitation, the young man made a futile gesture--he fumbled inside his backpack which was now stained with human sweat, and grime. Pulled out the study manual; took its attached electronic erase/pen. Began to sweep the tip of the erase wand over each sentence, page by page, each thought, idea, historic documentation disappearing under the ray of the eraser pen, turning the pages rapidly straight thru from the very beginning-- its index, on thru the middle until he was done. When finished, it had become a blank book.

That night set unusually fast. It was the longest night he could remember and dark, so dark & cold, so lonely without Mable. The heat pack was gone, having fallen off of his backpack where it was hanging, outside, to catch the sunrays, but had become dislodged during the escape. He had two warm tent sheets, that was all.

It was the winter solstice… unknown to Starvax. Calculated by wisdom of the ancients—which predates Christ, Mohammad, the odyssey of the

Hebrew children. A mystic knowledge. Our inheritance from those pagans who worshiped nature directly, not needing the intercession of priests, but by gazing up into the sky. …It was the lowest point of the year, when planet earth is furthest from the sun on its orbit. This block having the shortest sun hours, the longest night… a very magical time.

'I can't see anything.'

Moon had drifted into an almost total eclipse. It's barest edge illuminated in a faint light on the undermost curve of its dark belly.

A black sky & no stars of silver, shone. Nothing. S/he huddled sinking into the feeble heat of himself under the overspread tents.

Midnight dark.

Drank the last water. Had nothing to eat. Was so afraid, with no hope. There, Starvax spent the longest night of his life.

When dawn broke Starvax saw he was closer to the ocean then he'd ever imagined he could be!

He'd slept where he'd come to a decline in the land in a hollow of earth protected from blasts of wind by being between taller rises of land. Now, at dawns light, renewed, within a few minutes he'd climbed up the next hill and permeated the tree grove. With short bursts of Mable's space shoes plunged ahead thru the dense brush holding his backpack in his arms in front of him as a shield. Suddenly had driven himself thru the last line of twisted trees and shrubbery and broke out into a clearing. & there stretched before him the most beautiful sight—a limitless beach!

Now he began to run! Unhampered, straight down towards it! Dirt gave way to pebbles under his feet, then a strange substance he'd never felt before, compacted, thick, soft. 'Sand. This must be the sand.' Now his short run had brought him up to the edge of the vast magnificent liquid— water which licked up at his feet—the ocean itself!

Starvax plunged into the water! Dipped both hands in it, threw water over his face. Thoughts screamed inside his brain, '*why am I running? What am I doing? Why have I thrown my whole future away, my good record, my security? Why am I here, just to touch some water you hear about, but never see, and never would have seen if I hadn't run away? Why am I doing*

202

all this darf?' He thrashed about in the blue water! Excited, wild, afraid. Questioning from his deepest soul. *'Why?'*

And felt maybe he was doing it for those revolutionary fighters the study group had told them about, those resistance comrades separated by a generation of time. Yes! That's why he was risking his life! In a flash the reason became clear. Because he must, somehow, continue the good work. For their sake, prisoners stuck in the jail system for protesting too hard, too strong for animal rights, for environmental cleanliness, for minority civil liberties. The ancient struggles had been all for these things.... *'It's the same rights as the ones we have now...In this new Utopia, many of what they demanded have been granted, but one of the greatest of all rights — freedom, has been squeezed almost to death.....I want to keep the faith too! I gotta hold my head up high! I want my freedom! I can't go back on my word to Mable! I can't wiggle out of my new truth, even if they let me! I gotta hold onto what is real! I must! I must!'*

He knew at once he shouldn't be here. 'I'm going in the wrong direction.' Because there's no way out of this—he had no boat. Starvax took one last look; breathing deeply filled his lungs with the strong salty air of the ocean. His body wet with seawater. But as he turned to go, back up the pebbly beach heading up the incline suddenly there burst out of the shrubbery, a team of a dozen monstrous cyborgs, their broad metal physiques gleaming dazzling with sun.

STOP CITIZEN STAR1.VAX! YOU HAVE BEEN APPREHENDED BY THE UNITY OF UTOPIA, YOU ARE UNDER ARREST! STOP WHERE YOU ARE! DON'T TRY TO ESCAPE!

With gigantic steps shaking the ground under them they ran at superhuman speed clumsily towards Starvax over the stretch of sand.

As he stood trembling in fear, almost to death, frozen, seeing a thundering, bone shattering army of metal robots closing in, their monstrous basso profundo screams directed at him; all the young mans plans for flight immediately deserted. Each gigantic metal monster towered over him at 9 feet, outweighed him by 1,000 pounds. Nothing would stop these Frankenstein creations upon which no pain could be inflicted!—that being the purpose of their design.

'They can tear me apart, twist both arms out of their sockets, pull off my legs and rip my head off my body with blood spurting out from my neck and I'd be dead.' As he'd heard they could do.

Was it the hyper anxiety of his impending extinction which brought a final reasoning so it hit home in a flash! inside Starvax mind: *'The Unity wants me back, **because they want to silence me...** Because now I have the truth.'*

A cyborg who reached him first, a millisecond before the others, grabbed out at him—and with its huge 10 inch metal jointed fingers secured his shoulder with a surprising gentle touch. Immediately the second got to him, secured his other arm in its powerful ten-inch grab. They treated him very gently and with the utmost care. For like stock clerks in a warehouse it was their job not to mangle the merchandise any more then might occur accidentally in the process of capture. Surrounded by a forest of the huge machines they marched him back up over the sand, up into out of the clearing, back thru the grove of shrubs and trees which, by their immense metal bulk 4 feet wide at the shoulders they had easily cleared out whole trees and shrubs effortlessly, allowing them a free path to return.

'So it's all because the Utopia has got to silence me. To prevent me from telling the truth to other citizens.'

Chapter 18.

'Where am I?'

Awoke, s/he was in a hospital cell; there was no mistake about this.

The worrying had gone from his head, his mind felt magnificently clear. Lucid, he thought a moment: 'The Unity might drop me back in the wilds...where I want to go... Unity has given me truth serum I bet, which is why my head feels so clear... so they've found out! Discovered my utter resolution not to return to that darf Depot!'

Upon further waking up he felt he was in prison, could see the grim outlines of a confined, austere cell...maybe he'd finally get to enjoy terrarium walls, he'd pull aside the curtains once he got up... When his grey blue eyes finally fluttered fully open saw he was in a hospital bed, free, unrestrained. 'I'm climbing out...' But as he started going over the side rail felt his body wasn't moving! Furrows appeared over his-her forehead... Starvax's head lay on pillow this he knew but could not feel. Was fully awake now. Eyes moved back and forth. Realized his body was immobilized.

Starvax tried to yell, no sound came out! Arms, legs stiff! He couldn't even move a finger! Then a small sibilant hiss pushed out from his lips, snake sound... It was all the voice he had!

Once the medical observation team saw over the scanner that he was awake they rushed in in a hurry. Grim, eager to get on with it.

Starvax felt his throat open, his voice began to croak:

"Where am I?"

"You've been removed. Permanently." Said the pretty Ward Matron in a cold voice.

"Your trial will be happening shortly." Said a Tech. Both he and the Ward Matron were industriously checking his body for physical response.—There were no arm nor leg motor functions.

"We'll all be on TV. Spencer & Emerson are interviewing us staffers right now!" A young trainee Aid said blithely. "We'll hear their commentary live! Translation captioned—broadcasting out to all vax's globally!"

When a moment passed and the others were leaving, one Tech lingered beside him.

"I fixed it so they won't hurt you comrade." She whispered, while swiftly arranging the covers. Then, moving aside, leaned over him, now, speaking in a too loud voice guaranteeing it would be picked up by the scanners, while positioning herself at an awkward angle so that she could fuss with the sheets over his body while smiling into the observation cameras: "You're full of radiation now, you've been out there too long, —we can't allow you to infect the others."

"In more ways then one." From the doorway the cold Matron added--- ominously.

Then the last techs disappeared from the cell.

Starvax wasn't afraid if they might torture him as he felt nothing in his body.

Soon the interrogation would happen.

S/he must have dosed, because upon awaking again, Starvax saw he was in a different chamber. A courtroom, in which he was prominently displayed in its center. A bank of spectator seats containing citizens including the young, plus a balcony full of happy, excited drones. And a high podium for the judge—the Chief Investigator.

Spencer & Emerson were there as promised, flanked by many technicians outfitting the courtroom with all kinds of camera equipment to capture different angles, sonic beams to pick up each word.

What a production! It took the His Honor, the Chief Investigator a few minutes to flounce, flaunting him-herself fully and grandly from a private entranceway adjacent to the courtroom, to finally mounting the throne of his high podium, but only after having first traversed the chamber from one side across to the other—time-consuming what with all Unity's constituents bowing, saluting a familiar "Hello Your Honor," the genuflecting of drones, and other underlings, which greeted him/her as he-she passed by, and always always moved with a grand swivel of each hip rotating shaking her buttocks in a most provocative manner. —Until the casual observer was itching, simply itching to see the bitch finally come to rest—much as one may be relieved to see a gigantic ship sail into dock smoothly without upsetting any of its cargo or passengers, & also while not capsizing anything lesser in its way.

Enticing; finally he stepped up to podium with each proud foot in men's sensible shoes. "'La imitation." some observer in the spectator dock whispered.

First, out of hell, came one of hell's matrons, the Ward Matron who had fastidiously fussed about with his person, checking for any possible motor response. The Matron, skinny, ultra ultra feminine, as far to the distaff side as was possible to be, stunningly beautiful but hard, not lifelike face, high pitched voice, a cold machine, smile like a vampires sucking blood, obviously an oldster, she squeaked down the aisle to be examined on the bench:

"Your Honor, he confessed to me in his sleep. That he knowingly was a conspirator with the Mable.vax traitor, in league with Aliens to overthrow our planet. And I solemnly swear this is true."

Next came Dr. Seltzer, a silver ultrasound scope swinging at her neck; who gave a concise cold testimony, then rose and left the room, excusing herself for a moment. "Yes, Your Honor, Citizen Starvax was fully sane and in possession of all his mental facilities when we interviewed him on the date in record."

From his gurney in the center of the courtroom, Starvax could hear Dr. Seltzer throw an hysterical hissy fit as she flounced down the hall: "I don't care if he dies! Die bitch for all I care! Disrespect for me! For all of us in the Unity who tried to save you!"

Chief Investigator: Did the traitor Mable.473.vax have a secret plan for your escape Star1.vax?

Star1.vax: Uh, uh, I don't think she did. We got lost. It got dark. All we could see was one foot in front of us. Good thing we didn't fall off a hill and die.

The young man retreated back inside himself, fastened his mind to his total intent: *'I must keep the faith too! I have to hold my head up high! I must! I must!'*

The black drone who'd serviced his deluxe suite sub was called to testify. His shiny baldhead polished like a crystal ball. He was baring false witness.

Grandly and more in the manner of a marquise then a servant, the drone spoke in the simple terms which his vocabulary would allow:

"Mister, I mean Citizen Starvax's had a bad book hid away under his bed. I reported it to Unity Command to help the Unity."

However much of the small audience was ignoring the drivel which fell lisping from his ebony lips, in favor of admiring his fine physical attributes. A perfect sex toy for the princess & princes of the Utopia hoi poli. Not a few eyebrows raised among those attending... So handsome & well bodied .. and well hung.

"& then Mister Citizen Starvax—that man over there—told me... 'if the Registry comes looking for me, don't tell them I'm in. But he *was* in!'"

At this, in the spectator dock a young one squealed—"But mommy Starvax's not a citizen!"

"He is until he's proven guilty after the trial, then he won't be a citizen! Now shhhh!"

The child stared at Starvax, this man strapped down to the gurney by chemical restraints, not understanding.

"It's just a technicality. A simple technicality. Now shhh! You'll learn more that way." The mother hushed.

"Oh." The child was relived & turned to again to watch the proceedings in wonder.

The ebony drone finished the last of his lisping testimony involving a tedious rendition of difficult drape closings/openings, then came the final interrogation of prisoner Starvax.

"Did the Traitor Mable473.vax lure you into this stupid plot to conspire with aliens?"

"Tell us Star1.vax!"

Trembling with fear, s/he remained silent. S/he turned his head away. Eyes gazing into eternity which he had now seen.

"'Tell us.'"…the words still echoed in the courtroom.

As Starvax hadn't been afraid if they would torture him, feeling nothing in his body, now, he felt unafraid because he could feel nothing in his soul. Just an empty blank.

Perhaps comrade Starvax was untouched because of being fairly low-level player. He didn't know much.

Tell them!" Hissed Doctor Seltzer. She had composed herself and returned to court. Tell them! Save yourself! Don't be a total utter fool!"

***

Utopia. How high she stands! Having liberated herself entirely from past sin. How mighty she rises, spreading into the starry galaxy!

They had liberated humanbeings from their torn-apart hell war & failed social structure and turned it into a paradise.

'My mom never got to see me grow up..'

Deep seated and well rooted down in the very primal instinct of a human being interwoven with the drive to stay alive is some compulsion for freedom and truth, which can cause a human to give up their life.

And s/he knew he wasn't going to give up this passion.

'We all run the race, and begin to know at some point we're going to drop out of that race—realizing that stronger and stronger as we go further and further, it just remains a question of how long, how far we can travel, and upon what impulse.'

Now the courtroom was vacated, the drama done. His gurney being wheeled away too fast, by Aids who's only thought was to get it over with so they could go to lunch; propelled down the long white hall into a very special room.

Some anonymous white-coated nameplate said Doctor of Final Administrations, Utopia and bore the great seal of The Unity, blue and a yellow sun; a doctor he didn't know, now came to the side of his gurney.

Stronger then 8 burly soldiers holding him, two at each of his arms, 2 at each leg, there was no chance for escape, because of the paralyzing nureo-psyche meds, which had been administered to him full force.

Set on the gurney laying face up. A medical aid proceeded to cut away the sleeve on Starvax's arm, and left it exposed.

Then a medic came in, taped adhesive bands around Starvax's forearm in two places probed gingerly with rubber-gloved fingers for a blue/green vein, and stuck in a thick needle. Immediately he taped this needle down so it was permanently affixed to Starvax's arm—and would not be dislodged easily.

A technician came in last, pushing a machine which had a canister of some elements and a series of buttons to adjust the flow of those elements with a tube connected to it which lay in a coil. The technician pushed this machine along the floor directly up to the gurney, took one end of the tube opposite to the other end which snaked into the canister of the machine and this end he stuck into the receptor valve of the needle which had been placed into Starvax's vein so that they were connected and locked together, and said grimly, "You'll see that beach comrade citizen Starvax…"but not in the way you thought."

Sad. He'd ever get to find his mother. That woman who'd gave him life, birthed out of her own body in red bloody pain. He'd never see her again. But wasn't that how it operates? This very empire, which kills our plans and subverts our dreams? *'I'm never gonna see her again, ever!'* Young Starvax's last thoughts gone without a ray of hope of a heaven nor a prayer to who knows where for deliverance? The promise of Utopia having substituted itself in replacement for a god.

Sure enough, as the medication engulfed him he heard it....

Crash of waves in the background in his ears; sight of sand see and wind in his vision... At least they had courtesy to do that....

Outside hung a pleasant moon, hung, in a crescent.

Unity wasn't taking any chances this time.

***

"Sky's the limit! 800 floors!" Yelled the telly! Next would come a photo document of himself and excerpts from the trial being broadcasted already, down the hall in the lunchroom.

They built the new empire on the smoking ruins of the old.....

'Darf! I Sort of thought we'd hitch a ride on our space boots along one of those ancient winding highways which has traversed the old Am-Erica since the turn of the century...' Driving. Automobiles. Their 2 amazing headlights, their blasting horns in a cacophony of speed, weaving together; mesh of traffic flowing down turns of the turnpike... 'And just ride right off the whole bonk continent. I guess I figured the resistance would come in a space ship and then we'd fly away across the Milky Way!'

As he lay dying, thought: 'last darf thing I did was to stop & erase my study manual...' Then, swiftly a message returned to him out of the ethers of his soul in connection to the universe: 'Aw, that's OK. I've got all of it up here, in my head & in here, my heart.'

His Mable was being taken from him. Tears were in her eyes.

Somehow he'd known he wasn't going to give the Unity the satisfaction it so wanted.

He had the core of a persimmon, which meant no core at all! So thus had feared he'd be like one of those who turned in Anderson & their comrades,

210

way back in the beginning of his sojourn with the resistance, with that study class which had lifted the shades off his eyes and caused him to see! See for the first time what he'd vaguely known had been wrong with his life…
Turn them all in because they upset the Utopian plan, and the Unity was going after him to end it! But, in finality, he had not given in all the way.

Raw sunlight cast its rays along on the cave floor and s/he was a baby… playing with his parents who were free; but aging prematurely due to radiation killing them alive but him healthy still being so young…

As he lay dying drifting slowly into unconscious as a ship leaves shore each wave carrying it out at ebb tide…

'Maybe I can't help the resistance, but by my dying… like the old prophets spoke. Maybe we at the end must prefer some kind of returning to the universe what we have taken, especially when so many have taken so much and offended grievously.---Even if they have been forgiven by merciful forgiveness.'

Documents prepared by
Red Jordan Arobateau
for the RESISTANCE
Dec. 26, 2057
(Unity Of Utopia,
Lovely Hill View By The Bay)
Block 7/5:00 Hours

www.ingramcontent.com/pod-product-compliance
Lightning Source LLC
Chambersburg PA
CBHW030324020726
47493CB00004B/1150